WRAITH OF TALERA

WRAITH OF TALERA
THE TALERA CYCLE, BOOK 4

CHARLES ALLEN GRAMLICH

WILDSIDE PRESS

To the Readers of the Talera Cycle

Published by Borgo Press,
An Imprint of Wildside Press LLC.
www.wildsidepress.com

CONTENTS

WHAT HAS GONE BEFORE

Ruenn Maclang was born and grew to manhood on Earth. On the planet of Talera, he was reborn a swordsman and a leader of warriors. Through three previous volumes, Ruenn fought his way: *Swords of Talera*, *Wings Over Talera*, and *Witch of Talera*. He began as a man lost and alone on an alien world of savagery and beauty, but he found his path. He found friends who fought with him, and for him, and he found a woman to love. That woman was Rannon, a princess who became Queen of the island kingdom of Nyshphal after her father was murdered.

Ruenn and Rannon married in a bloody throne room after a desperate battle and narrow victory against the sorceress Vohanna and her allies, which included the brothers of both Ruenn and Rannon. But though the Witch herself is finally defeated, the Witch's War is not yet over. Rannon's air-fleet lies devastated; her army is nearly bled white. Nyshphal's remaining enemies are gathered with fire and steel. Amid the chaos a new threat appears, an apparition from Ruenn's past that warns of a deadly future, a future in which even honor and love can be corrupted by hate.

And now, *Wraith of Talera*.

CHAPTER ONE

DEATH OF A SWORDSMAN

My brother was pale, paler even than in the days when his soul had been owned by the Witch Vohanna. He lay on his back in a bed under soft covers, the rise and fall of his breathing almost imperceptible. Someone had crossed his arms on his chest and I pushed them down to his sides so he wouldn't look so much like a corpse. He was not dead yet. Bryce Maclang was not dead yet.

Looking to Bryce's left I saw another bed, another pale, still form. Only the hair had color, a copper-red foaming that set the white pillows afire. *Ahrethane*. She had been placed together with my brother here in Jystral castle so their care would be easier. Talerans named her efrinore, a term I translated as druidess, a wise woman of the forest. Two months ago she had saved my life and the life of everyone here in Timmuzz, the capital of the island kingdom of Nyshphal.

In the city's throne room, when Bryce was about to destroy us all after being turned into Vohanna's Bane-thrall, Ahrethane had thrown her arms around my brother, linking her earth magic with the *toir'in-or* sorcery of Vohanna and canceling both out. Ever since, the two had lain like this.

I thought of the *toir'in-or* crystals then, often called milkstones for their color. They are not stones at all, but a mind amplifying energy source manufactured by the Asadhie race who created Talera and populated it with life from many planets. Sometimes I wished all milkstones were buried in the depths of the world never to be found. But such a stone had opened the gate that brought me from Earth to Talera and I could not regret that eerie and wondrous journey. Because of it I had known great pain. But also great love. Because of it I had found Rannon. Now a Queen. And my wife.

I turned to go, for while Vohanna herself was defeated, some of her allies still tasked us and must be driven from our lands. Many of us were leaving soon for the coast to attend to that matter.

A low moan vibrated the air behind me and I spun around again, looking from Bryce to Ahrethane and back. For two months neither had made a sound, but surely they must have made this one. Yet, to my eyes they lay still as portraits beneath the faint light of the room's rundal-oil lamp.

I took a step toward them and the hair curled to life at the nape of my neck. Their mouths were open, though they had been closed moments before. Dark light bled from between their lips.

Now I took a step back, hand dropping to the sword at my hip. A crimson glow flashed between the two beds, swirled for a moment in the air like a dust devil. I bit my lip, with blade half drawn.

The light seethed, then settled. I could see through it to a place outside this room, as if I were trapped in a tarnished mirror looking out through the glass. The landscape in that other place was stark, with a harsh black sea breaking in foam on a beach of white sand. All around lay the color red, in hues of rose and ruby and saffron.

Along the white beach two men fought, blades of steel gleaming. It was instantly clear that one of the men was myself—Ruenn Maclang. The other I could not place. His face was hidden in shadow, but his build and movements seemed familiar, terribly, terribly familiar.

Now even sound and scent crossed to me from that other place. I smelled the briny sea and heard its waves assault the beach's tenuous hold. I heard the clangor of swords as they linked, crossed, shivered, parted. In the image, I was driven back. The other man was better than I with a blade.

Fear tightened my scalp, clenched my heart. In that moment I was no longer standing in a room in Jystral castle, in the city of Timmuzz. I fought for life instead against a swordsman whose skill I could not match. And still the lower half of his face was hidden, covered with a mask of ebon silk so only dark pupils and gray irises showed above it.

Sweat burned my eyes; my breath rattled with exhaustion. My opponent made no sound, only kept coming, swifter than thought, the point of his blade a nightmare that I blocked and parried. Then I stumbled, legs gone leaden, and missed a parry I had to make. A wink of bloody light stabbed through the buff leather of my jerkin, tore deep into the chest behind it.

I cried out, and was hurled back from the image, back into the room where Bryce and Ahrethane lay like the dead. My chest ached. I thrust a hand inside my shirt, over the heart. There was no wound. Yet, I felt the fatal blade in my flesh, cold, alien, evil.

I looked up. The red glow was shrinking in the room. Only the image of my opponent remained visible, limned in ghostly light. Then that wraith, too, was gone, and just a sound lingered, lingered and faded. And faded. The sound of laughter.

"Ruenn!"

The calling of my name startled me. At the room's door stood three men. They were friends—Valyan Tiersal, Diken Graye, and Kreeg. Each had taken wounds because of me, and I because of them. Best to say we had taken wounds *for* each other. We loved each other as brothers.

"Are you all right?" Diken asked. "We thought you cried out."

I straightened up, shook my head. "It's fine. Only...."

I shrugged, and they took the gesture to refer to the sadness that often whelmed me in this room. I let them think that, not wishing to tell them of my experience. There was naught they could do about a hallucination, and they might treat it as a warning, or as a premonition of things to come. They might think I was cracking under the strain. Then they would treat me differently, and perhaps put themselves at greater risk as they tried to protect me.

I looked back at Bryce and Ahrethane but spoke to Valyan and the others. "We should get to the ships. We don't want to keep our enemies waiting."

Valyan and Diken nodded; Kreeg chuckled. I followed them from the room, and they did not see me examine the fingers that had felt my chest. They did not see me wipe a faint mist of crimson off those fingers onto my breeks. This, too, I would not tell my friends.

There'd been no wound where the vision-sword struck.

There *had* been pain.

And blood.

CHAPTER TWO

ECHOES OF WAR

We came to Teleur, coastal city of the island kingdom of Nyshphal. We came bloodied and battle-hardened, with arrow and axe and more deadly weapons, to take the city back from the enemy who had seized it.

Vohanna's *sorcerous* armies had dispersed with her death, most fleeing back to their own worlds through sphere gates that opened at the Witch's passing. Her Human allies had not fled. Enemy troops from Ubai and Revenor had entrenched themselves along our coast, centered at Teleur, near the delta of the Vehr River where they controlled our best access to the sea and its trade routes.

So we came to Teleur. We came with the dawn.

In late winter along Nyshphal's eastern coast a morning fog rises off the Vehr and we used it to our advantage. Only as the prows of our airships thrust through the mist over the enemy's outer lines did they sight our maroon sails above them. Tocsins rang, cold and brazen. That alarm came too late. By then, iron-bounds casks and wax-sealed clay pots were already tumbling over our railings, each trailing sparks from a lit wick. The first explosions wrought screams from the ground below, screams cut quickly off by the sudden blossoms of orange flame that followed. Even from far above one could smell the burning.

Vohanna had introduced gunpowder to Talera. She'd stolen it from men of Earth, from friends of mine who had died for her greed. The soldiers below were from an army that had used the powder against my adopted homeland of Nyshphal. Nyshphalian scientists had learned from their enemies, and now we turned the weapon back on those who had come against us with it.

Our casks were bombs, with a gunpowder core packed inside myriad shards of pottery. To this we'd added an older weapon, clay pots of God's Fire, a combination of oil and pitch and sulfur that clung and cooked. Taleran warfare had gained a measure of brutality and lost a tithe of honor. I mourned only a little for that loss. We had to win this war others had started—for Rannon's people and mine, for the living and the ones who had died to preserve those lives.

Invaders or not, our foes were courageous. Even out of the carnage below, dark arrows and crossbow bolts leaped toward us. Our hulls rattled, but we'd plated the wood with metal and they'd have to bring up bigger weapons before they could hurt us—onagers and ballistas. They would not get that chance.

While the enemy's attention was turned to the sky, the second wave of our attack came in by water. Teleur lies within the delta of the river Vehr, and branches of the muddy stream snake around it on three sides with levees built high to hold back the seasonal floods. Those three approaches to the city are not walled because the channels are too shallow to float any ship of war. They were not too shallow for the swimmers our airships had dropped off just upstream.

Even in fading winter, few Humans could have stood the cold of those waters long enough to reach the enemy lines unseen. These swimmers were not Human. More powerful they were, with black and green scaled hides and lean tails that thrust them along far faster than a man could swim. Out of the river they clambered, and slunk, until some guard whose eyes were not drawn skyward saw them and shouted in fear. Then they drew free the steel blades strapped to their muscled limbs and came charging in with war-cries only Klar throats could utter.

Klar![1] Reptilian in race. They are named pirates and slavers, called arrogant and cruel. I know these things to be true. But also they are great warriors, and some of them do not care for the evil side of their reputation. Such a one was Jask, a comrade-in-arms from days past who had become High-Council of the Klar kingdom of Talen. He had outlawed slavery in his domain, taken steps to curb the Klar appetite for piracy, but had not even tried to tame his people's fighting heart.

Not long after Vohanna's death I visited Jask. He had been happy to see his old friend, Ruenn Maclang. We had relived past times. He still felt as if he owed me for helping free his people from tyranny, and though that hadn't stopped him from negotiating a favorable trade agreement with Nyshphal, his warriors now fought beside ours less for future commerce than for friendship and honor.

So, Nyshphal was no longer without allies of our own.

While the Klar struck at our enemies below, our air fleet forged on. As we passed over the outer edges of the city itself, the fresh sea breeze filled our nostrils with a salt tang and tattered our fog shrouding. Glimpses of Teleur peeked through and wrung from me a gasp. Much of the city had been burned.

---

1   Many alien races have appeared in the Talera series. See the Taleran Encyclopedia entry 1 at the end of this book for further information about them.

From visits here, I remembered the fishing shacks and taverns, the inns and family homes, built from the dense wood of the local chelaquin tree, often built on pilings as protection against storm surges off the Temeri Sea. A temple to the great god Sevarian had once stood in blonde bansul wood upon the highest point in the city. Now, the temple and many other buildings were gone, replaced with barracks-like structures of rough-hewn new lumber. Only the docks and the massive warehouses used to store trade goods remained largely intact, and those because they served the city's conquerors. The destruction done to my home country by the Witch's War was almost beyond bearing. But bear it we must. And more.

A foursome of Revenor air scouts sighted us as we broke from the fog. They were each twenty-five to thirty feet long, with tapered prows upon which sat a single ballista, and bearing flat-keeled hulls painted dark blue. These were not sailed ships, as were the airborne battleships of both Nyshphal and Revenor. They were driven by clear crystalline wands connected to rotors, the wands having been charged by contact with a *toir'in-or* power stone. As such, they did not require a trained Pilot, only a helmsman at the wheel.

The scout ships were nowhere near as heavily armed as we were, and though higher speeds dramatically reduced the range they could travel before their wands exhausted their charges, they could have outrun us easily over the short distance. Yet, they chose not to flee but moved to slow our advance long enough for their own sky galleons to take off. Since their air fleet greatly outnumbered ours, it was not in our interest to let this happen any sooner than it had to.

I glanced from the bridge of the battleship *Khiang*, which I commanded, toward the ship to my immediate left. A maroon and gray flag with a border of beaten gold flew from the mast there, with a striking trenkil, the Taleran eagle, at its heart. It was the flag of an emperor. Or an empress. It was Rannon's ship, once her father's personal warship, now renamed simply the *Raptor*, or *Jaikil* [2] in Nyshphalian. Beneath the wind-whipped battle standard could just be glimpsed a form resplendent in leather and steel with a maroon cloak about its shoulders. I caught a glint of light from a bronzen helm, and saw the figure had an arm raised.

A hundred images flickered through my thoughts, Rannon in a room where warriors clapped swords on shields to honor her, Rannon in a gown of white silk with her dark hair unbound, Rannon with a bloody blade and smudges of exhaustion beneath her blue eyes, Rannon weeping at her father's grave. I held these thoughts only a moment, and lost

---

2   See the Taleran Encyclopedia entry 2 for information about Talera's languages.

them when the figure's arm dropped. Scarlet pennants snapped open from *Jaikil's* mast, and then from the masts of the other ships within our fleet. We had four airships armed with cannons we had taken or copied from Vohanna, and they made up the "V" of our advance. At Rannon's signal, these four loosed their forward batteries in concert.

The deck beneath me shuddered as flame and smoke belched from our prow with a hell-borne roar. Three of the enemy scouts disintegrated in mid-air while the fourth had its bow torn off. Men tumbled free of the last craft, small specks that grew smaller against the rising curve of the city below. I felt for them, but not enough to change that which was ordained.

Sweeping above us now came a flotilla of our saddle bird riders, Human warriors aboard the backs of monster birds the like of which had never flown the skies of Earth. The eagle-like vullwings flashed by with their broad, muscular bodies, and then came the hawkish sabruns, as sleek in the air as a shark is in the water. Aboard two of those birds would be Valyan Tiersal and Diken Graye. I would not envy their wild freedom when battle came to blows.

Other saddle birds, massive hespern transports, would be landing soldiers behind the enemy's front lines to assist the Klar, but that portion of the battle was also out of my hands. Rajan Critus, a black-eyed duelist who led the imperial guard but who also served when needed as a field officer in the army, commanded those troops. I felt no worry for his skill with either men or blades.

Our own task was enough to trouble my mind. The protecting fog shredded completely away from us now. The blue-white winter sun crested the horizon as if the sea were foaling a star. Enemy patrol ships and swift destroyers, the latter some eighty to a hundred feet long and bristling with weapons, converged to meet our slender fleet. At least three Revenor galleons had also taken the sky. More of the enemy's great battleships were just starting to break free of landing places within the city proper. Those last would be loaded with Ubain troops and would try to close and board our woefully undermanned craft.

Again Rannon sent up a signal, and with command cries of "rish" and "jehas" our bird riders dove their mounts upon the rising galleons. The birds vented their hunting shrieks—a savage sound—and more bombs, smaller ones, and pots loaded with God's Fire, went flinging from their ranks onto the decks of the lifting ships. Smoke spurted up; fire followed.

But the enemy was not without the ability to bite back, and from the roofs of the higher buildings ballistas sang and arrows clove. I winced as saddles were emptied and wounded birds went spiraling down into the city. Our remaining riders struck at the ballista sites then, raining down flames on the archers' heads. Still our losses mounted and we had no birds and riders to spare.

Another signal flashed from Rannon's masts. I instantly ordered more sail and our pace quickened. The other three cannon-ships fell directly into line behind us. After, came seven other Nyshphalian battleships and some fifteen lesser craft, spreading out to form inverted "Vs" at our back, their catapults and ballistas loaded and ready.

The enemy had more of the bombs they'd used against Teleur and Timmuzz during their invasion, but our spies had discovered one thing that gave us hope. The bombs had been given to her allies by Vohanna, but she had not trusted them with the secret of gunpowder itself. Their arsenal of explosives was limited and they had no cannon. We had to use any advantage, and so I'd suggested a play from the history of my home world—Earth.

In traditional Taleran battles of air and sea the ships closed one on one in a melee of individual combats. But on Earth as early as the 1500s a naval tactic appeared in which cannon armed ships fought in a single file known as the "Line of Battle." This let each vessel bring its guns to bear without fear of hitting friendly craft, and allowed for concentrated fire upon a single target. For the first time in history, the Line of Battle appeared on Talera as we drove straight forward into the teeth of the enemy ships racing to meet us. Now, as Rannon and I had agreed, command passed to me in the battleship *Khiang*, which translates into English as *Warrior*.

Two Revenor destroyers flashed toward us from our starboard side, two more from port. These were primarily sail driven ships, though they also carried a secondary charged wand and rotor system to allow for quick bursts of speed over short distances. They called upon that speed now and were almost in range for their ballistas and catapults to fire when I snapped the order that loosed our cannon. We had just six guns to a side, but Rannon's ship behind ours had six more that could be brought to bear. With a monstrous bellow the cannons discharged, and the smell of black powder hammered away the tang of the sea. The enemy destroyers hit a wall of iron and tore apart.

Our men cheered, and I did not say nay. They had lost too many fights and too many friends in the past few months to steal even a small victory from them. But soon the cheers died and the men's focus fell to their tasks as more enemy destroyers rushed like dark wolves upon us, and as the main enemy fleet took to the air from the landing field at the city's north side. There were nearly forty vessels in that fleet, the core consisting of some fifteen Revenor galleons supported by half a dozen of their counterparts from Ubai.

It was the galleons we wanted.

Under my orders, new signals flashed from the *Khiang's* mast. We turned to starboard. The other cannon-ships followed. This brought us perpendicularly across the front of the enemy advance in a maneuver known as "crossing the T."

No doubt the commander of the Revenor fleet was brave and experienced, but he had never experienced the tactic we offered against him now. His ships leaped forward, white sails catching and bellying in the wind. We must have seemed an easy and outnumbered target.

Until he closed within our range.

Our first two broadsides were loaded with chain shot—small iron balls bolted together by metal links—and were aimed deliberately high. Enemy masts exploded into kindling. Shredded sails tumbled like falls of snow. Even across the distance between their vessels and ours I heard the tinny shouts of confusion as the galleons lost speed and directional control. One big ship plowed into another. A third yawed madly to one side and crushed an escorting scout craft.

We fired again, this time with round shot, with the barrels of our cannons cranked down. The decks of enemy galleons erupted upward, flinging men into the air. Now came screams that drove out the sound of the wind. Again we fired, and I ordered a turn to port so our battle line swept down their flank and we emptied our cannon into the chaotic mass of their broken vessels at point blank range, the sound of the big guns a continuous roar.

Palls of smoke clotted the sky. Cinders rained down, burning. I brushed them from my armor. We kept firing. *We* had no shortage of powder and ammunition. For two months the massed efforts of the people of Timmuzz had gone toward little else but making the materials of a new kind of war. Everyone knew our attack was a gamble based solely on our guns. We had one throw of the dice to win or lose.

Smaller enemy vessels stormed to the rescue of their bigger cousins. We hammered shot into them, the barrels of our cannons scorching with heat. We couldn't get them all; we took hits. A ballista bolt, eight foot long, weighing some twelve pounds, sheared one of my crewmen in half. A stone from a mangonel smashed a gap in our railing and I heard the clangor of shields torn from the inside hull where they are lashed on a ship in flight. But the rest of our warships were in action now, screening the attacking enemy away with catapults and ballistas constantly firing, firing.

One Revenor commander tried a ploy born of desperation. Their galleons could not close with our cannon-ships; our guns could outrange their catapults. But they had explosives. Now, an enemy captain ordered a set of bombs trimmed with longer wicks and used his catapults to launch them.

The bombs Vohanna had given her allies consisted of a sealed amphora stuffed with gunpowder and surrounded by a skin of leather into which nails and more powder had been packed. They were lighter than a catapult's normal stone ammunition and could be hurled further. I'd suspected such a trick and had stationed archers along our ships' decks as a possible countermeasure.

As the charges lifted toward us, our archers lit fire pots and used flaming arrows with barbed steel heads to shoot the deadly packages in midair. It worked—in some cases—where arrowheads met leather and cut through to the first layer of powder. The flat crack of the explosions and the twisted fingers of smoke in the air made it seem as if we sailed through a fireworks display like those on Earth.

Not all packets were hit, however. Some came down. One exploded off our port side, staving in several planks but otherwise doing little harm. Another struck Rannon's ship behind ours, blowing a hole in the foredeck and sending its package of nails scything through the crew around where the Queen stood.

I did not know if the scream I heard then was in my head or in the world, or even if it were a Human sound and not the shriek of ricocheting metal. But after it came silence. An awful silence.

CHAPTER THREE

NO VICTORY WITHOUT LOSS

In battle, no silence lasts. The enemy ship that had hit Rannon's *Raptor* with a bomb was reloading. We gave them no time to finish the act. I bellowed out: "Fire!" Our cannons boomed, the shells ripping open the Revenor galleon, spilling its crew into the sky.

Rannon!

I spun to look aft, toward the Queen's ship. My thoughts raged, ached, roiled. Was Rannon alive? There was activity on the other craft's foredeck. I could see it, a termite swarm of soldiers. What were they doing? There was no escaping such an explosion unscathed.

Was my wife alive?

Then the *Jaikil's* cannons fired into an enemy destroyer slashing in at them and it became clear someone was in charge on the vessel. The *Raptor* could still strike, but was it Rannon who gave that order? Or someone else? For a moment I stood frozen. The others around me did not seem to realize their Queen might have been injured, or killed. What would happen if they found out? Outnumbered as we were, we could not afford panic. I couldn't let my own fear show.

A young man stood near me, to carry messages if needed. He was a war orphan, and too young for his first battle. The name he'd enlisted under was Munt, which was not his real name. He looked no older than thirteen, or about fifteen in Earth years. We had lost so many warriors we'd had little choice but to pluck the youth. I leaned toward this one. His brown eyes were huge in a powder-stained face.

"Munt," I said, for his ears alone. "I need you to climb to the crow's nest. To see the deck of the *Jaikil*. I must know if the Queen lives. Tell *only* me. Raise a hand above your head to signal yes. Below your waist to signal no. Do you understand?"

The boy nodded, licking unconsciously at dry lips. He scrambled quickly into the rigging and thrust himself upward like the monkey he'd borrowed his name from.

I glanced back at the arena of battle. Some smaller enemy vessels fled now, harassed by our surviving saddle-bird riders. Only three of their galleons had any remaining capacity to fight, and they were being systematically pummeled by gathered knots of Nyshphalian vessels. I snapped out an order. Signal flags raced up our masts and the third and fourth cannon-ships in our line broke away to finish those fights. These were the *Harkest*, or the *Revenge*, and the *Gleene*, which means *Blade* in Nyshphalian.

Smoke eddied and swirled, staining the blue-white winter sky. I tasted cinders and soot. A broken raft of torn enemy hulls drifted slowly past us toward the south, their sails down and many of them burning. Some spiraled gradually toward the earth below. The ones floating had living Pilots, members of a Caste trained from childhood to use milkstone-charged crystals to provide lift for Taleran airships. In the other vessels, the Pilots were dead or dying and the buoyancy provided by their crystals was bleeding away. A few of our own craft had also been destroyed, and others damaged, including Rannon's flagship. Despite those losses, the air portion of the battle was over and we had won.

My gaze rose to the crow's nest of the *Khiang*. Munt had reached it but there was as yet no signal. Again I glanced toward the *Jaikil*. My fists clenched, fingernails daggering my palms. I had loved Rannon since first seeing her as a captive of the Klar, her wrists held in silver manacles. Love had deepened as I fought beside her and saw her courage and the loyalty she felt toward her people. I remembered our lodgings in Jystral castle, where we had come to live as husband and wife and where someday we hoped to raise our children. I remembered her feral laugh, and the blue wildness of her eyes when we made love. How could I live without her?

A shout brought my head around. White flags flashed from two of the remaining enemy galleons, and more such flags began rising above the decks of other ships. Strange that both Talerans and Earthmen use white for surrender, but perhaps it is because all Humans on Talera are originally *from* Earth, some apparently brought here during historical times. There are certainly other Taleran practices with roots on the home world.

The sudden bloom of white aboard the enemy's remaining vessels brought cheers from our own ships. I did not share in that joy, could not until it was clear Rannon lived. Too, we needed to turn our attention toward the city's harbor where the third and final wave of our attack should have begun.

Because of its mighty air fleet, Nyshphal had possessed only a modest sea-going navy before the war. Most of that was sunk by the combined Ubain and Revenor fleets during the invasion of Teleur. The Klar had a powerful navy, though, and they were our allies. My old friend Jask, who still carried the blood-red shield he'd once carried as a clanless Keshaki, would be leading his black-hulled longships into the harbor against the enemy shipping there. I knew the fear those wolfish vessels with their violet sails and flags of black could evoke, and though the Ubains, in particular, were unlikely to mount much resistance, our airships needed to be there if help were required.

I prayed Rannon would be there too.

Again I glanced toward Munt in the crow's nest. He had his hand up to shade his eyes, and then he jerked, as if struck. My heart jerked as well, and sped to a thudding pace. I gritted teeth to keep from calling out to him. His hand.... He had taken his hand from his face, had looked down at me. Then he flashed a quicksilver smile and lifted his hand above his head.

I sagged in my boots. She lived! Rannon lived!

"Saar, Vohn," I said to the relay man who conveyed orders to our Pilot, "ask Mr. Ostt to take us out over the harbor. We need to see." It surprised me a bit that my voice was steady. My heart certainly was not.

Vohn nodded, passed on the order. We came about, maroon sails booming, catching fresh winds. Another command sent up signal flags, and half our fleet moved to follow us while the rest prepared boarding parties for the surrendered enemy craft. We had attacked at the fifth dhaur,[3] the dawn hour, and by the movement of the sun barely two more dhaur had passed. It seemed scarce enough time for the destruction we'd wrought.

As we came over the harbor, with the wharfs standing out dark against the muddy brown water spilling from the mouth of the Vehr, I saw even more destruction—and realized our help was unneeded. Knowing the Nyshphalian navy offered little threat, our enemy had apparently recalled most of its warships. The tonnage at anchor or tied to the docks consisted almost exclusively of troop transports or supply vessels. The majority had not even tried to fight. The few that had were afire down to their waterlines while the swift shapes of Klar longships circled them like barracudas.

Now, more white flags began to appear, from enemy ships in the harbor and from buildings on the shore. Exultation swept me. We were going to win. Not just this battle, but the war. Finally we had bled out most of the venom the invasion had driven into Nyshphal's veins. And Rannon lived!

I ordered the *Khiang* to draw alongside Rannon's *Jaikil* and signaled a wish to come aboard. Ropes were tossed from ship to ship and tied off to bind the craft together. A long gangplank was laid across the vessels' railings, anchored by men at either end. I left Vohn in temporary

---

3   See Taleran Encyclopedia entry 3 for information on time measurement on Talera.

command and raced across the plank, hardly thinking about an act that once terrified me, and leaped down onto the deck of Rannon's flagship. She greeted me there, and even through the battle grime staining her face her eyes shown like blue diamonds. Then I saw the pain hiding behind those eyes and went still.

"Ruenn," she said. Her voice ached. Then came one more word, another name besides mine: "Kreeg."

Kreeg. My friend. Ex-rhanvin, ex-fighting slave. A man of incredible strength. His existence had been a brutal one before Valyan, Rannon and I had met him in the Lava Mines of the Klar. Then he'd learned what friendship and sacrifice could mean, and his true nature asserted itself.

I'd never known a man who could eat and drink more, nor one who would as readily shed his blood for those he considered brothers. I remembered the day Kreeg had offered me his fealty, and for years now he had served as a personal bodyguard, even though I had never requested it of him.

Two day ago I had requested something from him. I had asked him to serve in this battle as *Rannon's* bodyguard. Her own personal guard, Rhandh, had died in the final fight against Vohanna in Timmuzz. I'd wanted to make sure our Queen would be as safe as anyone could be in a war.

Kreeg loved Rannon. Because I did. But he'd been reluctant to leave my side. I had persuaded him, against his protests, had told him how important it was to me for Rannon to have the best shield-man she could. He had agreed. And now....

"When the bomb hit," Rannon said, "he covered me with his own body. He saved my life. His was taken."

I nodded, then lowered my head. Rannon put her arms around me.

"I'm sorry," she said.

"No victory without loss," I muttered. "There can be no victory without loss."

The words provided no comfort.

CHAPTER FOUR

OF THE DEAD AND THE LIVING

Kreeg. Heril. Rhandh. They had been friends and had died in the Witch's War.

Eric Ryall, my cousin from Earth. Dead at Vohanna's hands.

Hurnan Jystral, father of Rannon. Betrayed and murdered.

Before that, Jedik Ver Lha Yed, the best swordsman I had ever met. He'd taught me that a blade is not a weapon for a warrior's hand. It is the hand itself. He also was dead, in one of the early skirmishes of what turned out to be Vohanna's war.

These were not the only names on the parchment of the slain. Sometimes it seemed the dead outnumbered the living. And there were others who were not dead but were no longer fully alive either, among them Bryce and Ahrethane. Some claimed the *spirits* of those two had died, even though their bodies lived. I hoped that was not true. I did not believe it to be true. Even so, the Gatherers of Souls had been busy of late.

After a moment, I stepped back from where Rannon sought to comfort me on the deck of her flagship. I wanted to hold her, to kiss her and forget. But the clamor of war lingered. The burn of spent gunpowder and the oily stench of God's Fire yet tingled my nostrils. And Kreeg was still dead.

I looked over the *Jaikil's* railing. Many white flags flew throughout the city now. A very large one fluttered from a pole outside a recently erected building on the site where the temple to Sevarian once stood. From that building the conquerors of Teleur had ruled their holdings. They had not ruled long, but the damage they'd caused would take years to repair.

My fists clenched; I felt hate, like embers baking inside. That hate was not truly directed at the soldiers of Ubai and Revenor below. The hate was for Vohanna, who was finally dead and beyond any further vengeance.

"We should land," I said to Rannon, in a voice carefully controlled. "The Ubains outnumber our troops on the ground. We should take their surrender while they're in shock and haven't had time to count our true strength."

She nodded, gave the orders. Her hand squeezed my arm but she said nothing. There was nothing to say. Kreeg was dead, but because of that sacrifice, Rannon lived. I blamed myself for one, joyed in the other. And felt guilt over the joy. The Human mind is a twisted one. Is it any wonder we so often do the wrong thing, follow the wrong leaders, believe in the wrong causes? Perhaps that is what the soldiers of our enemies had done. Some at least. For that I could not hate them.

The ship's deck rocked beneath me and we began to descend. The crew made ready the sails. The Pilot, situated in an iron bubble about a third of the way back from the bow, would be channeling his mind into the *toir'in-or* charged crystals giving lift to the craft. This Pilot was very good. Despite our size, he brought us in light as a drifting thistle until we settled about a hundred tahng [4] from the enemy's headquarters. Here we would formally take their surrender.

A gangplank was lowered and Rannon and I strode down it with some forty gray cloaked warriors at our back. More ships landed as well, disgorging more Nyshphalian marines, but the remaining cannon-ships and the majority of our fleet and saddle birds stayed aloft as a threat. We did not expect treachery but were prepared.

A Ubain general in the finest armor came walking stiffly from his headquarters to meet us. Two younger soldiers accompanied him as assistants. One assistant waved a white flag while the other carried something dressed in purple cloth. The general bore no shield or weapon but wore a patch of black leather at his left shoulder embossed with the sun symbol of his empire. Five golden rays radiated from that sun, indicating his command rank.

The general was a short man with hard brown eyes. He smelled of rawhide and sword-oils. He removed his helm, revealing pale hair cropped close to the skull. As he reached us, he bowed to myself and Rannon. We did not return it.

"I am Ysteen ve—" the commander began.

"I do not care what your name is," Rannon snapped. "I care only that you are defeated."

The man's lips thinned but he did not reply. Instead, he jerked his head at the aide who held the cloth covered bundle. That soldier turned back the purple wrappings to uncover a sword snapped into two lengths. Ysteen picked up both halves, offered them to Rannon.

"The blade is shattered," the Ubain intoned ritually. "I surrender command to you. My officers and I will stand for ransom. I ask that you treat my men with mercy and allow them to return to their homes."

---

4   See Taleran Encyclopedia entry 4 for a description of distance measurements on Talera.

Rannon did not touch the broken sword. "Where is your Revenor counterpart?" she demanded. "The head of your air fleet? I require his surrender as well."

"He is dead." The general jerked his chin toward the sky where Revenor galleons burned. "Destroyed with his ship by your demon weapons. Our surrender includes the airships and the last of our warbird riders."

Rannon nodded, but still did not touch the sword of surrender. I stepped forward and grasped the two halves myself, then passed them to one of the Queen's Gray-Cloaks. Rannon did not even glance at them as the soldier carried them off.

"I will deal with your men far more mercifully than you dealt with this city and its inhabitants," she said to Ysteen. "Your officers and your men both will be ransomed, the money used to repair that which you destroyed. Your army forfeits all weapons, armor, ships, and saddle birds. *You* will stand trial for war crimes against the Nyshphalian people. If another citizen of this land is harmed by your troops, you will be immediately executed. Do you understand?"

The Ubain had stood in parade ground stiffness during Rannon's address, and now drew himself up even further. "I do."

"Then get out of my way," Rannon finished.

She brushed past the man to stalk toward the building he had come from, which would serve us now as our own headquarters in Teleur. I followed the Queen, knowing that her day, and mine, had but begun. For the moment the sword of war was broken, but I did not feel at ease.

CHAPTER FIVE

THE WAGES OF VICTORY

Fighting was easy compared with the work of the next dozen hours. Men and messages came and went. The last of the Ubain and Revenor troops surrendered and makeshift prisons were set up in the city's empty warehouses. Fires were put out and food distribution points arranged by our troops. A field hospital was thrown together. Rannon orchestrated it all. I helped where I could.

I also took a moment to seek out Diken Graye and Valyan and tell them of Kreeg's death. Valyan took it hardest—the two had known each other a long time—but as we stood there and began to tell stories about our friend, each one wilder than the next, the green skinned Llurn warrior at last began to smile. Soon, we three were laughing together at one thing or another Kreeg had said or done. Thus, in the Taleran way, we honored our lost companion, who had joyed in life too much to want his friends to weep. After, we all returned to duties that could not be neglected, though we'd never forget the good natured brawler known as Kreeg.

As for *my* duties, I rapidly grew tired of the paperwork involved in winning a war. How can a sword be so much lighter to heft than a quill? A visit from a band of Klar provided a welcome distraction. At the group's head stalked Jask. His blood-red targe hung over his back and the pommel of a well used broadsword rested beneath his dark-scaled hand. I strode to meet him. We clasped arms. He smiled, and meant it. Though few of his people either express or truly understand Human emotions, Jask was an exception. I did not know why. Nor did I ask. The one time I'd mentioned it to him he claimed to be insulted.

"I should renegotiate our trade agreement, Ruenn" Jask said. "You failed to deliver on your promises."

"Oh? What promises were those?"

"You claimed there'd be a fight and then went ahead and had all the fun yourselves. We scarcely got our ships into battle before the krutt-lovers surrendered."

"Guess we got carried away," I replied. "If you'd like, there's the remainder of the Ubain empire. We could always invade and conquer *them*."

He laughed and slapped me on the shoulder. "Humph. I've enough hassle governing my own people. I'd never want to rule a bunch of troublesome Humans. Especially not if there were more like *you* among them."

"There are no more quite like him," Rannon said as she came up beside me. "Of course, he is from another world."

"A world where the delicate flower of the Klar race never took root," I added

Jask shook his head. "A sad little place where there are no Klar," he said, before sketching a bow to Rannon. "But you, Milady. Your khi was surely once housed in Klar form."

"I think you've just been insulted," I said to my wife, grinning. "Maybe I should take this Klar outside and teach him some manners."

"Oh, ho," Jask said. "And still I'd not have the fight you promised."

Rannon laughed spontaneously. It was good to see. She took Jask's arm, and the three of us spoke for a while of lighter matters before the Klar commander returned to his ships and we returned to the work of setting things right in Teleur.

In late afternoon, a brief rain fell. After that the skies cleared and the temperature plummeted. It was only a few days before the spring passage, that ten day period when the blue-white sun turns green and ushers new life into the world. But while the days grew milder the winter evenings could still be brutal. The cold contributed to the harsh conditions for the city's civilians and Rannon had as many blankets distributed from our ships' stores as we could spare. In the headquarters building, where Rannon and I worked, fires were lit to hiss and crackle in the hearths. The flames could battle back the chill but did little to combat fatigue.

Rannon leaned back from one document among the many she studied and rubbed her eyes. "How nice of the bastards to record every bit of booty they shipped back to their empire. It's a wonder they left us the dirt."

"We'll demand reparations," I said.

She looked at me. "And if they refuse to pay? What threat could we use to force them? We don't have the food or facilities to hold their troops. I doubt they'll attack us again without sorcerous backing but we could never muster the strength to take the war to them. They know that."

She sighed and slumped a bit in her chair.

I rose and went around the parchment littered table to knead the tight muscles of her shoulders with my fingers. She sighed again, with a bit of pleasure this time, and let me work for a moment before reaching up to catch my hands.

"How do you manage it, Ruenn?" she murmured.

"Manage what?"

"To find the strength to comfort me when your own day has been as hard or harder than mine?"

I bent to kiss her on top of the head. "Responsibility is a heavy burden. The greatest responsibilities have been yours."

She turned to look up at me. Soot smudged her pale cheeks; ashes peppered her dark hair. It mattered not.

"I could never have done this without you," she said. "I'm not sure I would even have survived father's death." She looked down. "Or my brother's betrayal."

Squeezing her shoulders, I told her: "You should eat a bit."

Minutes earlier, one of her Gray-Cloaks had brought in two flagons of verhlis tea, fresh and warm from the brew pot, and a wooden trencher piled with meat, bread and a fragrant white cheese made from the milk of the taverel. I'd cut us each thick slices of buttered bread and layered strips of terval meat and cheese between them.

"I invented that just for you," I added, indicating her sandwich.

She looked at me and chuckled. "I seem to recall you saying some fellow on your home world invented it long ago."

"Did I? Well, that doesn't change the fact I invented it again here on Talera. I think I'll call it the Maclang. I'll become famous across the world. My name will be synonymous with exquisite dining."

She smiled and shook her head. "With adventurous dining, maybe." Then she took a bite. As I'd hoped.

I stroked her back, and the door thrust open.

A guard raced in. "My Queen! The sky! You must see!"

Rannon dropped her sandwich, jumped up. "What?"

The guard had already turned, leaped back outside. Rannon and I rushed to follow, burst through the doorway out into the chill night. It was early and only the smallest of Talera's four moons was aloft. This was Nimeru, the Blue Dreamer, worshipped by many as a goddess of poetry and love. But it was not toward Nimeru that everyone stared. Above the moon arced the "shield."

The Asadhie who created this world condensed Talera from the core of a gas giant planet and then placed an atmospheric shield high over the surface to block the toxic gases above from poisoning the life beneath. Sometimes, great displays of wild lightning flare behind the shield. At other times, static discharges build in the vast roiling clouds held at bay by the barrier, and they shift and dance across the horizon in waves of amethyst and ivory and rose, much like Earth's aurora borealis.

Tonight, neither bolts of lightning nor an aurora drew the eye toward the atmosphere's outer reaches. Tonight the shield itself radiated fire, and the whole sky above it was lit with ruddy flames. Towering weaves of orange and scarlet and superheated white swirled and whipped like monstrous tornadoes above the shield, crashing together, uniting, tearing apart again before dissipating themselves in awesome violence against the barrier that preserved life on the planet's surface.

It seemed even that I could hear, or feel, the terrific battle of the elements raging far above us. A low vibration passed through the very air; some vast but delicate pressure whispered against my eardrums. My skin itched, though no scratching would ease it.

"Sevarian!" Rannon exclaimed beside me. "It'll break the shield."

The Queen of Nyshphal trembled, and I held her. If the atmospheric barrier went, every living thing on Talera would die choking. I trembled myself. Others babbled prayers to their gods; some fell to their knees or their faces in supplication.

I'd told Rannon and a few more friends the truth about Talera's artificial nature. It was a truth I'd learned from Jedik Ver Lha Yed, who had been a product of a scientific culture. But though most around us did not know exactly *what* the atmospheric shield was, they held it in superstitious awe and were terrified by any threat to it. The truth of the barrier didn't matter, of course. The ignorant would die no more quickly than the informed if it ruptured.

"We—" I started to say, and froze as the sky suddenly quieted. The storm of flames above the shield snuffed out as if they'd never been. The vibration I'd felt in my bones decayed to nothingness.

I looked at Rannon and almost laughed in relief. Then a shout brought our gazes once more to the heavens. This time it *was* the moon at which everyone stared. Little Nimeru. Little Dreamer. A greenish-black stain had appeared in the upper right hemisphere of the small orb, and even as we watched a jagged tear erupted from that point and zigzagged its way swiftly across the moon's surface to the lower left quadrant. Nimeru had cracked clean across. To be visible from Talera that crack must be miles wide.

Rannon gasped beside me, and suddenly the ground bucked beneath us. I tried to hold onto my wife as the world around us shuddered and heaved, throwing everyone down who was still standing. I landed hard, on my back with Rannon on top of me. Her blue eyes were stark with terror. Mine had to match hers.

A quick wind whipped pebbles across us. A second wind followed, stronger, angrier. A grating sound rattled in my teeth and the front of the headquarters building crashed down behind us, sending chunks of wood flying. One man was struck, cried out. I rolled over, dragging Rannon's body under mine. She shouted something no one could have heard. I only held on as the earth rippled like a beast trying to stir flies from its hide.

For a minute, then two, then three, the brutal shaking continued. More buildings fell. Dust and debris buffeted past us and whipped away in the wind. At last the land quieted and the air moaned down to silence. I rose cautiously, drawing Rannon up with me. Others, too, got slowly to their feet.

"Is it over?" one man asked.

"Yes," said a second.

I knew the last man was wrong when I heard the humming, the sudden whine that battered the air. It was the sound of a sphere gate opening, of something coming through.

CHAPTER SIX

OUT OF THE GATES OF MADNESS

I drew my sword, and Rannon hers. She, too, knew the sound for what it was. A sphere gate swirled into existence before us. Such gateways had been used in the distant past to fill Talera with a bounty of plants and animals and races taken from many planets. Such a gate had first brought *me* from Earth to Talera. I had seen many others since then; I had seen Vohanna open them between worlds and between locations on the same world. Seldom had I seen anything but horror come through one.

This gate was big, bigger than any I'd ever known. Our soldiers milled about it. Though trained for war, they had not experienced the gates as I had. They did not know what was happening.

"Arm yourselves!" I shouted, just as the first…something came shouldering through the portal's mist into our world.

It was an insect, or much like one, like some cross between a praying mantis and a crab, with two arched front legs and three more slender ones to either side of its fluke-shaped body. It was the size of a locomotive.

The creature's huge forward pincers came down, smashed the earth into mud right before us. One of its hind claws caught up a soldier, scissored through his armor as if it were papyrus. I hacked my rune-blade into one of the big claws, felt the steel rebound. The creature didn't even notice, but slewed about as it plucked another soldier from his feet and tore off his lower half. I slashed at one of the thing's smaller limbs. This time the sword's edge bit, but not deeply enough to disable the leg.

Rannon came rushing to help and the creature flicked its flattened tail at us, caught us both a glancing blow and sent us smashing backward into the ruins of the building behind us. The impact stunned. For a moment I lay still, trying to breathe as I counted whether my bones remained in their beds. Then I staggered up, shaking off fragments of wood. Rannon climbed to her feet beside me, wincing as she plucked a six inch splinter from her shoulder. Her hair had come unbound in dark strands that fell across blue eyes.

My wife snarled, moved to leap back into battle. I caught her arm and pulled her back. The mouth of the sphere gate was only steps away. It was still open. And even as I imagined the possibility, another of the giant creatures came through. Behind it rushed a skittering horde of much smaller beings. These were also insectoid, but man-sized or bigger, armed with maces and curved swords and leaf-bladed lances. I had seen *these* creatures before.

Sporns!

Eight eyes glittered below a pair of chitinous horns on the Sporns' ovoid skulls. Their lower faces were full of feelers, their bodies naturally armored by a ribbed exoskeleton. They ran on four multi-jointed hind limbs, carried weapons in four upper ones. When last I'd fought them they'd served Vohanna. I wondered who they served now.

There was no time to wonder long. The bigger beasts struck at random, at whatever moved that was not monster or Sporn. The Sporns saw *us*, and four of them came leaping in our direction while others fell upon our disorganized troops. Rannon and I met the four with slashing steel. I ducked beneath a yataghan, hacked off both left forelimbs of one foe. Silvery blood sprayed. I dodged it, remembering. It burned like a weak acid, though about all it could truly do was raise welts where it touched.

Rannon killed a second enemy, was pressed back by two more, their weapons windmilling wildly as they tried to overwhelm her. I cut one down from behind; Rannon took out the other. There were plenty of fresh foes, however. Coming for us. At any moment the two big monsters might turn in our direction as well. Our swords would avail us nothing there.

"Gray-Cloaks! To your Queen!" I shouted, calling for Rannon's guards.

Men responded; some were already on the way. Before anyone could reach us a second sphere gate whined opened behind us. I spun, saw the gray swirling mist of the gate coalesce. A shadow moved in the gray and I put my back to Rannon's so we could protect each other.

A shape leaped through the new gate. A man. No, a woman. She wore an armor of bones, carried a rapier in either hand.

"I'm with you!" she shouted.

She rushed past me, threw herself at the Sporns who were moving against Rannon. Two beings followed her from the gate. Both were armed. One carried a crossbow and an axe; he was a Kaldi. Some call them bear-men. The other was Human, tall and gaunt, with a shaven head and twin short blades in his hands called kahnnas. I knew him. He fought for Chalathar, the sorcerer who had helped us defeat Vohanna and who had told me once of his hopes for bringing a lasting peace to Talera.

The gaunt one's mescal-eyed gaze met mine, burning. Then I turned with him, and with the Kaldi and Rannon and the woman with two rapiers. We met the Sporns face to face and hacked them up.

The huge mantis-like creatures were not so easily dispensed with. Both sphere gates had closed the instant our new allies came through. The first gate had already birthed two of the big monsters before it shut on a third, shearing the beast off behind the head, leaving its scythe-like mandibles clashing on air. The two that made it through caused enough damage by themselves as they stomped and crushed anything in their way. Their rampages did not seem directed, though. Their high, fluting calls suggested confusion and the paths of destruction they wove looked random. Still, they killed anyone who attacked them, or strayed too close.

We stayed back.

I looked at Rannon, and at the three warriors who had come from the second gate, and at the Gray-Cloaks who had joined us.

"Swords are less than needle pricks to the big ones," I said. "We need the ship. We can use the cannon."

"Or bombs," Rannon added.

"Yes."

Someone was thinking faster than we were. A shadow flashed above us. Another followed. I looked up to see a brace of sabruns sweeping over, men between their wings. One warrior stood in his saddle, hurled a sputtering package down onto the back of a rampaging monster. The bomb exploded in smoke and shrapnel, but the hard exoskeleton of the thing deflected most of the blast.

The creature certainly felt the blow. It bellowed, reared back onto its hind legs and hooked a long claw at one of the bird riders. That strike missed, but with great bravery the rider held the bird tight, wings buffeting in invitation for the monster to try again. It did, and as it bellowed once more a second sabrun rider swept in low and chunked a lit bomb directly between its mandibles.

The creature's roar aborted into a belch of black smoke. The forward portion of its head disintegrated. The monster's body shook itself like a wet dog, but it wasn't aware yet that it was dead. Its legs worked like a shuttle on a loom as it charged off through the streets, caroming off buildings and scattering anyone in its path before collapsing in a heap of threshing limbs.

One of the sabrun riders raised his fist to salute us. It was Valyan. The other would no doubt be Diken Graye. I had no chance to verify before the two were off after the remaining monster.

Rannon gave a long sigh beside me and I glanced her way. She pushed a strand of hair from her face. Dead Sporns lay like litter around us. A few living ones fled with soldiers in pursuit. Forty or so had burst through the initial gate, although I assumed more were supposed to do so before it shut down so abruptly.

I looked from Rannon toward the woman with two rapiers who had come through the second gate. Something told me she was the leader of the team that had raced to our support. She had certainly accounted for her share of Sporns, and had done so with speed and economy. She was tall, perhaps 5' 10" or better, and well muscled with shoulder-length brown hair braided at the back. Her face was thin, angular, with the lines of exposure to sun and wind etching the flesh below the light brown eyes. Her skin was dusky, almost golden, a shade I'd not seen before in a Human.

The woman wore russet leathers and her armor was indeed made of bone, or something much like it. Her breastplate resembled the base of a turtle's shell. Her greaves were fitted together from pieces of what looked like horn.

"Thanks for your help," I said to her. And then, "Chalathar sent you?"

She nodded, shook her rapiers free of the silvery blood that smoked along them and sheathed them at her hips.

"I'm Shai." She gestured toward her companions. "Volek and Rence," she named them.

Volek was the Kaldi. The gray tips on his brown fur made it clear he was no longer a youngster. He'd lost his crossbow and nursed a wound to his left wrist. Rence was the gaunt fellow with the kahnnas, he whom I'd seen before. His blades were sheathed over his shoulders and he looked bored.

"How did Chalathar know we were in danger?" Rannon asked Shai. "Or, a better question. Why did he send us help now all of a sudden? And not before?"

The warrior woman's brown eyes met the blue ones of my wife. "I'll tell you. You're not gonna like it."

CHAPTER SEVEN

WHAT PRISON CANNOT HOLD

"Vessoth," Shai said. "God-Husband to Vohanna."

Rannon frowned. As for me, my mouth thickened with cotton and my heart started to thud. I grasped hard upon the wooden arms of the chair where I sat.

"What about him?" Rannon asked, staring straight at Shai, her frown deepening.

We had returned to Rannon's battleship, were aloft in a night sky that seemed strangely quiescent beneath the broken moon of Nimeru. Shai and her two companions, and Rannon and I, had gathered in the ship's cabin around a table where an oil lamp burned.

"He's escaped his prison."

My hands tightened convulsively on the chair's arms. *No*, I thought. *It can't be*.

"I imagined that was a myth," Rannon said.

"No," Shai replied, her gaze never wavering under my wife's hard look.

"Nimeru was his prison," I blurted.

Shai said nothing, but she looked toward me at last and inclined her head in a brief nod.

"I don't understand," Rannon said, shaking her own head.

I thought she *did* understand, at least most of it. She just didn't want to give it voice, to make it real. Vessoth was an Asadhie, supposedly one of the twelve who had constructed Talera. They were often referred to as the First Gods, though they were not supernatural. Many Talerans doubted they had ever existed but Rannon knew the truth. She'd met Chalathar, who *was* an Asadhie, and Vohanna, who was another. She knew the legend of the God War, when the twelve had fought among themselves and half of Talera had fallen to ruins. She knew the story of how, after the war, Vessoth was imprisoned by an alliance of other Asadhie. What neither Rannon nor I had understood was how much reality there was to the legends.

Shai finally spoke again. "I only found out the truth of Vessoth's imprisonment tonight myself. From Chalathar. Just before he opened the gate and sent the three of us," she punched her chin toward her companions, "to aid you. Then *he* shut down the gates. All the gates."

"That would explain why they closed so abruptly," I said. "A good thing. It kept more of the Sporns from coming through. And those other big monsters. Whatever they were."

"The Sporns have a symbiotic relationship to the big bugs," the one called Rence said. He sat tipped back in his chair against the dark paneled wall, his long fingers steepled before his gaunt face. "The big ones are quattles. The Sporns use them as brooders for their young, and there would certainly have been more Sporns coming through that gate. They breed like heen."

I had neither seen nor heard of a quattle before, but I knew of the heen. They are rat-sized predators that hunt in huge packs. In appearance, they are like miniature monkeys with big heads, but they have the teeth and feeding habits of piranha. They are notorious for the rapidity with which they reproduce.

"Chalathar didn't shut the gates solely for us," I guessed.

"No," Shai said. "To keep Vessoth from getting off Nimeru."

"But—" I started.

"We think he was imprisoned *inside* the moon," Rence interrupted to explain. "He may have opened the door to that jail but he hasn't escaped the moon itself."

"The gates may not stay closed long, however," Shai added. "Chalathar promised he'd keep them shut as long as he could. That's why he's not with us. He's also trying to limit Vessoth's sorcery by blocking his personal *toir'in-or* power stone. When Vessoth was imprisoned, most of his milkstones were taken from him. The Asadhie cannot live without a stone to maintain them, however. Chalathar says he knows the stone left to Vessoth. Don't ask me how. He also said it would take all his strength to do what he's doing, and eventually that strength would fail."

"Other milkstones could have been smuggled in to Vessoth by now," I said. "It might be how he broke free after being imprisoned for so long."

"Possibly," Shai agreed. "It is likely Vessoth had help from some source. Speculation will do us little good at present, however."

Rannon gave a broken sigh and leaned back in her chair.

Now, the one named Volek spoke for the first time. "There's more. Chalathar didn't have a chance to confirm or deny this, but it's part of the legend that Vessoth was confined because he wanted to rupture the atmospheric shield and cleanse the surface of Talera of all life. He wanted to start over."

"We don't know that part to be true," Rence said.

I looked at Rannon. Her shoulders had slumped under this new weight of threats, and I reached out to stroke her arm. She glanced back at me, nodded slightly though she could not work up a smile.

"So what do we do?" I asked Shai then. "Surely Chalathar had a plan."

"One." Shai dropped her hands to the hilts of her rapiers. "We take the fight *to* Vessoth, invade Nimeru while the sorcerer is getting his legs under him."

"Why didn't Chalathar send you there instead of here then?" I asked. "He could have opened that last gate to anywhere."

"Because he fears Vessoth already has some of his servants with him," Rence said. "Maybe *that's* how he escaped. Besides, Nimeru may be the smallest of the moons but it's still a big place. We don't know where the sorcerer might be. We need an airship to search. Troops if we have to fight."

"We can't fly an airship to the moon," Rannon protested. "Besides, in case you haven't noticed, the Nyshphalian fleet is a bit battered at the moment. Not to mention busy with a war."

"We don't need a fleet," Shai said. "Just one ship loaded with fighters. And the right Pilot."

"You," I said to Shai, guessing it.

"Yes. I can take one ship that high."

Again I looked at Rannon, met her gaze. She shook her head at me, a very slight shake.

I turned back to the others in the room. "The Queen and I need to talk alone."

Rence pushed forward in his chair from where he balanced against the wall, let the front legs come down with a hard thump on the cabin's planks. He started to speak but Volek caught his shoulder and stopped him. Shai merely rose from her own chair and motioned for the others to follow her outside.

When they were gone, I stood and drew Rannon into my arms. I hugged her tight, then pushed her out to arm's length to look into her blue-on-blue eyes.

"Saysa," I said, calling her by the Taleran equivalent of honey. "It has to be done."

She closed her beautiful eyes for a moment. Her fists clenched by her sides. "I know" she finally said, her voice dry. "It's our fight too. If Vessoth was Vohanna's lover as the legends say, then surely he'll come after us for our part in the Witch's death."

"The legends have been unfortunately accurate so far."

Rannon nodded. "It will be the people of Nyshphal who suffer most."

She turned and walked away from me then, over to look out a port-hole onto the night. I did not follow.

The blue light of Nimeru, much diminished since its rending, slipped through the porthole to mix with the oil lamp's flame and paint Rannon's upper body with a martial glow. She was suited to this cabin, which had once been her father's. She had not changed the simple furnishings of dark oak, or the displayed weapons on the walls. Nor had she touched the flags, which included the old crossed-dagger battle standard of Teleur when it had been an independent state ruled by the Jystral family. Rannon's father had been born in Teleur, and I knew she must be thinking of that as she looked out upon the hard used city.

"I just want peace," Rannon declared at last, her voice almost plaintive. I knew from her tone the incredible toll she had paid over the last few months of violence. Rannon was the strongest woman I'd ever met, but in that moment she was close to cracking. I wanted to hold her, tell her "shhh, it'll be all right." That wasn't what she needed.

"We'll have to *make* peace happen," I said. "Beings like Vohanna and Vessoth don't fold their game unless they're forced."

She turned from the porthole and looked back at me, her eyes shadowed. I could see the faint glisten on her cheeks that marked the glide of tears.

"Here is where you tell me I can't go."

"You can't," I agreed.

"Rajan Critus could handle things here. For a bit."

"The problems of moving men and ships about. The material problems. Not the spiritual ones. Critus is a good man but he's not the Queen of Nyshphal. We have no idea how long we might be gone. The people need you now. Every day."

Rannon had been raised a princess, raised to rule. A sense of duty had been laid down with her bones. She knew the truth I'd spoken.

So now she walked back and put her arms around me.

"I don't want to lose you," she said. "I need something too. *I* need *you*."

"You won't lose me. I'll be back."

"Can you promise?"

I had no answer.

CHAPTER EIGHT

HOWL

Abruptly, I paused outside the door of my cabin aboard the battleship *Khiang*. Ruby light bled from beneath that portal. My first thought was fire. But when I threw back the door in near panic no flames licked out at me. The light was within the cabin but not *of* the cabin. I knew then what I would see as I stepped across the threshold.

I had left Rannon for the moment, gone to the *Khiang* to oversee the loading of men and supplies for a trip to the moon—to Nimeru. Despite the assurances of the warrior, Shai, it was a trip I was not at all sure we were capable of making. Although Talera's moons, and her sun as well, appear to rise and set much like Earth's companions, they orbit beneath the planet's atmospheric shield and are theoretically within reach of a flyer. Some tale tellers claim to have done so—for the moons, at least. I was skeptical.

Of course, I had once been skeptical of sorcery and had seen it many times since arriving on Talera. I saw it again now within my cabin. Before me, as in Timmuzz in the room shared by Bryce and Ahrethane, two men limned in raw red light fought each other with gleaming swords. They warred on a white beach with an obsidian ocean for background. One of the men was me. The other wore a black mask and moved with the fluid grace only a panther could match. I saw it all, like a play on a stage. The figure that was Ruenn Maclang stumbled; the other figure lunged with his sword flat and true before him.

Deep the blade went, into the heart. My heart. Once again I cried out, and for the moment could not say which was the real Ruenn Maclang, the man standing in the Captain's cabin of the *Khiang*, or the man who fell dying to his knees on that pale beach.

I grabbed for the wound and felt some cold, ghostly blade being drawn back through my fingers as it left my body. I looked down, tore back the laces of the shirt to probe for an injury. The flesh was whole over the heart, but the site flared with pain and there was a sheen of blood on the skin. I could smell the copper bite of it.

Taunting laughter made me look up. The man in the black mask, with the eyes of gray, was staring off the beach into the cabin, staring at me.

Only the thinnest membrane of crimson light separated us. Chill sweat slicked me. My hand fumbled toward the hilt of my rune-blade. The man lifted his own sword, licked the steel where it ran with blood. Maclang blood.

Hallucination! I thought. *It has to be a hallucination.*

Even as I thought it, I knew it was a lie.

Then the swordsman pointed the glittering tip of his weapon at me. The dark silk covering the lower half of his face fluttered. Once more came the bark of cruel laughter, followed by a single word.

"You!" the man said.

I heard the word clearly, snarled in a hoarse voice that dripped with anger. The voice was familiar, and yet unfamiliar. But it was very real. No denying that now. No hallucination, this. A sending instead. A threat.

I drew my own blade.

From somewhere came a raging howl, not from within the cabin, not from the world of the ruby haze where the gray-eyed swordsman lurked. Yet, the man from the scarlet-lit world heard it. As I heard it. He looked up, and around, then back to me. For the first time he seemed unsure.

Abruptly, the burning red light flickered and went out. I was alone in an empty cabin. The howl continued for a long moment, then stuttered to a stop. The swordsman's voice had merely haunted me with a sense of familiarity. The howl I knew at once.

Bryce. My brother.

He was awake.

CHAPTER NINE

AWAKENINGS

"The ship is ready?" Shai asked, her voice sharp with impatience.

She stood in my cabin aboard the *Khiang*, with her men Rence and Volek behind her. Rannon, too, was there, and Diken Graye and Valyan, who would accompany us.

"Ready," I agreed.

Most of the night had gone; few of us had slept. Food, weapons and other necessities had been packed into the *Khiang's* holds. A few necessary repairs had been made. Volunteers from other Nyshphalian crews had been chosen to replace the men we'd lost at Teleur. In a hastily constructed mew on the deck, six sabrun warbirds sat hooded. I wasn't sure we would need them but wanted them handy in case. Rannon had also suggested we strip our remaining cannon-ships of their powder and shot to feed the needs of my battleship. I'd declined. There was a reason.

"There will be one slight delay," I added.

Shai frowned. "We must not waste time."

"We have to return to Timmuzz first. We can get more powder and shot there, but the main reason is we have to pick up my brother. And Ahrethane, the efrinore."

I was surrounded by frowns now. No one understood.

"They're awake," I said.

Rannon gasped. "Awake!" She grabbed my arm. "How do you know?"

I met her blue-eyed gaze. I told her part of what had happened in my cabin. The smallest part.

"I *heard* Bryce. Heard him cry out. I don't know how. It was like...."
I shrugged, not having the words. "It was inside my head. But if he's woken up then surely Ahrethane has too."

"One more sword and a wood witch won't make any difference now," Shai snapped. "Time lost may."

"It can't be helped," I said. "I have a feeling we *will* need another sword. And a wood witch."

"A feeling!" Shai's nostrils flared as if she'd smelled something rank. "Well, I'm the Pilot and I say—"

"The ship and crew are mine," Rannon interrupted, her voice hard. "If Ruenn believes it best to fetch Bryce and Ahrethane then that is exactly what will happen. Else the *Khiang* goes nowhere."

Shai's gaze met Rannon's, the brown of good earth at war with the blue of a clear sky. The warrior woman was inches taller than my wife, heavier by at least thirty pounds. I knew from watching her in action against the Sporns that she'd fought many times with life at stake. One did not acquire such feral grace in a practice arena. But she did not know Rannon, and many times I'd seen warriors overlook the strength in my love's lithe frame.

Shai was gruff, a bit restive, and accustomed to command it appeared. But she seemed to realize she was not going to win a war of words against the Queen of Nyshphal. I did not think she was used to losing at anything, and was curious how she would take it. I needn't have worried.

She finally nodded. "You're right," she said to both Rannon and myself. "We've got few enough facts as guides. Perhaps feelings are the thing we need to rely on. Let's make it quick."

For a moment I glimpsed the real person inside the blunt shell of Shai's exterior. Behind the lean features and brown eyes, some worry goaded her. I wondered who it was for.

Rannon nodded as well, then turned and kissed me fiercely there before the others. When she broke the kiss she took my hands and stared into my eyes.

"Bring yourself home to me," she said.

I smiled at her. "This time I'll remember the flowers."

For a moment the comment confused her. Then she recalled the words I'd said to her once on the island of Talen after chopping her free of the Klar shackles that held her enslaved. It had been only the second time we'd spoken. I'd said: "I did not realize I would find you again so soon. Else I would have brought flowers."

Now, as she had done on that long ago day, she laughed. It was no dainty laugh. Her head tilted back and her humor roared to the rafters. I laughed too, as did Valyan, who had been there to hear the words first hand. In that moment we were all three young again, young as we had been before the Witch's War stole so much life from each of us.

I thought to myself then how dour we had all become, how intense and focused, especially Rannon, who was agonizingly young for the responsibilities now thrust upon her. In Earth years she was barely twenty-four. She had handled the stress better than could be hoped, but it had burned her. It had burned us all, and we'd grown a bit cold, a bit distant from our finer instincts.

I shook my head. Unless we hung on somehow to our Human warmth, our ability to laugh, the Witch would have won—no matter the outcome of our battles. I kissed Rannon again, then looked at the others. I put a smile on my face, felt it take hold.

"Let's go bottle up another sorcerer," I said. "The first one was too easy."

CHAPTER TEN

TO TIMMUZZ

The trip to Timmuzz would not take long. The wind was at our back and the *Khiang* glided along under full sail nearly as swift as any arrow. Needing the rest, I slept for a time. My dreams were of Rannon. At first I saw her as she had been when we met, bare of foot on a sandy beach, wearing a gown of white with her midnight hair falling long down her back. She had borne slaver's chains then, and she bore them now in the dream. For just a moment. She saw me, held her arms out, and the chains clattered free to the ground. She was smiling.

The dream changed. I ran toward her but could get no closer. Her smile faded; her arms dropped to her sides. Now came the glisten of tears on her pale cheeks. The sand where she stood changed too, became finer grained and pallor-white. Then a ruby light flared and the sea turned black where it crashed onto the beach. Rannon stared at something near her feet and suddenly raised both hands to her mouth. I heard her sob and looked to where she was looking. A figure lay there, half covered in sand like some debris from a wrecked ship. I knew the figure. Me. Dead!

I stopped running.

It's a dream. Wake up!

I looked up into a sky that was crimson on crimson, strained to lift my arms, strained to touch…something.

Just a dream!

The nightmare broke and receded like a river flood returning to its channel. I sat up, wiped a hand across my sweaty face. The cabin was empty save for a map table and some chairs. No strange ruby light this time. No taunting laughter.

I rose and went up on the cool deck, understanding there would be no more sleep for me at the moment. I passed men I knew but only nodded to them while striding to the prow to stand looking into the clear sky ahead. The fresh air finally began to wipe the scents of blood and gunpowder from my nostrils.

We had left Teleur near dawn and the sun was well up now. It was still generally blue-white, a winter sun, but a faint emerald circle girded it. We were very close to the spring passage, when the sun would turn green. Normally, it would be time of great festival in Timmuzz, but I did not think the war-torn people of Nyshphal would be much in the mood.

I thought then of the dream that had just visited me, and of the events that had surely given rise to its images. Although I hoped this dream was only a dream, my experiences with the world of the ruby light had driven home the fact that someone was sending me visions, visions that had the power to cause me physical hurt. It did not seem likely to be a friend.

Who could be behind such attacks? And for what purpose?

It reminded me of something Vohanna would have done, and with Vohanna dead my mind turned naturally to the one called Vessoth. He'd been her husband. Could he want revenge on a man who had been instrumental in his wife's destruction? The desire for vengeance is a powerful force, but on some levels the very idea of Vessoth targeting me seemed absurd. Many people had lent a hand in bringing down the Witch. I was not that important, surely not important enough for a would-be God to concern himself with.

Yet, if Vessoth was an Asadhie, as he appeared to be, he surely had the power to lay such a curse on my head. The question was whether he had the desire. For reasons unfathomable, it certainly seemed that his wife, Vohanna, had taken a keen interest in the brothers Maclang.

I spat over the ship's rail. Vessoth might be the logical choice for whom, but the why was a tougher question. Each time I'd been struck I had bled. Each time the resulting chest pain had felt colder and lingered longer. Was I intended to die from such ghostly wounds? Or was the sending meant merely to weaken me, to distract me, to break my spirit— the khi as the Talerans call it?

The last issue, of course, was to put name to the instrument being used against me, the swordsmen in the black mask with the gray irises. He *was* familiar. Something about the way he used his sword. Yet I could not remember any foe I'd ever fought who could wield a blade like this man.

At least I didn't think so.

A momentary chill hovered at my shoulders, settled between them like a parasite.

Bryce had dark grey eyes, at least before he'd been taken by Vohanna. I'd fought him once in the Witch's arena and knew his skill with a sword. But.... He wasn't *more* skilled than I. Not like the man on the white beach. That man had been my superior, far better than anyone I'd ever seen except my old teacher, Jedik Ver Lha Yed.

No, I did not think the man in the black mask was Bryce. *That* fellow had reacted with surprise when he heard Bryce's mental howl. He'd not been afraid. Not exactly. More wary than anything. It had still been good to see his absolute confidence shaken.

Bryce's face grew firm in my thoughts then, driving out any other distractions. What would I find when I saw him once more? He was awake. I *knew* this. The last time we'd faced each other he'd been Vohanna's Bane-thrall and had tried to kill me. A Bane-thrall is a sorcerer who is essentially a slave to another sorcerer. Vohanna had planned that fate for Bryce from the start, from the moment he'd come through a sphere gate from Earth into her lair. First she took him as a lover, then made him hate her. She'd used that love and hate to chain him.

She was dead. At last dead. But could Bryce come back from what had been done to him? Could he learn to be fully Human again, even with the Witch's influence removed? I wondered, also, about the milkstones Vohanna had implanted inside of Bryce? He'd told me of them. Were they still there? Or had they fallen away with Vohanna's death, as they'd fallen from the bodies of many others she'd corrupted?

"Timmuzz!" someone shouted.

Ahead of the ship, I saw the outskirts of the city looming—lovely, rose-stuccoed Timmuzz. She was bruised by war now, with ugly gaps where buildings had been torn down or burned during the recent siege by the Witch's armies. A wall was under construction around the city, where none had existed before Vohanna. As we passed over I saw people laboring under the sun to haul stone blocks to the wall, lever them into place, and seal them with mortar. Most of the workers were elders or children, for many of Nyshphal's men and women of fighting age were dead, or they were still soldiers who wielded other tools besides chisel and trowel.

The warrior Pilot, Shai, was not flying our ship now. Our regular Pilot, Cailif Ostt, a dark skinned young man from the Stone Cities, knew the landing field and brought us in. Aerial scouts had seen us coming and word had spread. Many had gathered. The crowd saw me at the prow as we set down and surged forward for news. I raised my hands. A hush settled.

"The Queen sends you her greetings!" I shouted. "She is well and—"

Cheers drowned the rest of the words. Rannon was much loved by her people. Deservedly so. They had feared because she was not at my side. Now they joyed. But some shouted for quiet, to hear what had happened with our counterattack at Teleur.

While the noise died, I looked across the worn but curious faces of the throng. Bryce and Ahrethane were nowhere to be seen. On a raised platform to one side stood Arca Heskern and Taskin Bhent. Heskern was our chief scientist. Gray haired and often severe, but highly intelligent, she would be eager to know how our new weapons had performed. Bhent was commander of the army. A stout man, once given to drink but who no longer touched alcohol, he'd been left in charge of our forces in Timmuzz. He'd not been happy and would want to know what he'd missed.

The crowd only waited for word of the battle's outcome.

"Teleur is ours once more!" I shouted to them.

There were more cheers, in a great swelling of sound. But among the masses some wept, and some collapsed to be caught and held up by their fellows. The horrendous strain of the war had taken a toll on every Nyshphalian. That strain had snapped now. Looking over the people, I could see: they took my words to mean the worst was over, that peace would reign. I could not tell them they were wrong. I could not mention Vessoth or our voyage to Nimeru. Not yet.

The gangplank was lowered and we went down from the ship into the crush. I touched hands, returned smiles, let the people touch me. It came home to me then. I was King to these men and women.

How strange!

I had never sought such recognition, never wanted this kind of responsibility. But it had come with marriage to Rannon and I could not shirk it. For a moment, the thought of it nearly overwhelmed me. My legs weakened; my heart stuttered. I tried to remember how Rannon behaved among her people. I put on a broader smile, walked slowly, nodded at greetings, touched hands and shoulders. No one seemed to find my actions unkingly. No one was more shocked at that than I.

At last I made it through to face Arca Heskern and Taskin Bhent.

"My brother?" I asked. "He is awake?"

"He is," Bhent said. "He wants to see you. He waits in the chapel of Sevarian. On the castle grounds. He said for you to come alone."

CHAPTER ELEVEN

ANOTHER SWORD, AND A WOOD WITCH

I entered the grounds of Castle Jystral through Thorn Gate, so named for the ancient thorn trees framing it. The thorn is sacred to the god Sevarian, who is the chief deity of the Nyshphalians. These trees had been transplanted from a holy grove far south in the Katari Mountains, where it was proclaimed that in ancient days Sevarian had lived for twelve years as a mortal Human. The castle guards did not bar the way. After all, it was *my* castle now. Mine and Rannon's.

Along cobbled paths where bittergrass roots had started to crack the stones, where too long unattended gardens grew riotous with safweed and redbriar, I strode with just thoughts for companions. Diken and Valyan had pressed to accompany me. I'd given them another task, to work with Arca Heskern on a modification to the ship and its cannon emplacements. Besides, Bryce had wanted me to come alone.

I was curious why.

Soon, I came to a red brick way, and as I turned down it the temple dedicated to Sevarian loomed into view. Of marble it was, polished to a high alabaster in the sun of early afternoon. Yet, I could see the scars of battle marring the polish, and the lamps that once would have turned the building into a glory at night had been emptied of fuel to warm the people of Timmuzz during a hard winter. Sevarian was not a jealous God; he did not demand sacrifices of his people when they themselves were barely surviving.

The temple complex was huge. There were two worship areas and quarters for many monks, though during the recent siege much of the space had been turned into a hospital, a phorosnex in the tongue of Nyshphal. The very back portion of the building had been left untouched, however. This was the smallest, most intimate of the two worship sites, often referred to as the chapel. It had its own postern. In contrast to the marble steps and great bronzen portals of the main entrance, the door to the chapel was of simple, brass-bound oak. I paused there.

Bryce would be on the other side of this doorway, but what should I expect from him? I found myself frightened for Bryce, for what his experiences might have done to his mind and body. I was honest enough to admit that I was also a bit frightened *of* him. Was he a man again? Or still a sorcerer? Was he brother or enemy?

The door opened softly under my fingers. I stepped through into the nave, saw the copper altar and the rows of snow-wood pews to either side. Light fell onto the altar through the stained windows of the clerestory. A single rundal-oil lamp contributed its own sweet glow and a smell that reminded me of beeswax candles. In the pew closest to the chapel's front, a man knelt. He heard the door open and rose to face me. It was indeed Bryce.

I strode down the aisle to meet him. He let me come. He'd cut his long hair but it remained white on white, as it had been when Vohanna owned him. Across his too gaunt face coiled the faded lines of old tattoos. But when I reached him, I saw his eyes. Though nested within dark circles, those eyes were grey again instead of the rust-red or silver he'd borne in unhappier times. I hoped that was a good sign.

"Ruenn," Bryce said, in a voice both hoarse and familiar. "It's very good to see you."

"Is it?"

He gave a slight smile. "I don't blame you for being cautious. But the Witch's influence is gone. This time, I'm sure."

"Forgive me. How can *I* be sure?"

He nodded his head several times, an unconscious gesture as he considered the question. Then he grasped the bottom of his thin cotton shirt with his left hand and pulled the cloth up above his stomach. In the hollow of his belly I counted four small wounds, each the size of an acorn. They looked almost like bullet holes and were just beginning to heal.

"The *toir'in-or* came out," Bryce said. "The milkstones Vohanna placed inside me. They came out and I awoke."

Only then did I realize how my jaws ached from clenching, how my eyes burned with seeing. A long breath shuddered from my chest, and I took one more step toward Bryce. He opened his arms and I folded him to me, hugged him hard. He hugged me back, fiercely.

"My God," I said. "I never thought to have you whole again."

"Not quite whole. But what is left is free."

I stepped back from him.

Not quite whole.

I looked to Bryce's right arm, toward the place where his wrist had been sheared through. I remembered the false hand Vohanna had given him to replace the one damaged when a revolver exploded in his grasp. Made of steel and copper and spiderweb-wires, that hand had been alive, an entity with a mind of its own. I was glad it had been destroyed, but it was hard to see the stump that remained.

As if reading those thoughts, Bryce said: "A small price to pay. I would pay it again."

"When this is over I'll take you to Jedik's Isle. The Emirians have worked wonders with artificial limbs. Because of their own handicaps."

Bryce nodded. "When this is over I will gladly go. But now...."

"Now what?" I prompted after a moment.

"Now I must tell you why I wanted to meet you alone."

My heart had started to slow; its pace picked up again. I frowned.

"All right."

"Do not be shocked," he told me.

Before I could promise anything he turned and called out: "Ahrethane! It's time."

A dozen strides behind the altar hung a set of braided gold curtains. They stretched from ceiling to floor, separating the priest's area from the rest of the chapel. Those curtains stirred and I looked eagerly for a glimpse of Ahrethane. I'd hoped for her awakening, had believed in it, but had not been able to completely shake away the doubts.

It *was* Ahrethane who pushed through the curtains then. I recognized her copper-fire hair, and her small stature. She was barely five feet tall. Slowly she walked toward me, in a kirtle of forest green belted with a yellow cord. Her eyes were focused on the floor.

I smiled, but she did not look up, did not meet my gaze. Bryce's comment came back to me. "Do not be shocked." Of what should I not be shocked? Why would she not look at me? What was wrong?

"Ahrethane?"

My voice stopped her, but still her face was turned down. On her pale cheeks I saw a reflection, almost a glow.

Some trick of the light, I thought.

Now Bryce spoke, his voice low, so gentle as to startle me. "Ahrethane."

I glanced at my brother, intrigued at the affection in his tone, and when I looked back to Ahrethane she was also looking at me.

"God!" I said, as I stumbled an unthinking step backward.

"Ruenn!" Bryce snapped. "It's Ahrethane! There is no danger here!"

I could not spare another glance for my brother, but I saw Ahrethane tremble and knew my reaction had caused it. A knife blade of regret stabbed me. I'd hurt her, though not by intent.

"I'm sorry," I said to her. "It's just...."

"It's all right, Ruenn." She responded in a voice soft and lilting and fully familiar. "Now you know why we did not meet you at your landing."

"Yes," I said. And, "Can you.... Are you able...to see anything?"

"Strangely enough, better than before. If differently."

"How did this happen?"

Bryce it was who answered. "During the confrontation between Cha-lathar and Vohanna in the throne room. When Ahrethane clutched onto me to thwart my attack. There was some kind of transference of power. *Most* of it went from me to her."

I noted Bryce's emphasis on the "most" but did not question him on it now.

"For me, it's not solely the eyes," Ahrethane said. "My magic. It's changed. Not earth magic anymore. Not *toir'in-or* sorcery either. I... haven't quite learned to use it. Only for small tasks. I have a feeling that when I do I'll be much more powerful than before." She gave a wry smile. "I'm not sure I like that."

"Can you handle milkstones now?" I asked, remembering a time when she could not.

She answered with a demonstration. From a pocket in her kirtle she drew out four small white stones and showed them to me glistening on her palm. I imagined they were the *toir'in-or* that had come out of Bryce's body.

Ahrethane focused her attention on her hand, her lips thinning with concentration. Then the stones...floated. My eyebrows lifted.

The milkstones began to spin. Fast. Faster. Blurring.

Ahrethane looked up again. The tiny smile playing around her mouth bothered me. Her strange new gaze bothered me more. I recalled the molten silver flame that had filled Bryce's eyes when he served as Vohanna's Bane-thrall. The same light glittered now in Ahrethane's sockets, but that was not the worst of it. Ahrethane *had* no eyes, merely black holes filled like cups with horrid light.

"Only for small tasks," she repeated. "But the power is coming to me. You'll need me against Vessoth."

I wondered how she knew about Vessoth. I wondered many things.

CHAPTER TWELVE
JOURNEY TO NIMERU

I watched the woman, Shai, seat herself in the *Khiang's* iron encased Pilot room. There had been a time in Nyshphal's history, not long ago, when these rooms were often made of glass and stood on the open decks of ships. The Witch's War had changed that. According to long standing tradition on Talera, the Pilot Caste, consisting of those who were selected and trained from youth in the use of *toir'in-or* charged crystals to guide sky craft, was sacrosanct. No nation attacked or threatened Pilots deliberately, on pains of having all their own Pilots refuse to fly for them.

Vohanna's armies, many of whom had come from outside Talera, had not honored tradition. They had killed Nyshphalian Pilots wherever they could. Too, cannon loaded with explosive shot were not as discriminating as arrows or blades, or even ballista. More Pilots had begun to be killed by accident. As a result, the old style Pilot chambers had been mostly replaced with spherical iron rooms embedded in a ship's upper deck and supported in a framework that allowed the sphere to rotate left and right. A large viewport was the sole vulnerable point, but it was often made of triple reinforced glass that offered considerable protection. Grills to either side of the viewport allowed in air, and sound so the Pilot could hear commands from the deck.

It was into such a room that Shai now tucked herself. I was curious about her training as a Pilot, and how she had come to abandon the Caste to serve Chalathar. The Pilot Caste is a force unto itself on Talera, wealthy and influential far beyond its numbers. There is a Pilot's school in Timmuzz, for example, but it owes no allegiance to the empress of Nyshphal. Nor did one hear much about the secretive Caste. I knew only that the elders of the society had some way to detect those children who showed promise for the life, and to be so selected was both an honor for the child and a financial windfall for the parents.

Very few Pilots ever left the Caste once they were members. In fact, I'd never heard of one until Shai, although I understood selectees sometimes washed out during training and were dismissed from the society. Diken Graye was one such. Diken was a brave man, a skilled warrior and intelligent. Yet his mind had proved unsuitable for whatever reason to the talents and disciplines required of a Pilot.

Shai was also unusual in that she was a woman. The vast majority of Pilots were males. They might be from many species, but they were males. I didn't know if this was because of some cultural bias, or something biological, or for some other reason entirely. Perhaps one day I would find out. Not today. I didn't think asking Shai would do any good. The Pilot Caste is notorious for being closed mouthed about their society. In fact, to 'Pilot' something is sometimes used as slang for keeping it for yourself.

With muscular hands grown strangely delicate, Shai reached to the four *toir'in-or* charged crystal wands that powered the ship's lift and stroked them to brilliance. Under her touch they began to spin, and power flared through the network of steel cables running from the Pilot's chamber to the rudder and the flaps that helped our sails control angles of ascent and descent.

The flaps were a new innovation developed in Nyshphal by Arca Heskern and her fellows. In peacetime, such could not have been done without permission of the Pilot Caste. But many of the Caste members at the college in Timmuzz had been killed during Vohanna's siege. No one had time to follow proper procedures, or to insist that they *be* followed. Heskern had informed the Caste of the changes after most of our ships had already been fitted with them.

Even though there'd been a war going on that would affect all of Talera, the issue had still ruffled feathers among the Caste leadership. Both Heskern and Rannon spent quite a lot of time soothing those feathers. Ridiculous, yes, but very Human, I suppose. In this case, "Human" meant most all of the intelligent races of this world.

Under Shai's caress, the ship vibrated, then rocked slightly in its berth. I felt the moment when she broke free of the ground, when she became a creature of air rather than land. Shai grasped the wheel then, her face a picture of intense concentration. It was interesting that she seemed completely familiar with the new flap designs. I'd not thought the word of them had spread widely yet. It wasn't the first time Shai had surprised me; I doubted it would be the last. As we began our climb toward a rendezvous with Nimeru, I shut the heavy door of the chamber and left the woman to her work.

Up on the battleship's deck, I joined Munt, Diken Graye and Valyan Tiersal near the bow. Not far away stood Shai's companions, Rence and Volek. Full canvas filled our masts, the maroon sails stretched taut with the early afternoon wind. I heard the creaking of the rigging, the occasional flap-flap of canvas in the breeze. Nothing unusual.

We did not go straight up toward where the moon of Nimeru would rise in half a dozen dhaur. The ship could not manage such a steep ascent and we would not reach the height needed the first night anyway. Instead, we spiraled in and out of scattered clouds, climbing higher with each round toward the upper reaches of Talera's atmosphere.

The first few dhaur fell behind us and we went below to eat terval steak and bhurl. The terval is a type of Taleran cattle whose ancestors had certainly originated on Earth. Bhurl is a nut with a meat that tastes like black beans. I imagined nothing quite like it ever grew on my home world.

The lure of our strange voyage would not let us linger after the meal in conversation over cups of Verhlis tea, however. Soon, we returned to the main deck, where some of us diced or played other games of chance while the rest paced and watched and waited with restless minds. The moments crawled.

We passed the highest point any Nyshphalian vessel had ever recorded. The clouds dissipated, leaving behind a pure expanse of turquoise sky. The temperature grew steadily warmer. Valyan wiped a trickle of sweat from his brow. Diken and I shed the rawhide dusters we'd worn against the chill of the lower altitudes. I had experienced this phenomenon before, but never so strongly. On Talera, because one is getting measurably closer to the sun as you mount up through the air, it gets hotter instead of colder.

Also unlike Earth, there is no drop off in oxygen content as you climb through Talera's sky. I had been informed of a possible reason for this, although I'd not seen the phenomenon myself. There is apparently a species of Taleran plant that actually floats through the air in vast, cloud-like masses. The plants produce a bladder that functions much like a balloon filled with helium. The reason I'd not seen them is that these masses are located solely around the equator and I'd never crossed it in an airship. Who knew why the plant's range should be so restricted.

I gave some consideration then to greater mysteries of Talera. To create this artificial world the Asadhie had performed miraculous feats of engineering. They had built a sun, for goodness sake, one that looked and performed much like a true star but which they'd leashed to their own demands. How did that sun generate heat? How did it change colors, as it was changing now toward emerald to usher in the spring? How could it appear to rise and set like a normal sun?

What were the moons? Were they rocky orbs, like Earth's Luna? Or something else? How had the atmospheric shield holding back the poison gases of the outer atmosphere been constructed?

I knew gas giant planets could be many, many times larger than Earth. If you were to form a world the size of Earth at the center of such a giant, there would still be a vast area of gas surrounding it. Room enough, I imagined, for fake moons and a fake sun. Of course, I did not know the actual size of Talera. Perhaps it was larger than Earth. Perhaps smaller. I knew the gravity was not recognizably different between the two planets.

It occurred to me then, if the Asadhie had made a sun they could surely alter gravity. That meant comparing Earth and Talera on the basis of relative gravity was useless. I shook my head. Such questions could not be answered through reason. Facts were needed. I had to see for myself. If we were indeed able to reach Nimeru then the first facts about the underlying nature of this world and its creators might finally begin to appear.

There was, as well, another issue troubling me, and I did not think a landing on Nimeru would help settle it. If Vohanna had truly been an Asadhie. If Chalathar and Vessoth *were* Asadhie. Then how was it that they seemed immensely less powerful now than they would have had to be to construct Talera? Had they *forgotten* what it was like to be Gods? Had something happened to strip them of their once vast powers, or of at least some of those powers? Or were the beings who claimed now to be Asadhie merely imposters? Was even Chalathar lying? I'd liked him when we met, but in truth could not say I knew him.

"Look below," Valyan called from where he stood by the *Khiang's* railing, and I put aside my impossible-to-answer questions and joined him there.

Though the setting sun still lit our ship, night had fallen on the land far below. An occasional wink of lights marked cities and towns, but Talera was only sparsely populated and between the faint signs of civilization stretched swathes of blackness where wild climes predominated. Against the dark lands washed the seas, and from here those waters glowed faintly blue with phosphorescence. It was beautiful, but also a little frightening.

Night eventually caught up to us on our journey and the moons rose, one after another, then fled the sky again far above us. Nimeru was first, arriving at dusk, when the darkness is not yet complete. Afterward came Sieona, dressed in turquoise and known in many cultures as the "Storm Queen." Sieona rises at the Taleran eighteenth dhaur, which corresponds to about ten o'clock at night on Earth. At midnight, the 20th dhaur, Tisiminna took the sky in golden majesty. Her name means "beauty," and like many beauties she has her courtiers, two smaller orbs that circle her constantly. Last came Rath, largest of the moons and shedding a light of brutal red. Rath is known as the "Warrior," and his color does remind one of war. He rises at the second dhaur, at what would be two o'clock on Earth.

Rath's appearance reminded me that too few of us had slept much lately. I ordered everyone but a skeleton crew to bed, although I don't know how universally the order was obeyed. I tried to obey it myself and tossed and turned for just a little while before drifting off. No dreams disturbed me this night.

Not long after dawn, the noises of an awakening ship brought me back to consciousness. I finished the usual morning rituals quickly and ate a bit of fruit and cheese for breakfast. Then I returned to the *Khiang's* deck to find the sun burnishing the ship's sails and planks with a tinge of emerald. The spring passage was upon us, and the sun would grow more and more green over the next ten-day. I was glad for the people far below us in Nyshphal; they'd suffered a rough winter and warmer days would be welcome. It did not seem likely that the coming of spring would make much difference to those of us embarked upon this journey.

I saw Cailif Ostt, our usual Pilot, standing near the bow and looking both intrigued with our journey and a little uncomfortable that he wasn't at the controls. Cailif hailed from the Stone Cities, far south of Talera's equator. It was a land I'd never visited but of which I'd read much. The Stone Cities were considered one of the more advanced Taleran societies. The people I'd met from there had all been dark of skin and with other physical characteristics that reminded me of sub-Saharan Africans on Earth. The Asadhie had sampled widely of Earth's population when they first brought Humans to Talera.

"You look like a man with nothing to do," I said, coming up to him.

He shrugged. "I feel displaced. Being out here. But," he gestured at the sky, "I'd never have been able to take us this high. Officially, no one ever has. Shai is quite amazing."

I smiled at the admiration in his voice, then left him to his considerations and walked the deck to see how the rest of the crew was doing. Once in a while I glanced over the *Khiang's* side. Still we were climbing, with Shai somehow managing to keep us in position for the wind to push steadily at our sails. Our pace had slowed, though, and the ship moved more sluggishly than before. I wondered how our new Pilot was coping with the strain that must be tearing at her.

Passing Rence near the Pilot's chamber, I stopped to speak with him. He appeared rather miserable.

"How is she?" I asked.

He shrugged. "I took her more water. At least she's been drinking some. The food I left her was untouched."

"Did she say anything?"

"No. I didn't want to interrupt her, break her concentration." His gaze met mine. "She's tough. She's…just never tried anything like this before. Dhaur after dhaur. I don't see how she stands it."

I wished there was something I could say to give Rence a little confidence. I wished more there was something I could do for Shai. I knew of nothing. Our fate lay in the woman's hands, or, more precisely, in her mind as it powered the *toir 'in-or* wands.

Not only our fate. Perhaps the fate of all Talera.

CHAPTER THIRTEEN

LOOMING THREAT

The day passed and tensions grew as our pace slowed further. I spoke desultorily with friends and crew. I nibbled at terval jerky and gnawed at passal. Passal is a Taleran "travel" food, somewhat similar to pemmican, though it is fish based rather than red meat based. Fish, fat, and various kinds of berries and nuts are ground together into a fine mixture and then packed tightly into rawhide sacks to harden. The resulting mixture is not terribly tasty but it will keep for years and is relatively light to carry. That last was important on a trip such as ours.

Only certain fish are suitable for making passal, most commonly the slab-sided jergal, a huge, ugly, bottom dwelling river fish that I did not think descended from any Earth species. The iskit is the most common berry used in the food. This resembles a small, hard blackberry and grows wild all over Talera. The nuts included are often walnuts or pecans, which are little changed on Talera from their Earthly origins. Bhurl is sometimes used but gives the mixture a very different taste, and not one I much liked.

Frequently, I glanced toward the Pilot's chamber. There was little to see of Shai except for a vague shadow behind the viewing port, but I sensed the titanic battle she waged there in that small iron room. Piloting an airship is no routine, mechanical act. It requires near constant attention. No wonder a relative few are suited to the task.

As evening began to seek us out, an impatient Munt climbed to the crow's nest to keep watch for Nimeru. If our trip was to be successful, this should be the night we would reach her.

"There she is!" shouted Munt suddenly.

We all lifted our eyes to heaven then. The sun was sinking steadily, painting multicolored bands of rich light along the horizon. Through that light the mist-blue moon came crawling quickly skyward. The crack in its surface was visible as a black, jagged tear, and I could make out features on the surface I had not previously noticed.

Diken saw the same thing. "What are those dark areas?" he asked from beside me. "I've never seen them before."

I shrugged. "They look like seas but they're too regular. Almost perfect circles."

"Maybe that's why Nimeru seems dimmer than usual," Valyan said.

I nodded. "Could be. We'll know more soon enough."

"What do you think we'll find there?" Diken asked.

The warriors Rence and Volek had come up to us as we stood talking, and it was the gaunt one, Rence, who answered.

"A prison."

"And Vessoth?" I asked.

Now it was Rence who shrugged. "I almost hope not."

"What exactly does this Vessoth look like?" Diken asked.

Rence shrugged again. "They call him the Snake God. I suppose there's a reason."

"I've seen a statue of him," I said. "Definitely snake like. With a head somewhat like a cobra [5]. The Asadhie can switch forms, though. I saw Vohanna do it. She had extra bodies stored in her pyramid."

"They would not have imprisoned Vessoth with any of his surrogate forms," Volek said.

"If Vessoth has found himself allies as Chalathar suspects, he may have obtained some of those forms by now," I said. "Besides, Vohanna could also *possess* beings. Do we need to fear that from Vessoth as well?"

Rence nodded. "Most likely. But after what happened with Vohanna in the battle at Timmuzz, Chalathar developed a test for such a thing."

"A test?" I asked, feeling skeptical. I remembered how perfectly Vohanna had mimicked Rannon's brother, Kuurus Jystral, at the end of the Witch's War. Not even Rannon had suspected the exchange.

Rence held up his hand, the back of it turned toward me. I saw he wore a ring with a small ruby stone at its center.

"Milkstones respond to milkstones," he said. "A speck of *toir'in-or* is embedded in this ruby. The ring will warm when brought close to Vessoth's *toir'in-or*. This way, we can identify him. And know if he takes someone over."

"How close is close?" I asked.

"A few paces," Rence admitted. "It's not perfect but is better than nothing."

"You have more of those?" Diken asked, rather hopefully, I thought.

"Shai has one. Chalathar didn't have time for more."

"Then I guess we'll have to rely on you two if there's any question," I said.

---

5   Cobras are among the animals brought to Talera from Earth by the Asadhie. See entry 5 in the Taleran Encyclopedia at the end of this work.

It occurred to me, though, that perhaps there was something better than these rings aboard for detecting *toir'in-or*. Below decks in my cabin, Ahrethane waited. In Timmuzz, where I had spoken with the efrinore and Bryce, we had considered ways to get her aboard the *Khiang* without anyone noticing her sorcerous eyes. I'd eventually remembered a heavy veil Rannon once wore to a fete. It was of dark grey lace, thick enough to hide most of the glow from Ahrethane's sockets. I was thinking now, however, of the milkstones Ahrethane had brought with her. Could they not also be used to detect the presence of Vessoth? It seemed likely.

"Captain!"

Startled from my ruminations, I looked up toward the crow's nest where Munt kept watch.

"Captain," the lad called again, and pointed. "Ahead of us!"

I strode toward the bow, the others with me. The last light of day hung in the sky but was quickly giving way to the blue sheen of Nimeru. In the distance, above us and between our ship and the now looming orb of the moon, a very large…something drifted toward us, spilling smaller objects behind it as it came.

Valyan shaded his eyes. "What by the hells are those?"

In a leathern holster nailed to one of the forward cannon mounts hung a spy-scope for ranging targets. I grabbed it up, thrust it to my eye, then jerked it abruptly down again.

"Prepare for battle!" I shouted. "The fight's coming to us!"

CHAPTER FOURTEEN

KILLING SKY

Someone handed me a longbow. It was of yellow wood, of the traentha tree, reinforced with terval horn and strung with a silken cord. I hooked a quiver of scarlet arrows over a shoulder, nocked one and let three more dangle between the fingers of my left hand for quick reloading. Valyan and Rence had similar bows, and Diken and Munt and Volek carried crossbows locked down on bright quarrels. Around us, too, other warriors were armed and ready. The cannon and ballistas were loaded, as well, the cannon with grape shot for close range work.

We would need all the weapons we could muster.

Through the spy-scope I'd measured our enemies. First there was the strangest thing, a long, wide ribbon of pale flesh that undulated through the sky high above us. From that monster's back spilled a horde of smaller creatures, winged beasts like dragonflies grown to the size of buffalo. Mounted on these rode Sporn warriors, and worse things.

The dragonflies came down toward us in swift free fall, until they reached our level and caught themselves in a blur of wings. They surged toward us then, hundreds of them, and I saw a last flash of sunlight stab from the weapons of their riders. Then the sun was gone and by the watered moonlight of Nimeru we waited for war.

A clot of darkness swept upon us where we stood in armor. I saw only outlines against a dim blue glow. But I heard the thrumming of terrible wings, close enough to echo among our sails.

I let free a first command. "Light!"

Torches and lamps burst awake at my shout, flaring up brilliantly, throwing the ship and its surroundings into stark relief. The giant dragonflies shied back from the flames, their many faceted eyes glittering. I saw their riders, lances lifted for hurling.

I shouted for a different form of light. "Fire!"

Readied fuses hissed into life; the cannon let loose. Grapeshot tore hellish holes through the massed ranks of our foes. At the same instant, I snapped up my bow and let fly an arrow. The tlatel wood shaft punched through a dragonfly wing, tore a Sporn from its back. I heard the high pitched ululations I'd learned to recognize as Sporn screams.

There was no time to reload the cannon and the flying insects came surging back with the Sporns mounted in ivory saddles upon them. Our enemies still outnumbered us. Their spears began to crash around us. A lance headed with bone splintered up fragments of deck at my feet. Another took Volek through the throat and hurled him back, his crossbow falling from dead fingers. I shot the one who had launched that spear between his eight eyes with a crimson arrow.

Now the Sporns began dropping upon our deck from the backs of their mounts, the heads of spears and the curved blades of their yataghans flashing in the torchlight. I sent two more arrows flying but could not see if they struck true. With no time to raid my quiver for fresh shafts, I threw down the longbow and ripped free my sword. I'd taken this blade—etched in silver with alien runes—from a dead Minotaur warrior in the forests of Vohan. Though made from some incredibly hard metal whose origins I did not know, it was slenderer and lighter than its three feet of steel would suggest. It had served me well.

Two Sporn warriors came skittering toward us, claws clacking on the wooden deck. Diken and Valyan leaped in front of me, caught the attackers' weapons on their own in a chingle of clashing steel. I almost laughed. There were many foes; no one could protect me from them all.

A Sporn with four blades in its four arms sprang over the heads of its companions and dropped toward me. Munt shot it with his crossbow, the quarrel tearing half the thing's face away. The beast kept coming, blades hacking. Insects are hard to kill, and Sporns are more insect than anything else.

"Leave some for me, lad!" I shouted, stepping past Munt.

I caught the flailing blades of the wounded beast against the rune-sword, sent them snapping back from the impact, then spun my own weapon up and around with both hands on the hilt. The creature's body was open to attack and I cut him up from abdomen to thorax. Silver blood and silver intestines came spilling. The smell of ammonia and other corrosives exploded in my nostrils. I stepped around the gore, caught one of the beast's curved swords as he dropped it.

Now I had two blades.

The Sporns are taller on average than men, but not as heavy. Not, I believed, as intelligent. They do not fight like men. They do not wear armor. Their sole strategy is to overwhelm with numbers. So I had imagined.

I heard a strange keening begin to grow as we cut our way through Sporn after Sporn. They outnumbered us three to one but it was not going to be enough to overcome us. I thought the weird sound marked their rising fear. Then something tore a man apart not three steps from me.

Through the spy-scope earlier, I had glimpsed other things besides Sporns on the backs of some of the giant dragonflies. I saw those things up close now; I'd been wrong about them. They *were* Sporns, but of some new type, bigger even than the norm of their race. Eight feet tall, perhaps, and built far heavier. Their eyes were green rather than the pus-white of their fellows. They wore armor. They carried targes. They fought in concert, like soldiers in a shield wall. I sensed the keening, somehow, held them together.

"Munt!" I shouted to be heard over the racking din. The boy stood at my shoulder, as he had since fight's beginning. "Tell Bryce it's time." He nodded, raced off.

I gathered Valyan and Diken to me. And Rence, and others. We charged into the enemy's battle wall. They had already taken a grim toll of our ranks and now they met us with blooded steel. Our blades hacked, blunted against the enemy shields. But we drove them back. I felt the burn of Sporn blood, saw smoking droplets spatter. The stench was like a slaughterhouse wetted with acid. I snorted to clear the sting from my nostrils.

The keening of our enemies spiked louder. Their eyes began to glow; my sweat turned cold. I'd seen such a lambent green often enough on Talera. It was generally associated with sorcery. I did not like it.

Where's Bryce?

The Sporn soldiery charged. Soldiers is how I thought of them. They were nearly alone now. Most of the typical Sporns had fallen to our blades. Enough of the new kind remained to give us hell.

We retreated slowly before their advance. They were cutting their way toward the iron bubble in the deck that marked the Pilot's chamber. I recognized then their intelligence. Or the intelligence that guided them. They wanted Shai but could not be allowed to reach her. Without her, Nimeru was unobtainable. Even a break in her concentration might mean the end of our journey.

As I was about to yell out for a desperate countercharge, I heard Bryce's voice bellow: "Clear for fire!"

Our crew knew what that meant; we'd trained it into them. Everywhere on the deck, they threw themselves flat. The Sporns paused. For an instant they were confused, and an instant was all we needed. I'd held Bryce in reserve for just such a surprise moment. He'd balked at what he called "hiding below decks." But without his good right hand he was no swordsman or bowman for a face to face fight.

He didn't need a right hand for what he did now. His left grasped a lanyard and pulled it.

In Timmuzz, before meeting with Bryce and Ahrethane, I'd made a suggestion to Arca Heskern, our resident scientist and engineer. Why not place a few cannon on lifts that could be raised from the hold onto the deck for use in repelling boarders. In scarcely a dhaur she'd gone me one better, had not only put in the lifts with an easily operated pulley system, but had set the cannon on swivel plates to aid in aiming.

Bryce stood behind a pair of such cannon now, Munt by his side, and when my brother pulled that lanyard the guns unleashed a storm of nails directly into the packed mass of Sporns. I had seen brooms sweep more cleanly, but never more effectively. Armor and shields could not with-stand that blow. Flesh disintegrated. The coordination of the enemy's attack made our counter even more effective.

I rose slowly to my feet, smoke drifting across me. The deck streamed with entrails and limbs. The stench was hellish. Not one Sporn soldier remained alive. Only a few of the other kind were left, and those not for long.

I went to Bryce, clapped him on the shoulder while nodding at Munt.

"Well done, gentlemen," I congratulated them.

Munt looked a little ill at the carnage. He stumbled away to be sick over the rail, and I did not embarrass him by appearing to notice.

Bryce gazed at me. "Those green eyes," he said. "On some of the Sporns."

"I noticed," I replied. "That luminescent color. It smacks of sorcery."

"The Thye Vessoth."

I started. *Of course*. I remembered of a sudden a temple on Earth, and a creature I'd come to know as a Thye Vessoth. A reptile. A bat-eared devil with stone blue eyes. They were priests of the Vessoth cult. Such a creature's death had played a role in bringing Bryce and I to Talera.

"*Thye Vessoth* sorcery," I said, as much to myself as to my brother.

Bryce nodded in agreement. "I think they were controlling these Sporns somehow. That's why they fought so differently from the others."

"It makes sense. But why not come themselves? Their magic might have turned this battle."

"Vohanna always called the Thye Vessoth 'cowards.' She never trusted them in her armies."

"Cowards? Maybe so. I *hope* so. Maybe they just had different goals than Vohanna."

Again Bryce nodded. "Could be."

I shouted an order then for the men to clear the deck of the battle's aftermath. Too, I wanted to count our losses, find how badly we'd been hurt. I also wanted men in the rigging to watch for any reappearance of the monster dragonflies. The dragonflies themselves had not behaved aggressively and had been left far in the ship's wake during the fight, but I didn't want to discount any danger, including the possibility of more Sporns remaining with their huge mounts.

"I think something's wrong," a female voice said.

I turned, saw that Ahrethane had come on deck, wearing her obscuring veil so as not to frighten the men with her uncanny eyes. It was she who had spoken. Bryce paled at her words.

A dash of cold caressed my own neck. "What do you mean?" I asked.

I heard her sniff at the wind. "The air. It's…changing."

I looked around. The ship was still rising, sails straining in the strong breeze. The sky was dark, though brightening bit by bit as Nimeru climbed higher in the sky toward us. I took a sniff myself. Other than the acrid bite of gunpowder and the acidic tang of Sporn blood mixed with Human gore and sweat, I smelled nothing. I felt nothing.

Then I saw, just above the highest reach of our masts, a thin and wavery line of blue mist.

"I—"

Some force reached out and took hold of us.

CHAPTER FIFTEEN

A STRANGENESS OF AIR

The very tip of our highest mast struck the line of mist and disappeared. The ship shuddered, then lurched hard upward. I was thrown to all fours; others went tumbling around me. I heard screams of panic, a few more of pain. One of the cannon Bryce had used to such good effect broke its moorings and plunged through the railing in a shriek of tortured wood.

Again the ship lurched upward. I was tossed over onto my back. The top of the mast was gone now; the crow's nest struck the blue mist next. A milky light flared at the point of contact and the wooden structure winked out. I realized suddenly what was happening.

Bryce grabbed my shoulder. "Tell Shai!" he shouted. "We have to abandon—"

"No!" I shouted back. "It's a gate. We're going through a gate!"

Bryce looked up. Recognition rushed into his face.

I thrust to my knees. "Stay calm!" I shouted at the crew. "It won't hurt—"

Sound stopped. I could feel my mouth moving but could hear nothing. Beside me, Bryce was frozen. A tingling coursed down my body. The air turned to gel and for an instant bands of iron wrapped around my chest. I couldn't breathe. Then the instant passed.

Sound returned. Movement returned. The ship gave a last shudder and, like a cork coming out of a bottle, instantly surged higher into the sky.

I found my feet. "It's all right!" I shouted to the panicked men and women around me. "We're safe. We passed through some kind of barrier." *Like the atmospheric shield*, I thought. I didn't say that part out loud.

"A transition layer," Ahrethane said, coming up beside Bryce and myself. "Some strange variant on a sphere gate. Smeared out in a thin sheet. It must separate the level at which the moons move from the normal atmosphere below."

"*Normal* atmosphere?" I asked, then realized what she meant.

We were no longer in any kind of normal sky. There were no more clouds anywhere except below us. The ambient light had taken on a brassy sheen. The air seemed less rich with oxygen than before and it smelled and tasted metallic. It *felt* different, almost…greasy. There was no wind either, not even the faintest breeze, and the sails hung limp on our masts. Our climb was leveling out as well.

Our climb was leveling out!

Immediately fearful for the success of our mission, I spun about in search of Nimeru. I found her. Little Blue Dreamer was no longer little. She'd swollen to fill half our horizon and the crack across her face showed as a black chasm much wider at top than bottom. She appeared to be rushing swiftly upon us, but it did not seem to me that we were high enough to catch her. With no wind for our sails, how could we make the rendezvous we had come so far to make?

I turned, thinking to ask Shai what we should do, but Rence waited there and seemed to read the question from my mind.

"Don't worry," he said, looking calmer now than he had throughout most of our trip. "Shai knows what she's doing. Chalathar told us we only had to get close to Nimeru and would then be drawn into her wake. We can figure out after where to land."

"Land!" Bryce said. "How will we possibly know where? How do we begin to seek Vessoth?"

Rence glanced toward my brother, his gaze flat, his irises the color of mescal. "I expect he'll find us."

CHAPTER SIXTEEN

ONCE UPON A BLUE MOON

I hoped Rence was wrong in expecting Vessoth to find us before we found him, but he was right about the effect the passing moon would have upon our ship. Shai might have been able to provide the *Khiang* with more lift through her manipulation of the *toir 'in-or* charged wands, but with no wind for our sails we had no control over direction. We were adrift. But, as Nimeru crossed the sky no more than half a dozen ver-langs above us, ten miles or so in Earth measurements, the prow of the ship turned and we were drawn inevitably along in the small planetoid's wake.

I knew about gravity, of course, but Nimeru was literally surrounded by the nameless gas giant planet from which Talera and its sun and moons had been formed. How would gravity work in such a situation? But, whatever force was involved, we were now within Nimeru's orbit and I figured Shai could land us. Then I received a pleasant surprise as a gust of oxygen-rich air rushed over us and filled our sails. The moon had its own atmosphere, separate from the strange sky we had crossed through to get here.

So, with our sails once more bellied full of wind and Shai at the controls, we began our descent toward the orb many worshiped as the goddess of poetry and love. I did not expect to find either of those things here, and it was for other reasons that I closely studied the surface of this new world we fast approached.

I already knew Nimeru was artificial, but its nature became absolutely clear upon close examination. For as far as the eye could see, hexagon after hexagon of what appeared to be vast tiles nestled flush against each other. Each tile was made of a polished, clear substance much like cut crystal, and somewhat more than half were lit with an inner glow of pal-est blue. The rest were smoky gray, like the burnt glass cover of an old lantern. These were clumped together in large dark circles and ovals, re-minding me of the Sea of Tranquility and the other lunar maria of Earth's moon, which had at one time been mistaken for actual seas. Even though we could see pretty well by its remaining light, Nimeru was definitely much dimmer now than before it had cracked. This must be the reason. The hexagons were the source of the orb's glow.

We were dropping swiftly but were still far enough above Nimeru's surface to see the curve of its horizon. As far as I could tell, the moon was perfectly round, and almost perfectly smooth except for one massive feature that marred the picture. A great ridge, like a mountain range freshly thrust up into the sky, ran the length of the planetoid, growing higher and more jagged as it zigzagged toward the moon's north pole. It was the crack itself, and from the way the material was rent outward it was clear the explosion which birthed it had come from inside.

Inside Nimeru. Vessoth's prison.

Young Munt stood behind me where I leaned against the *Khiang's* rail. Vohn Carbiz, who'd been relay man for the *Khiang's* Captain long before I took over command of the ship, had been killed in our recent battle with the Sporns. As a result, Munt had gotten his first battlefield promotion, and now I gave him his first order to pass on.

"Go for me and tell Shai to follow the rift as far north as she can. Tell her I believe we'll find what we seek at that point."

He nodded and sped off to do as I'd bid.

Bryce also stood near me, and Diken Graye and Valyan had joined us after having some minor battle wounds treated by our Phoros, our healer. Rence had wandered off. I knew not where. Ahrethane had gone below decks to avoid the questioning stares of the crew, many of whom seemed curious about what she hid beneath her rich veil.

"You think we'll find Vessoth at the end of the rift?" Bryce asked.

"I think we'll find him inside Nimeru," I said.

Bryce and Diken nodded.

Valyan pointed to something below us on the moon's surface. "Look there."

We looked, saw an irregularity, something surely not natural to the moon, something not caused either by the crack that had so recently torn it open. I leaned over the rail for a better look, and thirsted to know the story behind what I saw.

"It's an airship!" Diken exclaimed.

Indeed it was, though wrecked and scattered across half a verlang of Nimeru's surface. I saw broken planks, shattered masts and shredded sails. The vessel had snapped in twain and the bow and stern lay a good hundred tahng apart. I could see no bodies but doubted many of the crew could have escaped such a crash. Of course, there was no telling how long ago the wreck had occurred and the dead might have simply decayed to dust.

"Anyone recognize its nationality?" Diken asked.

"It is a ship of my people," a voice said, and I turned to see Shai standing behind us.

The woman's gold-dust skin was pale, her eyes sunken. Sweat had plastered her hair to her skull, though it was drying now. She looked gaunt as a starving wolf. Rence hovered protectively beside her, as if afraid she might collapse at any moment. Despite the strength the voyage had leeched from her, however, her voice was strong as she continued: "I've turned the *Khiang* over to your Pilot. The flight from here on should be no more than he is used to."

I nodded. "You should rest. Regain your strength."

"I am regaining it now."

I felt one eyebrow threatening to arch but managed to fend the gesture off. Had I gone through what she'd gone through I would have wanted to sleep for a week. But my ways were not hers. She was, as Rence had declared, "tough." Or could there be something more to it? After all, she had a powerful friend in Chalathar the Asadhie. Who knew what skills he might have taught her.

The wrecked ship was falling behind us but was not forgotten.

"You spoke of your people," I said to Shai after a bit. "If they sailed that ship here, I'd like to know more about them."

"You know where lies Thresh?"

"Yes. Though I've never been there. It's a continent far west and south of Nyshphal."

"The southernmost tip of Thresh is part of a broad peninsula called Zaiapeth. Three big islands lie off its coast, each larger than the one before. Turani, Yesarth, Urash. There are smaller islands as well. My people were born from the volcano that built Yesarth." She smiled. "So it is proclaimed. We have settled most of the isles, though. Also, Zaiapeth. Our capital is Sarthia."

"I've heard of the Sarthians," Diken said. "Not quite an empire but more than a federation of cities. They are considered a power in the south. Even the Klar leave them alone."

Both Shai and Rence smiled.

"Rence is also of your people," I said, making it a statement.

Shai nodded. "His family and mine have long been linked."

"So. You knew that crashed airship was here?"

"Yes."

"Is that why you felt confident in being able to Pilot an airship to Nimeru?"

"Yes."

"Any...information you'd care to add?"

"What kind of information do you seek?"

I smiled, not without a bit of frustration behind it. "Where I come from we have a saying about trying to pry details out of someone as closed mouthed as you. We compare it to 'pulling teeth.' I'd like to know the *story* behind that ship."

Shai watched me for a moment, then vented a puff of air that expressed her own frustration. It was clear she didn't want to talk about the airship, but also clear I wasn't going to leave it alone.

"My mother was the Pilot," she said at last. "We Sarthians have long been explorers. About twenty years back our government decided to systematize those explorations. To keep records, bring back samples, produce maps. It was for the good of all intelligent kind, we told ourselves. But we are not without our pride.

"Some fifteen years ago it was decided that a journey to one of the moons would show the world what we were capable of. Nimeru was chosen. No one had any inkling of its legendary connection to Vessoth at that time. Nor would anyone have believed it to be true if they had.

"Mother was selected as Pilot because she was the best in our family. We overstepped. We did not have the techniques for rigging and maneuvering ships that are available now. Some of those, you Nyshphalians invented just recently. The ship made it this far before someone apparently made an error and it crashed. Mother died on impact. We assume most of the crew did as well. Nothing more was ever heard."

I frowned. "If no one ever returned, how do you know what happened? How did you even know they reached Nimeru?"

Shai hesitated for a long moment. "I…. I felt the moment when my mother died. I was…in contact with her."

In contact?

My first thought was "radio." I rejected that idea quickly. I doubted anyone on Talera had anything approaching that kind of technology. So if not radio, then what?

"Telepathy!" I exclaimed.

Now Shai frowned. "I do not know that word. We call it sendahtia. Mind to mind communication."

I nodded. "Same thing."

She shrugged.

A thought occurred to me. Could some kind of telepathic faculty explain the abilities of the Pilot Caste to work the *toir'in-or* charged power wands? Could it even be the reason behind the ability of Talera's sorcerers to manipulate milkstones themselves? But then, Bryce had used such stones. As Vohanna's Bane-thrall he had demonstrated incredible power. Yet he had no telepathic talent. I certainly had none. No one in our family had ever shown such aptitude.

Icicle fingers suddenly caressed my neck. That last wasn't true. I'd heard stories of family members who "sensed" things. Especially on our father's side of the family. The Scottish side. I'd never given it any consideration before, had imagined it no more than tall tales. There was another thing, too. When Bryce and I had first been separated after being hurled to Talera, I had felt very intensely that he was alive. Had that feeling been no more than a refusal to accept the possibility of his death? Or had there been more to it? And if not through some telepathic like connection, how had I so recently 'heard' the howl indicating that Bryce had awakened?

I remembered something else and the icy feeling at my neck spread. I'd often wondered why the Witch Vohanna had taken such a strong interest in the brothers Maclang. Not Bryce alone, but myself as well. Obviously, she had known what kind of being she could turn Bryce into. What she could bring out of him. Could it have been because of some natural telepathic ability inside him? Did that mean I—

"Dihmus vishka!" Munt cried out. "Look!"

I looked. We all looked. I heard Shai moan. It did not take any mysterious power to know now that the crash of the Sarthian ship had been no accident. The missing crew I'd thought decayed to nothingness by time were not missing at all. Nor were they decayed. They *were* dead. Broken. Twisted. Fresh. As if slaughtered moments before.

Just ahead of us on the surface of Nimeru, I saw a bloody mandala arranged from the bones and flesh of once living beings. At its center, at the point of reintegration where the power of the symbol is considered strongest, there lay the image of a coiled serpent made from decapitated heads, the image of *Vessoth*!

CHAPTER SEVENTEEN
THROUGH THE HAZE

I looked away from the horrid mandala and toward Shai, whose mother was surely part of that brutal exhibit. After a single moan of heart-rending pain, the woman had fallen silent. Now, her face was completely empty of the emotions I would expect to be roiling inside of her.

How young had she been when her mother died? Judging from her appearance, she was no more than about twenty-five years old now. That was in Taleran years.[6] It meant she would have been around twelve on Earth when her mother was lost. Incredibly young by any standard. The worst thing for her had to be that the wound had healed, only to be torn open again in a way no one could have foreseen. It was hard to even imagine the pain of finding out that a mother you believed had died doing what she loved had really died in horror, and had then been "preserved" in some sorcerous fashion so her mutilated body could be used against you fifteen years later.

"We can…land," I said into the void that must fill Shai's being. "Bring the bodies home."

She shook her head. "No! We can't waste more time. The people from that ship are no longer hurting. Vessoth must be stopped before he does worse to others. Then we can see…to the dead."

The name "Vessoth" almost came as a hiss from her lips, and I was glad to know her hotter emotions were still alive inside her cold exterior.

I turned to Valyan and Diken Graye. "We need to get men watching everything. Ground, sky, the ship. Whatever force destroyed the Sarthian vessel must have taken them by surprise. We don't know if the same force is still operating but let's be ready for anything."

Both men nodded and hurried off.

I glanced back at Shai, spoke quietly: "I'd long heard rumors that airships had reached the moons. I guess at least some of those rumors were based upon your mother's journey."

Shai nodded, as if relieved to turn her mind outward to a conversation with me instead of inward to her own thoughts. "Probably. There were

---

6   See Taleran Encyclopedia entry 6 for information on Talera's calendar.

those who knew of the trip. After the failure, it was not much spoken of, however."

"Why?"

Her gaze found mine, bore in. "Do you brag about your mistakes?"

"I suppose not."

"Just so."

"Did your people make any other attempts to reach Nimeru? Or the other moons?"

Shai shook her head. "I would have known."

I nodded myself. Her comment sketched in one more piece of the map I was drawing about Shai. From things she'd said, and from the way Rence acted toward her, I was becoming convinced that she, or her family, or both, were important figures in Sarthian society. How important, I couldn't be sure. I hoped that missing information wouldn't be necessary to the success of our mission.

* * *

Though I feared an attack, whatever had struck down the Sarthian airship so many years before—whether Vessoth or something else—did not put in an appearance? We followed the widening crack in Nimeru's surface until we came to its source, a vast black pit surrounded by jagged peaks of torn moon-crust, which appeared to be made out of some alloy of steel and ceramic. Testifying to the incredible power of the explosion that had raised the peaks, some of them stood nearly as tall as the Lesser Katari Mountains of Nyshphal.

Although the crack had been wide enough in places for the *Khiang* to attempt passing through, there'd been too many ragged edges to risk it. Here, the inside bottom edge of the great pit itself was almost smooth, and the peaks of destruction above were all curved out and away from its center. It was as if a cork had been ejected with tremendous force from a bottle.

A breeze blew steadily from the interior of the moon and I ordered our sails furled so we could hover over the entrance into the world below. A light seeped up from within, a bluish-white glow that hazed the air like fog gathering around streetlamps. The haze shrank one's vision. Even with a spy-scope I could make out nothing of what lay inside Nimeru. I didn't like that.

I glanced questioningly at Shai. She shrugged.

"I vote we don't go in," Diken Graye said, smiling wryly.

"At least there's life inside," Valyan remarked. "I smell it."

I took a whiff of the breeze, caught the scent Valyan was talking about. The air coming out of the interior was damp, and redolent with the odor of growing things, of flowers and mosses and other plants, though I could not have named the varieties.

"Maybe we should consult Ahrethane," Bryce said.

"What if she tells us not to go in?" I asked my brother. "I don't think we really have a choice."

Bryce shrugged.

"Fetch her anyway. I'd feel better with her on deck. Still…" I turned toward Munt. "Tell Cailif to take us in. Slowly!"

Bryce nodded and moved off on his task. Munt relayed the command to our Pilot and within moments we began drifting downward *into* Nimeru. The haze gathered around us, closing us in. Visibility fell to twenty feet, to fifteen, to ten. Shai's hands dropped to the rapiers at her waist; others gripped their weapons, as well, seeking comfort in a place where little was to be had. My own hand found the hilt of the rune-sword.

A hawk-like shriek from something unseen carved the mist, making me jump. At least a dozen similar creatures answered from farther away. Droplets of the haze swirled over and around me, coating my face. The droplets eddied, as if stirred by the movement of something large passing through. I hoped the "something large" was us.

Rence suddenly cursed and spun around, half drawing his kahnnas before halting his movements. I glanced at him and he shook his head sheepishly.

"Nerves," he said.

Then we broke through the mist, came out into open sky. I looked down into the interior of Nimeru. Below us in the air floated a huge face cowled in the hood of a cobra. Its eyes wept blood.

CHAPTER EIGHTEEN

WHEN THE MOON IS HOLLOW ONE CAN TOUCH THE SKY

A collective gasp of fear raced through the crew as the face of the god, Vessoth, loomed below us. In the next instant the image broke apart into hundreds of winged forms that scattered every which way. I saw that the "face" had been made up from the serpent-like bodies of some species of flying reptile. Each of the beasts had four lanceolate wings tipped with talons. "Claw-wings," my mind dubbed the creatures. Their legless bodies were broad, python-like, and mostly brownish-black, but some carried a bright splash of red down their backs bright enough to be mistaken for blood.

For an instant I wondered if the face had merely been some trick of the eyes. Just as quickly I rejected that thought. The formation of the flying creatures had been too precise. The face had too perfectly resembled the statue I'd once seen of the Snake God. Vessoth was sending us another warning. Strangely, I felt this might be a good sign. If he had the power to destroy us, why didn't he? Perhaps he was warning us away because he didn't have the strength to do anything worse. I could hope.

"It's very lovely here," said a voice beside me, and I turned to see that Bryce had indeed brought Ahrethane on deck.

The efrinore wore her grey brocade veil, but though there were no eyes beneath it she was staring straight off from the ship into the heart of Nimeru. She must have missed the image of Vessoth and was focused on something else instead. I turned to look for myself.

I'd been distracted by the illusion of the Snake God's face and what it might mean. Now I *saw* this new world we'd come to. Despite the tension and terror of the voyage we'd completed to get here, one had to admit this was a lovely place. There was no sun but a satiny yellow glow suffused the moon's interior. That light felt warm, like the summer days of childhood I recalled from Earth.

The haze that had fogged our entrance became no more than an ephemeral mist elsewhere inside Nimeru. A good quarter of the interior surface of the sphere could clearly be made out, and where I'd expected to find more of the tiled hexagons packing the moon's outside, I found instead a lush and living jungle. Most of the inside walls were covered with a dense, tropical forest—at least in the visible sections. The trees were not tall but spread broadly in shades of orange and yellow-green. Vines as thick as a man's body threaded their way through that wood.

Under the strange warm light, lakes that gleamed like molten gold dotted the landscape, and between them rushed foaming rivers as big as any I'd seen on Talera. It seemed Vessoth had been imprisoned in a paradise, and I could not help but think of the snake in the Garden of Eden.

Above the vast forest, and in the air all around our ship, thousands of flying forms wheeled and dipped. They were mostly the claw-wings I'd noted before, but there were many others, including something resembling a parrot with an emerald green head and purple body. All avoided the immediate vicinity of the ship, as if wary of a potential predator.

At places in the riotous jungle arose massive struts of metal that thrust straight inward toward the moon's center. Letting my gaze follow one gleaming strut to its other end, I found that the heart of Nimeru was another sphere located within the greater sphere of the moon itself. This lesser orb, perhaps the size of a small city, was also densely wooded, though I scanned one large clearing in which a bright scarlet building squatted.

Not just a building, I realized quickly. *A pyramid!*

The sight drained the warmth from the light around me and cast a pall over my thoughts. Although dressed in red, the structure reminded me too much of Vohanna's black pyramid in the ruined city of Vohan, a place of which I had no fond memories. I was reluctant to point out the building to my friends, who were caught up now in taking in the beauties of the world inside Nimeru. When I did, the same pall came over their faces. All chatter ceased.

"Perhaps we should start our search for Vessoth over there," I said into the quiet. "From what I know about the Asadhie, they like their pyramids."

A few grumbled but no one argued. They'd all come here prepared to face such things. Even if they did not wish to.

"Should I tell the Pilot?" Munt asked.

I gave him a "yes," heard him relay the command, then looked at Ahrethane. "You get any sense of *toir'in-or* magic from that place?"

She sighed. "Only the faintest impression. I don't really know what that means. I'm still learning how to recognize my new...abilities."

I nodded.

Once again our ship began to move with purpose. We hauled up a few sails to catch the light breeze that whispered around us, and Cailif Ostt guided us deftly toward our goal. As he did so, the claw-wings started to take more notice of us. A squawking flock of the ugly horrors began to gather some hundred tahng off our starboard side. It made me uneasy.

We came down out of the interior sky of Nimeru and sat down gently as a floating thistle in the clearing of the great pyramid. A field of dark yellow grass further cushioned our landing, though nowhere did the blades of that grass lift more than a finger's breadth above the ground. This sward was carefully tended. I would have liked to know by whom, or by what?

While leaving most of the crew aboard ship under the command of Cailif, ten of us disembarked to approach the pyramid. Among those ten were Shai and Rence, Valyan and Diken, myself and Bryce and Ahrethane. Three other crewmembers joined us—Daik, Oleg, and Taren. All were experienced and steady warriors, not prone to panic when facing the unknown.

Beneath the yellow grass, the soil looked rich and I squatted a moment and stuck fingers in to see how deep the richness might run. They went in only to the second knuckle before meeting some denser surface. If the soil was this thin everywhere, how had the great trees of the jungle taken root?

Although we all half expected some kind of attack, nothing bothered us as we crossed the golden sward toward the pyramid. There were no steps leading up into the structure. A large iron door, banded with bronze, stood wide open at ground level. As if by mutual agreement, we drew our weapons as we approached that portal. Shai and I were the first through, with the others following closely.

Inside we found what can only be described as some combination of a cathedral and a mausoleum. The interior walls, of darker crimson than the building's outside, soared high above us, reaching to a vaulted ceiling pierced by huge clerestory windows. The golden light from outside fell through those windows like soft rain, illuminating intricate carvings that etched nearly every square inch of stone in the place. The carvings looked curiously mathematical in form; I wished for time to study them but now was not the moment. Someone else was in here with us.

Just inside the entrance lay half a dozen steps leading down into what resembled the nave of a temple. There were, however, no pews for a congregation to sit, only a mosaic of small, multicolored tiles on the floor that created an image of the Snake God himself. So cunningly wrought was the image that it appeared to have depth. I did not like the way the eyes watched us, or how the fangs seemed to drip venom.

Beyond the image stood a crimson altar, and in front of it a cathedra, the type of chair upon which bishops and popes are seated. The chair was not empty. The figure occupying it wore scarlet plate armor. A closed helm covered the head, and from it branched a rack of antlers. A thin slit in the helm marked where the eyes would be but I couldn't tell if anything living watched us from within. There was some effect of the thing's presence, though. My chest began to ache in the same place where I'd been struck by the vision-blade of the black masked swordsman. With an effort of will, I forced the pain away.

"We seek Vessoth," I called across the cavernous space to the thing upon the chair.

It did not respond and I looked about at my friends. Shrugs greeted me.

"Rence?" I asked softly, knowing he had a ring that was supposed to detect the presence of any Asadhie.

He shook his head. "Not close enough."

I puffed out a breath of air, then glanced at Ahrethane. Her veiled gaze was focused intently upon the scarlet shape, and when I called her name, she started.

"What do you sense?" I asked her.

She turned her head toward me for a moment. "Nothing," she replied, then turned away again.

I chewed my lower lip. Perhaps the seated figure was no more than an empty suit of armor. I didn't believe that, though.

An elevated marble walkway, which began at the pyramid's entrance, circled much of the interior of the building. I pointed it out to Diken and Valyan.

"Ready your bows and see if you can work around behind the thing. If it attacks, arrow it for me."

"Happily," Diken said.

Valyan only grunted assent as the two moved off.

The thing in the chair made no response.

"Not quite what I expected from a first meeting with Vessoth," Shai said.

"Appearances don't mean much with an Asadhie," I replied.

"Aye."

I started down the steps into the main part of the temple. Shai and Rence and the others followed. We'd crossed barely ten feet of tiled floor before Ahrethane shouted fiercely.

"Get off the image!"

I glanced down, saw my feet treading on the mosaic of the Snake God's face. Some thought registered. *Something wrong with the floor.*

I threw myself sideways, landed hard on my left shoulder. With a crackle, the tiles where I'd stood gave way. A scream tore from someone's throat. I couldn't see who.

I twisted over onto my other side. Shai and Rence had been close to the outer edge of the collapse and had pulled Ahrethane between them to safety. Daik and Taren had not yet stepped into the trap. I could not see Bryce.

Then I glimpsed fingers, white with strain, gripping the marble edge of the hole. I dropped the rune-blade and lurched toward them. My hands slapped down, latched onto the wrists of the man hanging there. With the strength of terror I pulled him up onto solid ground. It was Bryce.

"Oleg," he said, gasping. "I tried to grab...."

I did not wait to hear the rest of his words but came to my knees to look down into the pit. The tiled physiognomy of Vessoth had collapsed into a subterranean chamber perhaps a dozen feet deep. Oleg, an older man, a farmer before he joined the defense of Timmuzz against Vohanna's hordes, had served on the *Khiang* for barely a year. Now he lay dead at the bottom of a hole; the fall wasn't what killed him.

Standing up from the floor below were dozens of fang-like spikes, each no more than two hands tall. One stabbed into Oleg's shoulder; another pierced a leg. They would not have killed him either, except the tip of each spike was discolored a sickly violet that spoke of venom. Oleg's poison-swollen body shrieked of the same thing.

"You were warned!" a metallic voice said, sending echoes booming across the pyramid's interior.

I glanced up, saw that the motionless figure in scarlet armor was motionless no more. It had risen from its chair. With one crimson armored hand, it pointed at me.

"You were warned," it said again. "You were given a chance to turn back. This death is a stain upon *your* khi."

By khi, it meant "soul."

The thing's words stung because there was truth in them. In the pattern made by Nimeru's flying reptiles I'd seen Vessoth's face, with blood marking it. Now that same face had collapsed beneath us, taking one of my men to his doom. The trap had been plain to see. Only Ahrethane, without eyes, had seen it. Yet, the fault was not all mine. Not primarily mine.

I scooped up the rune-blade from the floor and came to my feet in a rage. "Even if the responsibility is shared," I shouted at the armored being, "you're the one who's going to pay!"

Brazen laughter boomed. I charged. The creature did not move as I came for it.

Six strides away. Five. Four.

A yellow-fletched arrow struck the being from the left; the black quarrel of a crossbow hammered it from the right. Valyan and Diken had each fired, but the arrow and bolt caromed away from the thing's steel plated form.

It didn't matter. I was one stride away. Still the thing had not moved.

I brought the sword around, hacking the heavy blade into the juncture where scarlet helm met scarlet armor. Sparks leaped as the weapon bit. I heard the awful screech of metal grinding through metal. The helm went spinning, crashed to the marble floor and bounded away. There was no body inside the armor.

There was something else instead.

CHAPTER NINETEEN

BLOOD-RED WORLD

For an instant, I saw only black nothingness down the neck of the suit of armor. Then vine-like tendrils of scarlet light whipped out of that darkness and latched onto the suit's steel plated shoulders. Static electricity grabbed at my sword and arced down into my body. I staggered back, hair standing up all over as the stinging discharge surged through me.

The scarlet tendrils thrummed like a hive of monstrous bees, then contracted like muscles to pull some whorl of burning light out of the empty carapace of the armor and into the open air. The thing that appeared in front of me was about the size of the condors I'd known from my California home on Earth, but it resembled some bizarre blend of a mollusk and a ball of St. Elmo's Fire. It wore a pyramid-shaped shell on its back, but a shell formed from sparking electricity rather than calcium. The only fleshy parts were a soft white mouth, like a snail's, and bulbous crimson eyes slit right down the middle by the black pupil. The eyes were those of a viper.

I raised the sword. The scarlet tendrils, which had acted something like the tentacles of a cuttlefish, released themselves from the armor and the creature soared into the air out of reach of my blade.

"Arrow it!" I shouted to Diken and Valyan.

I heard Valyan's bow and Diken's crossbow release shots but the thing was already moving by the time they fired. It dove past me and into the pit that had opened up moments before with the collapse of the floor. I turned in time to see it disappear down a head-sized hole in the center of the pit.

"Krutt!" I cursed.

"Was it Vessoth?" Shai demanded as she rushed up beside me.

The others gathered around too.

"I'm not sure it was Vessoth," I said, "but I think so. I saw Vohanna in her true form once. At least what I believe was her true form. She was like…" I gestured toward the hole in the floor, "that thing. Not exactly. But similar. As if they belonged to the same…race, maybe." I threw up my hands. "I don't know how to explain it."

"Dihmus vishka!" Taren muttered, her voice strained.

"No god involved in this one," Diken responded. "Maybe a demon."

"Neither!" I snapped. "Just another meddling Asadhie!"

Shai stiffened at mention of the Asadhie. I suddenly knew why. *Chalathar*! She was thinking of Chalathar, who was also an Asadhie, though one who seemed to be at war with the rest of his race. I wondered in that instant if Shai were in love with Chalathar; I wondered if she were thinking now about what kind of being he *really* was—inside.

A mad and mechanical giggling started behind me and I spun around, the others with me. The helmet I'd cut from the suit of armor Vessoth had inhabited was glowing. It looked molten, waxing so intensely with vermillion light that I had to shade my eyes. The sound originated from it.

Then the giggle shut off, and a voice followed like the whisper of a razor cutting silk.

"Will you join me, Ruenn Maclang? At the white beach by the black sea? An old friend awaits you there. Walk the dead river to its end. Bring only those you don't mind losing."

The voice stopped; the giggling resumed, threatened to continue forever.

"Lend me your crossbow," I said to Diken Graye beside me.

He passed it over and I raised it quickly and fired a black quarrel into the helm. The metal shattered like porcelain, as if the glow that had filled it had burnt it to fragility. The giggling stopped and I handed the crossbow back to Diken.

Shai was looking at me strangely. "What did the voice mean about the white beach by the black sea?" she demanded.

I hesitated, but finally said, "In Timmuzz. Before this all started. I had a kind of…waking dream. Or something. I saw a vision of myself fighting a masked swordsman on a white sand beach beside a black ocean."

"You didn't think it important to tell us this?"

"I didn't know what it meant. Or if it meant anything. I thought it most likely a symptom of the strain we'd all been under with Vohanna's War."

"Apparently you were wrong."

"Apparently," I agreed irritably.

Suddenly, Ahrethane lifted her head as if she scented something. "The light is dimming," she said.

I glanced up high to the great windows, which provided illumination for the building. The light *had* lessened; the strange mathematical symbols on the walls had fallen mostly into shadow now. Even as I watched, the darkness spread.

"We better get back to the ship," Bryce said. "If the light goes while we're in here…."

"Yes," I agreed.

Before any of us could move, the light failed completely and a cave black night enveloped us. From outside the pyramid, from the inky sky, there came a great, spreading shriek. It was like the cry of a many-throated beast but it did not sound afraid of the dark. It sounded furious, and hungry.

Then a new radiance bloomed. It came stabbing through the windows like freshly wetted swords. It was red, red, as if all the world had been reborn in blood. I knew that light; I'd seen it twice before in the land of visions, where I'd fought the swordsman who was my master with a blade—where I had fought him and died.

The shriek of beasts came again from beyond the pyramid. It sounded to me now like the howl of hunters who seek to coordinate an attack on their prey. I thought it must come from the throats of the flying claw-wings we'd seen watching us ever since our entrance into Nimeru. Then another sound burst upon our ears, the hoarse shouts of desperate men and women fighting suddenly for their lives.

"Something's attacking the *Khiang*!" Shai shouted.

CHAPTER TWENTY

CLAW AND WING

My ship! Under assault!

The bronze-banded door to the pyramid remained open. I hurled myself toward it and through, then froze in shock. The sky outside was awash with the same virulent scarlet filling the interior of the temple, but that wasn't what turned me to ice. The crimson air seethed with thousands of winged forms—all wheeling, dipping, shrieking, diving upon the grounded *Khiang*. Already the ship's sails were in tatters. Now the masts began to shred beneath the onslaught.

Men and women from the *Khiang's* crew fired into the mass of beasts with crossbows; it was as useless as fighting a swarm of mosquitoes with a rifle. The claw-wings were nearly the size of jackals and attacked in packs of half a dozen at a time. I saw one such swarm snatch a woman into the air, her arms flailing as talons tore the life out of her in streamers of red.

"Get below decks!" I screamed at the crew, knowing they could hear nothing over the frenzied rage of the reptiles.

I drew sword, took a step toward the ship. Diken and Valyan grabbed my arms, pulled me back. I struggled.

Bryce was shouting into my face. "No! In the open they'll tear us apart. We have to get back inside the pyramid."

I stopped fighting. My brother was right. Even as I realized it, two things happened to make a final decision for me. First, the crew abandoned any attempt to defend the ship and began rushing for the *Khiang's* hatches, striving to get out of the open, to get below decks where they'd find walls for protection against their attackers. Second, hundreds of claw-wings suddenly took note of us standing outside the sheltering pyramid.

They came for us.

We ran.

I was last through the door into the temple and already Shai and Rence and others were straining to close it. The claw-wings were nearly upon us; the cacophony of their shrieks tore at our ears. I threw my own weight against the heavy portal and it slammed shut. There was a latch for a door bar but no bar to be seen. Taren thrust her spear into the latch just as the reptile horde crashed against it from outside. The door shivered and the spear shaft of good oak bent but did not break.

For a moment, a savage hissing came pouring through the closed portal. Then silence fell.

"They'll try the windows next," Shai said calmly.

Her words came true in the next instant as the great windows far above us shattered and hundreds of snake-bodied monsters surged through in a thrash of wings. All of us covered our heads with our arms as a rain of crystalline glass pelted us. Then we straightened and readied our weapons for what seemed a hopeless fight.

"Into the corner," I shouted. "Put the wall at your back!"

The claw-wings took a bare moment to find us within the dimmer light inside the pyramid, giving us the time we needed to back into the corner by the door and place a shield of stone behind us. Then the horrors came shrieking to the attack.

I sliced the head from the first beast to arrive. Its blood sprayed red across me, smelling like hot, sheared metal. More of the things surged in. I gutted another but a third slammed into me and one of its wing talons hooked hard into my left side. Grunting with pain, I brought my sword across to hack through the creature's neck. Its talon tore free as the thing fell away, but now my own blood mixed with that of our enemies.

There was no time to worry about how deep the wound was before a fresh monster replaced the dead one. Its wings buffeted. Its jaws opened on a hiss, and a mouth full of what looked like shards of bone struck for my face. I caught the thing by the throat, snarled as my fingers twisted and dug into scaled flesh. Blood burbled over my nails as the vertebrae beneath the hide snapped. I hurled the corpse into a beast attacking Daik to the left. Both creatures went tumbling.

I raised sword for the next clawed assailant. Suddenly, a bare step in front of me, a sheet of emerald fire leaped from the floor toward the roof. Several claw-wings were trapped in that conflagration. They went up like torches impregnated with pitch.

Instinctively, I thrust back away from the heat, then cast about desperately for the source of the fire. To the right stood Bryce, and next to him—Ahrethane. Her whole body blazed like a prism with green light. Her hands were out in front of her, and in each palm a pair of *toir'in-or* power stones whirled around each other like mad dervishes.

An icy sweat slicked me. I had seen Ahrethane's earth magic before. Her life magic. But this! Nothing living inhabited it. And I had seen Ahrethane cast her nature spells before. I'd seen her mouth moving with strange words, seen her draw skeins of power in the air with her fingers.

Now she did not speak; she did not draw. Her body poured out naked sorcery like a dam blowing wide to some titanic flood.

Every claw-wing in the temple erupted with fire from within its own body. Flesh and bone and muscle scorched to ash. The beasts' blood did not burn. It exploded outward, bucketing the walls, running like vermilion paint down the strange mathematical symbols, lending them a sheen of glory. Other than the drip of blood, an utter silence filled the pyramid, and the world outside it.

I stood gaping at Ahrethane. She turned her head toward me. Her veil was gone, as if vaporized. Her empty eye sockets were no longer empty. The silver light that had come to live there in place of Human eyes had hardened into the tight and intricately laced threads of spider webs. At the center of the webs I glimpsed some jittering movement in jade I could not identify. Nor did I want to.

Ahrethane's hands lifted and there were no milkstones clutched in them. I wondered where the *toir'in-or* had gone, and was afraid I knew. The woman I'd once called an efrinore brought her hands to her face, and a fresh veil wove itself around and through her fingertips. It came out of the very air and fell like shimmering green silk down to hide her new eyes and the smile that carved her lips.

"The winged are dead," she said. Her voice throbbed like a drum. She sounded nothing like the woman I'd known.

CHAPTER TWENTY-ONE

SNOW OF ASHES

For a long moment after Ahrethane spoke, none of us responded. None of us even moved. Then she sagged where she stood and Bryce quickly grasped her arm to lend support. He glanced at me, his eyes challenging. I kept my face carefully neutral and said nothing.

"I'll take her to the ship," he stated.

I nodded.

Diken stood on the other side of Ahrethane, and Bryce gestured for him to help. Between them they guided her to the door, which Valyan and Rence threw open. I watched as they walked her out. Her legs barely supported her and it was clear the use of sorcery had weakened her. I doubted it would take her long to recover, and I wasn't quite sure how I felt about that.

Through the doorway I could see that not a single claw-wing remained anywhere in the sky around the pyramid. Instead, a light but steady snow came drifting down. It was the ashes of the beasts Ahrethane had destroyed outside the pyramid as well. The very air smelled singed.

The *Khiang* had been mauled but its hull looked intact. Not so for the masts and sails, which were shredded beyond repair. Some of the crew came trekking back onto the main deck now, looking around at the damage. No doubt they were curious as to what had happened to the claw-wings that attacked them. I don't think they understood about the "snow" falling upon them.

"I thought she was efrinore," Shai said from beside me, and I glanced over to see the woman's chin jut toward Ahrethane and her escorts.

"She was. But surely Chalathar recounted to you what happened in the throne room of Timmuzz during the last battle with Vohanna? When Bryce had been turned into the Witch's Bane-thrall and was threatening to undo all we'd fought for?"

"He told me she used her body to cancel out your brother's sorcery. I don't see how that explains what she did to these flying reptiles."

I met the warrior woman's gaze, and so tall was she that our eyes were nearly level. "Bryce believes she absorbed some of his power when she grabbed him. I think he must be right. You saw her manipulating milkstones. An efrinore could never touch a *toir'in-or*. The Asadhie magic is alien to them in every way. Ahrethane can use them and that means she isn't efrinore any longer."

"How strong is she?"

"Barely a dhaur ago she told me she was still learning to recognize her new powers."

"She seems to be a fast learner."

"Yes."

"Aren't you worried?"

"She saved our lives!"

"I don't deny it. What has that to do with my question?"

"Nothing," I said, and strode away.

* * *

"The masts and sails are a loss," Cailif Ostt reported. The Pilot and I stood on the *Khiang's* forecastle and it saddened me to see the damage done to the ship by the attack of Vessoth's claw-wings. "We've got spares," Cailif continued, "but the mast steps and cleats on deck were damaged and will have to be repaired. We can cut wood for that in the forest but it'll take me a few days to work it to fit. I'd like to cut some potential replacement masts as well. We can rough them out here and finish them under sail. I don't want to be left helpless if we're attacked again and lose our spare masts too."

I nodded. "How long?"

"Six days. Five if we're lucky in finding the right woods."

Unlike any other member of his Caste I'd ever known, Cailif had been apprenticed in childhood as a shipwright before being selected for Pilot training. He also bore a natural air of command, and the two skills together made him highly valuable to anyone lucky enough to contract his service.

"All right," I said. "Take the six days. I'm leaving you in charge. I'll be gone. The sabrun saddle birds we brought along will let us scout out Vessoth's trail by then. I hope. As soon as the ship is under sail, follow us."

"How will I know where?" Cailif inquired.

"I'm leaving Bryce and Ahrethane here. Ahrethane will be able to track us."

Cailif frowned but did not argue. I left the man then and went below decks to my cabin. Shai and Rence waited there. Bryce as well.

"How is Ahrethane?" I asked my brother upon joining the three.

"She's resting. Saving us took a lot out of her." His tone was harsh, his words almost a reprimand for a slight that had not thus far been offered.

"I'm glad—" I started.

"Yes," Shai interrupted. "We appreciate what she did but now the question must be asked. Is she herself a danger to us?"

"No!" Bryce said hotly. "She—"

"Stop!" I snapped.

Silence followed, though both Bryce and Shai bristled. Rence was a rather mercurial fellow but seemed slightly amused at the moment. I rather liked him for that.

"We're not going to fight among ourselves," I ordered. I looked at Shai. "Ahrethane has been a friend for a long time and her heart has always been pure. But," I glanced now at Bryce, "she *has* changed since she awoke. Given our recent past, it is reasonable to be cautious about those changes. None of us are immune to taint."

Bryce opened his mouth, then closed it again with a snap of teeth. He caught my meaning. *His* heart had always been pure until he was corrupted by Vohanna and the power of the milkstones. It had taken Ahrethane's sacrifice to save him from that evil. Despite his wish to protest on behalf of Ahrethane, who I was quite sure he was in love with, he understood better than any of us the potential dangers of the situation.

"Here's what we're going to do," I said. "We've got six sabruns on deck. Shai, Rence, Diken, Valyan, and I will take them. Maybe include Daik, as well. We'll scout. See if we can find this 'dead river' of which Vessoth spoke."

"What about me?" Bryce asked.

"You stay here. Help Ahrethane all you can. If we find the river we'll follow it. Cailif says the ship will be ready to sail in six days. If we're not back by then, you get Ahrethane to track us, bring the ship to us. I know she can do it."

I expected at least a token argument from Bryce; it didn't come.

"All right," he said.

"I take it Diken and Valyan are saddling the birds now," Shai said.

"Yes," I agreed.

"Then let's find Vessoth and finish this."

I nodded, thinking of friends and companions, of those who would accompany me now, and those who would stay behind a few more days.

"Walk the dead river to its end," Vessoth had said. "Bring only those you don't mind losing."

There weren't any I didn't mind losing.

CHAPTER TWENTY-TWO

BROTHERS AND FOES

"Ruenn!"

I was headed for my cabin aboard the *Khiang* when the voice called out behind me. I turned to see Bryce. There was little time to waste; I wanted to fetch something from my sky chest and then quickly begin the search for the dead river. But Bryce was my brother, and the look on his face could not be ignored. It occurred to me then that I had something I'd been intending to speak with him about anyway.

"Walk with me," I told him. "Tell me what you could not say in front of Shai and Rence."

He joined me as I strode ahead. "You'll need Ahrethane when you face Vessoth," he said.

I eyed him.

"In Nyshphal," he continued. "Against Vohanna. You were defeated until Chalathar brought his wizardry into the battle. Swords of steel cannot best an Asadhie. Not alone. No matter the courage of those who wield the blades."

I knew he was right. I'd seen Vohanna "die" once impaled on a steel spike. She'd come back. I started to speak of it but Bryce held up a hand to silence me.

"Let me finish. Before I lose my own courage. I know I tried to use sorcery against Vohanna and it ended up turned against me. Against you and Rannon. That was part of the Witch's plan from the beginning. I was drunk on the power Vohanna fed me. Drunk because I'd never had any experience at wielding magic. Ahrethane has been a witch woman her whole life. She is struggling now, but she *will* master this."

"I hope so," I said, striving to keep the doubts out of my voice.

"She is a true 'unforeseen' in this game. She alone will not be what Vessoth expects her to be."

I nodded, then could not help but add, "*Nobody* knows exactly what to expect of her now. Not even her friends."

Silence held for a dozen heartbeats, but as we arrived at the door of my cabin Bryce suddenly grabbed my arm and pulled me around to face him. His grip was tight, almost painful. His eyes blazed with emotion.

I suspected for a moment he might strike me, and I would not allow myself to strike back. I had done so before and could not forgive myself.

For half a dhorrin our tableau held.

"You don't understand, Ruenn," Bryce finally grated out. He released my arm, gently. "If you go up against Vessoth without Ahrethane's help you won't live to know you've lost. I don't want to see that. I love you, brother!"

I blinked. A dampness misted my eyes. I reached a hand to Bryce's shoulder, then pulled him into a hug. He returned it.

"I love you too," I told him, before releasing him and meeting his grey-eyed gaze. "And I believe you about Ahrethane. We'll continue our plan to scout out the dead river. You and Ahrethane are inextricably linked now. Help her as much as you can to deal with what she's facing. When the ship is ready, bring her to me. We've come this far together. The lot of us. We all have a stake in ending Vessoth. If there is any way to avoid the final confrontation with the sorcerer, I'll do so. Until...."

I didn't need to finish. Bryce understood and flashed me a smile that reminded me of years gone by.

Behind me, the door of the cabin creaked. Bryce and I turned. Both our hands dropped to the swords at our sides. The door bulged slightly, as if pressed from within by some intolerable force. My eyes widened; my heart quickened. I drew the rune-sword and with an oath grabbed the latch of the door and threw it open. At my shoulder, Bryce gave a gasp and I knew he was seeing the same thing I saw.

Inside the room, the very air steamed in scarlet. A man stood amid the red, as if born from it. Above black silk, his eyes stared into me like the points of knives. All around him lay a ruby haze that hid everything except the strange warrior's lithe frame and the rapier filling his left hand.

"Soon, Ruenn Maclang," he said. "Your life will come to its inevitable finish."

"Who are you?" I snarled.

The silk over his mouth twitched and I knew he smiled.

"You'll learn it at the end. Your end."

"Only a coward hides his face from those he threatens," I sneered.

The cold gleam in his eyes quickened into flame and again the silk trembled over the lower half of his face. This time I did not think it from humor. His hand lifted and for a moment it seemed he was going to strip away the concealing cloth. Exultation swept me. Then I heard a single word spoken out of the air from somewhere above the strange warrior.

"No!" was that word.

The swordsman froze, and in the next instant the entire scene disintegrated. The ruby haze dissipated and the form of the warrior...went.

Once again the cabin was simply a cabin. I stepped across the threshold; my nostrils stung with a faint lingering scent of something acrid. There was nothing else.

Bryce followed me into the cabin. "So that's one of the visions you've been experiencing?"

"Yes. I'm glad someone besides me finally saw it. Lets me know I'm not going insane."

Bryce said nothing, though I could practically see the questions churning through his mind.

I turned toward my bunk, took up the rawhide duster lying there and slipped it on, then knelt to unlock and open my sky chest. Inside, beneath a layer of linen to keep away the dust, lay six artifacts from another world. On the day of Vohanna's death in the throne room of Timmuzz, I had gathered them to myself.

Vohanna's ally on that day had been Kuurus, the brother of Rannon. It had taken me a while to figure out that Kuurus had used the sphere gates to travel back and forth to Earth. He'd brought back knowledge for Vohanna to use as a weapon, and had even recruited six mercenaries from Earth to fight for her. They had been gunmen all, and armed with modern pistols that wrought awful havoc among us. In the end, though, they died with the Witch whose gold they'd taken. I got the guns.

I took out such a pistol now. It was a nickel-plated Smith & Wesson .357 with a four-inch barrel. I popped open the cylinder, saw it was loaded with five shells, with an empty chamber left to lie under the hammer so there'd be no accidental discharge. I clicked it closed and handed the weapon to Bryce. He took it with a look of both surprise and recognition in his eyes.

"How?" he asked.

"You probably never knew Kuurus was smuggling mercenaries and weapons from Earth into Timmuzz. After the Witch's death, I collected these. There's also," I rummaged around and pulled out a leather gunbelt and holster, "this." I held it up for my brother and he slipped the pistol into the holster and then took the belt.

"I found the gunbelts in the mercenaries' rooms after. There were extra cartridges as well."

Bryce nodded, his thumb rubbing against the gleaming brass of one such shell.

I withdrew a second pistol from the chest. This one was a Colt double-action revolver in blue steel. Written in engraved letters along the left side of its six-inch barrel were its make and caliber—Trooper Mark III, .357. I opened the cylinder, took out one of the five cartridges. It was a hollow-point, a frightful load meant to mushroom dramatically inside a target, thus causing maximum tissue damage.

Replacing the shell, I closed the cylinder on the empty chamber. Gathering the gunbelt for it, I shut and locked the chest before rising. After holstering the Colt, I buckled the belt around my waist under the duster. Then I turned and helped Bryce do the same with his gunbelt.

"Even has a left handed holster," Bryce remarked. The edge in his tone made me think he was remembering the day when a pistol had blown up in his right hand and taken it from him. On that day we'd both ended up on Talera.

"That's why I chose it for you," I said carefully.

"You think we'll need these?"

"Hope not. But we'll have them if we do. I've been intending to train Diken and Valyan in their use but haven't had the time. There aren't a lot of shells anyway. Our two favorite bowmen would be worse than useless with these weapons without some experience. You already know how to use one. And it'll be easier to handle than a sword."

"With *one* hand, yes," he said.

"Keep it close. I saw against Vohanna that a bullet will rupture a milkstone. When that happens you get one hell of an explosion."

"I'll hold that in mind," he said, then changed the subject. "The strange warrior we saw in your room a few minutes ago. Who is he?"

"I wish I knew. He looks familiar but I can't tell with most of his face hidden. I hoped for a moment he was going to reveal himself."

"It must have been Vessoth's voice that forbade it."

"I imagine."

"Will you have to fight him? Before you deal with the sorcerer?"

"I believe so. But unlike Vessoth, that warrior is Human. I know that much. Steel can kill him. I intend for it to."

I did not tell him that I still felt the steel in *my* chest from previous visions. I did not tell him that in those visions it had been me who died.

CHAPTER TWENTY-THREE

DEAD RIVER

The wind whipped my hair and clothes as I soared through Nimeru's red sky in the saddle of a sabrun warbird. Despite all that had happened in the past few days, there was exhilaration to be found in such a flight. I relished the freedom of moving in any direction I chose. I enjoyed the ocher gleam of the jungles far below, the friction of air whispering past, and even the chill generated by our swift passage, which was enough to raise gooseflesh across my body despite the duster I wore.

A sabrun saddle bird resembles a hawk grown to the size of a horse. It is sleek and swift and seems to joy in speed as much as any Human rider might. This particular mount was steel gray except for a ruff of feathers around its neck that was almost silver. My weight on its back did not trouble it as we arrowed along.

Riding a saddle bird is not unlike riding a horse, except that one moves through three dimensions instead of two. In well trained birds, such as mine, a hackamore is used to control the animal. Loops of rope or leather are fitted over the beak, with four reins running from there through a neck collar and into the rider's hands. The reins are for left, right, up, and down. The rider's left hand works the left and down reins. The right hand controls the right and up reins. Drawing back on all the reins slows the bird; letting them lie slack gives it its head.

The hackamore is loose enough for the bird to open its mouth partway. This allows it to emit cries often used among bird riders as signals. They can be heard over much greater distances than a Human shout could be. For a bird in training, the hackamore is replaced by an external metal bit that locks the beak closed. It is not uncommon for novice birds to try and eat their riders. A wing-stick, an iron-headed baton about the length of a man's arm, is also provided to bird riders. Before my first flight, which involved some "emergency" training, I was told the stick was for beating the bird about the head if it tried to eat me. That is not its sole purpose, however. In well trained mounts it can be used as a substitute for the reins in case they break.

Bird saddles are normally of light leather sewn around the edges with bone or steel rings through which cords are looped and tied off to riders' belts to help keep them in their seats. Falling off a horse is bad enough; falling off a saddle bird is far worse. Most saddles come with sheathes for swords and many have leather skirts where lances or other weapons can be hung. Beneath my sabrun's right wing rested six lances. A crossbow and bandolier of bolts hung beneath the left wing.

Of course, I had about me daggers, as well, and from its scabbarded place the hilt of the rune-sword arched over my right shoulder. I also had a pistol. My friends on their own sabruns, spread out in a search pattern across the crimson sky, were equally well armed. Except for the gun. We were prepared for war, though, as Bryce had argued, Vessoth would be hard to defeat using weapons as mundane as ours.

A distant shriek caught my attention. It was not the wicked cry of the claw-wings, of which I'd seen no sign since we'd taken to the skies. This shriek was purer, piercing. I recognized it as the "announcement" call of a sabrun. One of my companions had found something.

Turning the head of my bird in the direction of the call, I soon came upon Valyan. He stood in his stirrups as I approached and pointed. My gaze followed his arm. I saw what was surely a good candidate for the "dead river."

As I've mentioned, the interior surface of Nimeru is largely covered by a jungle, though its growth is less green and more orange and yellow than jungles I was familiar with. Now I saw another color threading its way through the vast ochre forest—a serpentine track of gray. It began as a thread in what I thought of as the north of Nimeru and wound its widening way south until it abruptly disappeared as if cut off with a knife. The very hue of the thing looked sickly. That could have been due in part to the red atmosphere but I had a feeling there was some truth in my instinctive response to that strange track.

"Looks like a river!" Valyan shouted to me.

Perhaps the "scar" of a river, I thought. I could see no water but we were a long distance away.

"Worth investigating, at least," I shouted back at Valyan. He nodded.

Within a dozen breaths, Shai, Rence, Diken and Daik arrived to join us and Valyan pointed out his find to them. By mutual consent, we took off to investigate, with the other sabruns falling into formation behind mine.

It was hard predicting distance inside the moon but it did not take long to reach what I judged to be the "headwaters" of the strange river. It had already become clear that the floor of the moon's interior was not all one level. There were ridges and valleys, though nothing too dramatic. The gray river, if river it was, began in a narrow decline between two ridges but quickly began a sinuous meandering back and forth across the landscape.

I still couldn't see any water, but that might have been because the gray color of the region was produced by the unconstrained growth of some fungoid plant that almost completely dominated the land beneath it. Here and there the barren limb of a forest tree stabbed out of the gray, reminding me of a man's hand poking up out of the quicksand that has choked him to death. That image wasn't comforting, but it also helped convince me this was indeed the dead river we sought.

On Earth, I had seen oak trees almost crushed under a load of Spanish moss, a kind of parasitic plant that resembles the pale beards of drowned men. The phenomenon below reminded me of those oaks, though this "moss" was far heavier and less like hair than like...entrails. There was an odor coming from the site, too, even as high in the air as we were. It smelled like rotted things.

I felt very fortunate that with the sabruns we could fly above this fetid clime and not have to land and make our way on foot. That feeling didn't last long. The instant we crossed directly over the gray region my sabrun vented a high shriek and twisted wildly against its hackamore. I snapped the reins hard against its neck, striving to turn it again in the direction I wanted. It fought me, backing its wings savagely as if the air above that foul place was physically painful to endure.

Around me I heard the cries of other sabruns and saw everyone facing the same struggles with their mounts. I drummed heels in beneath the saddle bird's wings and sawed at the reins. Its head came around but then it shrieked again and spun its whole body away from the swath of gray growth. This time I let it go and it fled straight back over what my mind was already calling the "living" jungle.

After covering nearly a verlang at high speed, I was able to regain control of the bird. The other riders soon joined me and we circled around each other while trying to figure out what to do. Eventually, Shai pointed out a clearing and we brought our sabruns into land there. I tethered my bird to a tree and gathered with the others.

"Ivid Yaal shei?" Diken asked, which would translate into English as, "What the hell?"

I shrugged.

"Do you think the sabruns sensed some kind of predator?" Rence questioned. "Or were they responding to the general repellant stench of that place?"

"The stench," Shai said. "I wanted to vomit myself."

Valyan stated the key problem. "So what do we do now?"

"We could try flying along parallel to the track of the river," Diken said. "If that's what it is. Keep it in sight but stay far enough away so the birds don't spook again."

"I'm remembering Vessoth's exact words," I said.

"Walk the dead river to its end," Shai quoted.

"Yes. Walk it. Not fly over or beside it."

Diken's fingers tap tapped against his sword belt; Valyan murmured something under his breath; Daik shook his head and spat on the ground. I felt much the same as they did.

"It'll be a trap," Rence pointed out.

"That's stating the obvious," Diken added.

I spoke again. "It's not that I want to do what Vessoth tells us to. But every time he's communicated with us he's also been giving us information. The image of his face we saw coming in to Nimeru. It showed us something about the danger in the pyramid. The very name of the 'dead river.' It helped us find this place. Maybe if we play his game he'll reveal a weakness we can exploit."

No one said anything but I could see the idea taking hold. I opened my mouth to add more, then paused. I wanted to give everyone a chance to turn back now. I *wanted* to tell them it was no cowardice to avoid venturing into a trap from which it seemed impossible for all of us to emerge alive. I couldn't say those words. I knew these men and women around me. They would be insulted.

"I don't want to leave the sabruns here," I said at last. "I've never seen a jungle where there wasn't something that would eat a tethered mount. If someone takes the lead bird. Heads back to the ship. The other sabruns will follow. Then whoever goes can guide the *Khiang* back here so *it* can follow the river behind us."

"I'm going with *you*," Shai snapped.

She was first to say it but the others quickly made similar statements. As I expected.

"We'll draw straws," I said. I pulled a knife and walked over to a smallish thorn tree at the edge of the clearing. The black-tipped thorns were all nearly the same length already. I cut five, trimmed one of them short and left the others long. Hiding the barrels of the thorns between my fingers, I returned to my friends and held out the hand for them to make their choices.

"Short thorn loses," I said.

"Loses? Or wins?" Diken asked.

"Depends, I suppose."

Shai reached out and pulled a thorn. It was a long one. Rence got another. And Daik. Diken chose next and his was short. He threw it down in disgust. His dark eyes met mine, then scanned around to the others.

"Try to stay alive until I get back," he said to us all.

CHAPTER TWENTY-FOUR

TURNED TO STONE

We watched Diken take flight on his sabrun and then shooed the rest of the saddle birds off in his wake. He circled above us until the other birds joined him, then turned his mount's head back in the direction we'd come from. He left us with a disheartened wave. I wondered if he was afraid he'd seen the last of us.

I glanced around at my remaining companions. Their gazes were resolute and I saw no need for a fancy speech to stiffen their spines; nor did I have the taste for it. These were seasoned warriors. They knew the risks.

"Let's go," I said, and we grasped our weapons and picked up the saddlebags of supplies we'd unloaded from the sabruns, and went.

Except for the color of the foliage, the jungle we found ourselves in was not dissimilar from others I'd experienced. It was certainly as tough to navigate through on the ground. None of the bigger trees were much taller than twenty or thirty feet but they were generally very broad at the base. Some were too large for all five of us together to reach around. Each of the giants provided a haven for a wealth of other plants, from mossy ferns to what looked like miniature cacti.

Most of the space between the big trees was filled with thick underbrush. Whatever animals lived here would probably have to travel through the canopy above us, along tree limbs broad as a horse's back and across waist-thick vines that sewed the whole forested world together. *We* had to work a crooked way forward, resorting more often than I would have liked to the edges of our swords and daggers to cut a passage.

I recognized the names of none of the trees and bushes we passed, but knew their types from other jungles. Flowers grew riotous as well, and one yellow striped ivory bloom the size of a man's head had to be some kind of lily. The air was practically a stew of smells.

Many of the trees bore fruit, the largest a kind of purple oblong that looked like a skinny eggplant. The smallest fruits were marble sized and bright orange. They grew in such massive clusters that the sturdy limbs of the trees bearing them were bent nearly to the ground. A variety of insects gnawed at both of these fruits and that bit of information went into memory. If many different bugs could eat them, we probably could as well. If necessary.

The insects themselves were numerous but did not come in the myriads that might have been expected. I saw ants and spiders and a dozen variations on those types that didn't look like they'd ever originated on Earth. Of the flying bugs, only a few were biters. For that I was grateful. Perhaps the incredible density of bird life kept the pests to a manageable level. At least, I used the term "birds" to refer to the numerous, darting, flying things sweeping through the trees around us. Many appeared to be something less—or more—than avian.

Some were clearly reptilian, although not the claw-wings we'd seen and fought before. Most looked like lizards with double sets of dragonfly wings. Other fliers I could swear were amphibians, though there didn't seem to be any water nearby. These were larger than the reptiles, with salamander shaped bodies and rows of what looked like "feelers" on their undersides. They had broad, flattened wings that thudded the air as they flew, and moist and glistening skins, like a frog. Those skins were brilliantly hued in scarlets, purples, and golds.

I'd always heard bright colors in nature generally mean danger. The thought intrigued me that these creatures might be Talera's equivalent to the poison arrow frogs of Earth's South America, whose toxins are used by the local tribes for hunting and warfare. It was another item to remember. There'd be much here to explore and learn if we could ever return in a time of peace.

I did also see some true birds—the green and purple parrot we'd all noted before, and several big-beaked creatures the size of buzzards but with the habits of woodpeckers. There was also a very strange flier I couldn't get a close look at. It whipped in and out between the trees at tremendous speeds, leaving behind no more than glimpses of a stream-lined form and four wings that appeared to spin completely around its body as it traveled.

Only once did I see anything that might have been a mammal, and that was a fleeting impression of something monkey-sized brachiating away through the trees. Several times, however, one or more of us noted big, yellow-gold snakes slithering along the branches above us. I wasn't happy about that, though there was nothing other than paranoia to tie them to Vessoth.

At first as we moved through the jungle we were accompanied by a constant mélange of whistles, calls, and cries. Gradually the cacophony faded and we began to see less life around us. Even the trees grew shorter as we progressed, and the vines less profuse. I soon realized why. We were approaching the gray region, where I felt sure the dead river began.

A throb of pain passed through my chest at that thought. For an instant, it felt as if a tine of frost had been plunged into my heart and then withdrawn. I paused, and the others stopped as well. They looked at me curiously.

I shook my head at them, continued on. Within a hundred paces we came upon the place we sought. We'd been making our way up a gentle grade, recognizing it only by the extra exertion required from our legs. Then we topped the rise, and halted. The breeze blowing at our backs ceased now, and several of us snorted as the fetid stench of what lay ahead began to curl its way up our nostrils. In front of us, the trees grew short and twisted, covered over by a mass of thick gray growth that looked unpleasantly like coiled intestines. There was an opening in the midst of that growth, a shadowy tunnel that beckoned like the bony forefinger of death himself.

Shai put the back of her hand across her mouth; Rence made a face and spat.

"Yaal's breath would not stink as much as this place," Daik said.

Yaal is the God of the underworld in some Taleran religions. Believers say he leaves the stench of corpses wherever he goes.

"Maybe we'll get used to it," I said, not very confidently.

"Wait," Shai said. "I brought something that might help."

Our warrior-Pilot squatted down and thrust up the flap of one of her saddlebags to pull out a long rectangle of fine green linen. When she unfolded it, I saw it was a flag with a white pattern in the center that resembled an hourglass open at both top and bottom. A sewn wreath representing the teslit vine formed a halo over the hourglass's open ends, completing the symbol.

The image is called a zaidoch and I knew what it meant. Teslit vines have broad, three-lobed leaves often used in painting and sculpture to illustrate wisdom. The leaves resemble Earthen ivy and the plant may be a variation. The open hourglass represents both knowledge and mystery. The whole of the symbol is used by both Taleran philosophers and scientists to suggest an ideal toward which they strive. There is an opposing symbol, called a naidoch, which lacks the teslit vine halos and has the curves of the hourglass turned inward toward each other. Instead of knowledge and mystery, the naidoch represents the dark unknowable. It is sometimes used as a symbol for the gods.

As Shai took up the flag and a knife, I realized what she was about to do and spoke to her. "Are you sure?"

She glanced up and nodded: "It's my family…banner. I always carry it. I think now it will serve better to help protect us from the miasma of that place." She jerked her chin toward the dead river.

I spread hands in acknowledgement and within a few moments she made efficient work of slicing out five bandanas. We each tied one around our necks and pulled the linen up to cover our noses and mouths. Thusly armored, we ventured toward the dark portal marking the entrance to what was almost certainly Vessoth's dead river.

Two by two we passed through that gateway, with Shai and me first. A few steps beyond it we came upon a short stretch of dry channel that curved out of sight farther on. I'd been afraid the fungoid growth that overlay the place would make it too dim for our eyes, but the light filtering through was merely diffused and we could see clearly enough. I didn't like being trapped completely underneath that awful gray canopy, which was low enough so we could reach up and touch it if we chose. Even my skin wanted to crawl away and hide from the thought of doing so.

Cracked plates of dried mud filled most of the channel bed, indicating that water had run here before. My guess was it had been long ago. The mud flakes were nearly as hard as stone.

"This is no natural river," Shai said.

I nodded. "Far too regular. Though I see where the banks have eroded in places."

"Made by some intelligence then," Shai said.

"Perhaps," I agreed, though not feeling quite ready to commit to any theory regarding this strange place.

"The trees along here are all dead," Daik blurted out.

I glanced at the barren woods lining the river banks and saw he was right. In fact, the trees were more than dead. A rap on a couple of random trunks with the hilt of a dagger revealed the truth; they were petrified. Maybe "mummified" would be a better word.

"The fungus growing all over them must be parasitic," I said.

"Let's hope the same thing doesn't happen to us," Rence added.

I glanced at him, shrugged. "Maybe the lesson is not to stand still."

We strode forward, rounded the first bend to see another ahead of us. This one curved in the opposite direction. The next bend switched back the other way. The river, or whatever it was, seemed to resemble a large "S" drawn through the landscape by a giant's finger. And its channel widened steadily as we proceeded, though our gray roof remained intact.

At least the walking was easy. No plants grew in the river bed and the patches of hardened mud were so dry our boots barely raised any dust.

The stench of the place hadn't moderated any but the bandanas helped us tolerate it.

"Ruenn!" Daik called out, his voice filled with an uncharacteristic tremor.

We all joined the older man where he stood near one bank of the channel. He pointed at something on the ground and it took me a moment to see it. Wherever the mud covering was scraped away, a pattern filled the river bed. It consisted of overlapping diamond shaped scales.

Shai got it before I did. "Snake skin!"

CHAPTER TWENTY-FIVE
BELLY OF THE BEAST

I glanced around. Now that Daik had pointed out the snake skin design in one place I began to see it everywhere. The entire channel seemed to be marked the same. Only the deposits of mud had kept us from seeing it before.

"Why would someone engrave this place with such a pattern?" Rence asked.

I went to one knee, used the tip of my dagger to pry up a few of the scale-like structures. They were hard but clearly not made of stone. The material felt more like…fingernails. Beneath them lay normal looking soil.

"It's not an engraved pattern," I said. "It's real."

"Impossible!" Rence exploded. "A paving maybe."

"Look at it," I said. "Some scales are bigger than others; they don't all overlap the same." I pointed out what appeared to be a scar cutting across half a dozen scales; I pointed out a pair of missing scales. "Snake skins are like Human fingerprints. They're all subtly different. I've never known an intelligent race to engrave things like that. Or to make paving materials like that. Intelligence demands order, consistency, symmetry. This is unique. And it's real. Like a skin that's been shed."

"This…river is verlangs in extent," Shai said. "If the whole thing is like this, that's a very big snake."

"Bigger now," Daik said. "If this is its *shed* skin."

I made no response other than rising to my feet.

"Impossible," Rence said again. "There's never been a snake that size. There can't be. No way it could survive."

"A few years ago I lived on another planet," I said. "With only one intelligent race. With one moon far too distant to sail an airship to. A planet without knowledge of the sphere gates, or sorcery, or the Asadhie. I'm afraid my sense of what is possible has been expanded of late."

"So," Rence spoke, "you're saying a snake as big as a…river lay here, created this channel with its titanic weight, I guess, then shed its skin and slithered off to…somewhere?"

Rence sounded angry but I knew his words weren't truly directed at me and that they came more from frustration—and perhaps fear—than from actual anger. I'd seen his bravery in battle against foes Human and inhuman. But we all have things that threaten our courage.

"I'm saying the skin right here in this place is real," I replied. "I don't know anything beyond that."

"Ruenn is right," Shai said. "We're facing a being who considers himself a god. Who has something of that kind of power. There's no telling what terrors he's brought to life to destroy us."

"It doesn't matter anyway," Valyan interrupted. "We can't turn back now. We're being watched."

"From where?" I asked.

"Everywhere. Though there are more behind us than in front."

I looked around, studying the petrified trees and the thick gray fungus that overlay them. Only an occasional twitch of movement showed in the gray canopy. It might have been the wind but almost certainly wasn't.

Daik had seen the same movements. "Maybe some kind of bird," he said.

"I don't think anything as normal as a bird lives in *these* trees," Valyan said. "And whatever the watchers are, they're good sized."

Daik shrugged.

"Let's move," I said. "Everybody keep an eye on your surroundings and keep your weapons handy."

We headed on up the dead river, along a channel left—apparently—by some monstrous thing that could not in all logic exist. The heart of dread darkness lay before us.

CHAPTER TWENTY-SIX

HERE LIE NIGHTMARES

The tree-covering gray fungus thickened along the banks as we threaded our way along the river, but the channel also widened so the reddish sky began to peek through again above us. Despite that sky's bloody color, I felt better for being able to see it. The opening up of our path even brought a lessening of the river's stench.

"Shouldn't it be night by now?" Daik asked after a while.

I looked around, startled at the question. I shouldn't have been.

"I mean," the older warrior continued. "Even if we arrived at Vessoth's pyramid in earliest morn, it's been more than ten dhaur since."

"Quite a bit more," Shai said. "Other than that instant of total blackness back in the pyramid, we seem to have eternal day inside Nimeru."

"Or eternal twilight," I suggested. "Given the color of the sky."

Shai snorted an agreement.

"Perhaps we should camp," Valyan said. "We won't find the end of this river without a stop or two along the way."

I studied my companions. Talera's day is two hours longer than Earth's, and those who live here have adapted. But we'd been without much sleep for quite a few days now. Tiredness had come to dwell in the eyes of my friends; I suddenly felt it in myself.

"Right," I said to Valyan. "We need some rest. There's nothing to light a fire with but we've all made cold camps before."

"We could try burning the fungus," Daik suggested.

I shook my head. "No telling what kind of smoke it would give off. I don't want to end up looking like the trees here."

Daik grimaced. "Good! I didn't want to touch the stuff anyway."

"I'll want two sets of eyes open at all times," I said. "Valyan and Daik will have first watch. Then Rence and myself."

Shai's nostrils flared. "What about me?" she snapped. "If you think—"

"You've had the least amount of sleep of any of us," I interrupted. "You Piloted us all the way to Nimeru. You'll get your turn at watch next camp. There's going to be enough exhaustion to go around before this is through."

The glare in the woman's eyes softened and she gave a curt nod. I wasn't sure the two of us would ever become friends, but I was beginning to like Shai. There was no retreat in her but she was fair minded and intelligent, a good warrior to 'walk' this river with.

"We'll camp as far from the banks as possible," I continued. "That'll give us about twenty paces on either side of us for a buffer zone."

Within a few moments we had our supplies unloaded and made a cold meal of jerky and passal. After, we spread out our sleeping rolls and Shai, Rence, and I turned in while Valyan and Daik began their watches. I had expected it to take me a while to fall asleep. It didn't.

* * *

When I awoke it was dark. I didn't understand that, or why someone hadn't called me when the light changed so unexpectedly. I sat up. There was enough ambient glow from some source that I could just make out Shai and Rence as humped shapes laying in their own bedrolls. Daik and Valyan were nowhere to be seen.

I pushed to my feet, stood listening for a long moment. My ears detected a distant…murmur, which sounded a bit like a quiet sea brushing against a beach. I had no idea what it might represent, and didn't care at all for that sensation in this place.

Feeling increasingly alarmed, I was about to waken Shai and Rence when I glimpsed a shadow standing about a dozen paces away and realized it must be either Valyan or Daik. Quickly, I moved toward it, right fist resting on the hilt of my sword.

The shadow was bulky, meaning it was probably Daik. He appeared to be staring very intently at the far bank, and, not wanting to startle the older warrior too much, I called out softly. No response came back and I moved a few paces closer and called again. Again there was no response, and my sense of alarm turned into something much more intense.

I rushed forward, then froze as my eyes made out how Daik was standing. He looked like a stunted and twisted tree, bent to one side with his arms up like the broken limbs of a lightning-blasted oak.

I shouted now. "Daik!" He didn't hear. Or couldn't respond.

I closed the distance between us, saw then that he was completely clothed in the horrid gray fungus from the banks of the dead river. The stuff wrapped thickly around him, bulbous as links of sausage. It covered his face, his whole head. It…pulsed.

Without thinking, I thrust hands into the stuff, began clawing it away. A dark serum spattered across my wrists and onto the ground. I uncovered one of Daik's cheeks, one of his eyes. The skin of his face was desiccated, the corner of the mouth drawn up into a rictus. The eye was milky and sunken—mummified.

"No! Damn it! No!"

I backed away from the man, spun on my heels, called out: "Valyan! Shai! Rence!"

No one answered. I rushed back to our camp, dropped to one knee beside Shai and jerked back the hide covering her. She was worse than Daik. Tendrils of the fungus had grown up her nose and into her eyes. Fluid flowed down those tubules as if the fungus was feeding from her. Yet her chest rose and fell. She was alive!

A ruby radiance bloomed around me. The sand beneath me turned black.

I surged to my feet, drawing the rune-blade. An alien chuckle brought my head jerking around and I found myself facing Vessoth. The strange being floated in the air some twenty feet away, his body sparking like stirred embers from some hellish fire. Before him stood the man with the black silk mask, held literally upon a leash of gleaming silver. The man's mask quivered with what I took to be barely restrained rage. For a moment, my mind registered something nebulous about their outlines, as if they were half reflection and half real. Then rage took over.

"You're both dead!" I snarled, and charged.

The disguised swordsman's leash fell away and he came to meet me. A blade leaped into his left fist, a rapier, a glittering length of steel sharpened to an evil edge. My rune-sword was broader, heavier. I brought it swinging with all my strength behind it, hoping to snap his blade where the two struck.

It didn't work.

Swift as a striking snake, my foe slid to one side, parried my attack at an angle that deflected the force of the blow away from his steel. Then his own sword came licking across and I felt the sting of a cut across the meat of my shoulder.

I ignored it, bore in. Anger over the loss of my companions gave me a swiftness I could not normally tap and I drove him back in a flurry of blows. I still could not pierce his guard. His technique was superb.

As is inevitable in such a fight, one man's attack falters and the other rallies. It became my turn to be driven back. But the unidentified swordsman had no better luck beating my defense than I had his. All the while, Vessoth cackled like some insane crimson harlequin.

Then my enemy paused. His eyes widened with startlement. He took a step back from me.

For a moment I stood rooted in my boots. Confusion swept me. Sweat drenched me. It was hot, broiling. I felt a tingling in my left hand and wrist and looked down. Below the elbow, across the tanned flesh, pustules of gray had sprung to life. They began to spread.

The fungus!

I cried out—an inarticulate sound of fear. I backed away from where I'd been standing, as if I could escape from something that was already a part of me. The pustules of fungus burst, releasing streamers of tissue that began to curl their way into tubes around my forearm. Through those tubes, pale ichors pulsed.

Cut it off!

The words screamed themselves into my mind. I had to cut off my left arm before the corruption spread further, before it consumed me. I raised the sword.

"Ruenn."

"Ruenn!"

I looked up. Vessoth was gone. For a moment I saw the swordsman struggling against the leash that once more encircled his neck. His eyes raged as he fought the chain like a war hound surging for the kill. I was the prey he sought. In the next instant a smear of intense purple light swirled over him and he was gone too.

Something like a sphere gate, I thought. *Almost.*

"RUENN!"

I turned to see Valyan sprinting toward me.

I looked down at my left arm. The flesh was clean, unsullied.

Valyan reached me, grabbed my shoulder. "Are you all right?"

"I…I don't know."

Beyond Valyan's shoulder I caught a glimpse now of Shai and Daik and Rence. They joined us. They too were fine, though their faces showed concern. I knew it was for me.

"What did you see?" I demanded of Valyan. "Just now. When you called to me. What did you see?"

"I saw you…fighting something. A shadow. I couldn't tell what. I called out. Then a flash of light, like a reflection from a mirror. And you were alone."

"Maybe Ruenn just had a nightmare," Daik protested. "Maybe he sleepwalked."

Shai shook her head. "No, I saw something too. Heard it. The sound of sword against sword. Something was here."

I reached to my shoulder where a thin cut oozed blood through the linen of my shirt. I held up a red finger to show.

"It was like the other…sendings from Vessoth," I said. I glanced down once more at my left arm, rubbed at it; it looked and felt normal. "But stronger than any before. Must mean we're getting closer to the source."

"Good news," Rence said dryly.

I glanced at the gaunt warrior and found myself suddenly grinning. "You sound like Diken now."

He grinned too. "Then Diken's a smart fellow."

I sobered. "I think Vessoth was using some kind of sphere gate," I said to them all. "It didn't act like it was fully open. Even so, that means—"

"Means Chalathar's hold on the gates is weakening," Shai interjected. I saw her face tighten with worry.

"Maybe," I agreed. "Could be it's something else. It didn't look like any gate I've ever seen. If it *was* a sphere gate then it could be that Vessoth is planning to escape Nimeru soon."

"Then all our efforts will have been in vain," Valyan noted.

"Yes."

"We better move," Shai said.

"Yes," I said again.

"I think we're being strongly encouraged to do so anyway," Valyan remarked.

I glanced at him and he pointed back along the way we'd come. We all turned to look. The watchers in the petrified trees, those who had been following us along hidden ways, had shown themselves.

CHAPTER TWENTY-SEVEN

SACRIFICE

The river bed behind us seethed with creatures. There were perhaps a hundred of them. Maybe a few more. They vaguely resembled spiders grown to the size of Dobermans, but they were no descendent of any Earthly species. They had the swollen abdomens of spiders, but also twelve legs instead of eight, and two eyes only, which stood above their wedge shaped heads on stalks.

The things were see-through. Their exoskeletons were faceted, like cut diamonds, and nearly as clear as crystal. Inside their bodies floated strange, milky organs, with nothing resembling a heart, or stomach, or intestines. Near their mouths were long tubes of gray liquid connected to twin sets of fangs that lifted the corners of their jaws. Their venom was the fungus material itself, I realized. A shudder passed over me.

The creatures moved more like spiders than anything else, in fits and starts, darting now to the left and then to the right, but generally coming steadily toward us. Spurts of dust rose from beneath their myriad feet.

"Bows," I said. We drew them into our hands.

All of us except Valyan had chosen crossbows for this expedition—for the quickness with which they could be fired and for the fact they could be triggered with one hand. Valyan had his usual longbow and was still faster with it than the rest of us with our crossbows. Of course, he was the best archer I'd ever seen.

At the instant our weapons were loaded and ready, however, the alien spider-things stopped moving toward us, only stood jittering in place on their dozen legs. Their fangs drip-dripped but they did not attack.

"Don't tell me they know what bows are for," Rence said.

"I doubt it," I said. "Whatever is controlling them does, though. And it doesn't want a fight yet. It wants us to move on down the river."

"You know," Daik said. He paused to reach into a pouch at his waist and withdraw a good pinch of jit-leaf [7] to stuff into his mouth. Then he continued talking around the wad of ground up material, "I'm really beginning to wish I'd drawn the short straw back at the beginning of the

---

[7]   See Taleran Encyclopedia entry 7 for information on Talera's native plants and animals. All entries are in alphabetical order.

river." He spat yellow juice onto the ground, then glanced toward me and smiled.

I returned it.

I looked around at the others. "These things are here to keep us from turning back, but that ship has sailed for all of us anyway. We go on."

With the spider-things following us like scavengers waiting to pick our bones, we continued forward along the river. Now, pools of stagnant water began to appear here and there in the channel bed. They bubbled and steamed, as if heated from beneath, and soon we strode through what felt like a furnace. Sweat poured down us; breathing became a chore. I took off my duster and draped it over a shoulder. The air grew even more foul and I was grateful for the bandana covering my mouth and nose.

"How long since we left the ship?" Daik asked.

"You mean," Shai said, "how long before they come after us?"

"Yes, I suppose I do," Daik admitted.

"Cailif told me five to six days before they'd be ready to sail," I said. "We're well into our second day now."

"Given what we saw of the river from above, we'll reach the end of it before they can get to us," Shai said.

"Probably," I agreed.

"Maybe we should wait for them," Daik said.

I gestured toward our nasty looking pack of escorts. "I'm guessing that would mean a fight with our friends back there. That's probably gonna happen anyway but I'd rather choose our ground. I've been looking for something we could use as a barricade against their numbers. We could pick them off with arrows then."

"Vhish!" Daik cursed.

"Speaking of which," Rence said. "Unlike the rest of you, I don't have a bladder the size of a ship. I need a stop."

With the exception of Shai, we all laughed.

"All right," I said. "We'll take a break. Let's keep one eye on our 'rear guard.'" I jerked my chin toward the spider-things.

By instinct perhaps, we all moved toward the bank of the river and found a depression in the channel where we could take care of our bodily needs. The top of the bank was about head high to me and I noticed something strange there. I leaned closer to examine it.

"Damn!" I said to the others. "Look at this."

In a line along the bank, each separated by a heka or so, red thorns had been embedded in the ground, their tips reaching about a finger's length above the surface. That was odd enough, but many of the thorns were not empty. Once living things were impaled upon them, mostly beetles and worms.

I knew there were birds on Earth that impaled small tidbits of food on thorns around their territory to attract mates. But surely a bird would not have been so orderly in its arrangement of offerings.

"Anyone ever seen anything like this?" I asked, uneasy.

Head shakes came from all around.

The Human capacity to adjust to fear is often amazing. Despite all that had happened to us: the fire and blood of the battle at Teleur, swords and cannon against the Sporns, our fight against the claw-wings and the loss of friends, the evil stench of the dead river and the spider-fanged monsters following us, I had not tasted of despair. Nor had I felt true horror outside of those moments when I believed I'd been contaminated by the gray fungus. Now, the simple fact of small creatures impaled for some unknown purpose raised gooseflesh across my entire body. I knew horror once more that I did not think would dissipate with the passing of time.

Without speaking we took up our journey again, but our eyes watched the banks. Horror grew. Because the thorns got steadily taller as we progressed, and the things impaled upon them grew apace, first little creatures like tadpoles and minnows, then frogs and small turtles, then birds and bigger fish.

Soon the thorns became sharpened stakes, two to three feet tall and set farther apart along the ground to accommodate the bigger sacrifices. We began to see creatures the size of rabbits and cats upon the spikes. I stopped walking when I came upon what had to be a descendent of an Earthly baboon. It must have been placed very recently. Its red blood ran down the stake; it still breathed and its eyes were open, though it seemed incapable of any physical movement. Angered at the cruel display, I drew a knife and cut the beast's throat to give it peace.

Daik stood beside me. He lifted the bottom of his bandana, spat out his chew of jit-leaf. Rence looked confused, Valyan speculative, Shai furious.

"I fail to see the purpose in such a thing," she said between gritted teeth.

"Vessoth has a purpose," I said. "Maybe just to threaten us. Or to break us. Maybe something else."

Where we had stopped was right before another of the S-shaped bends in the channel. From around that bend now, I heard a sound I recognized, the click of clawed feet against the hardened snake scales lining the river's bed.

"Sporns!" I said.

We spread out slightly and drew our bows as the Sporns came into view. At their head strode a Thye Vessoth. It wore a scarlet loin-cloth and one hand rested upon a long staff of ash. Embedded in the staff's upper length was a jewel-green wand that burned with an inner fire. There were perhaps sixty of the Sporns; it was the Thye Vessoth I watched.

The Thye Vessoth. Servants of Vohanna when I'd first learned of them. Servants of Vessoth himself no doubt now. They were reptilian, but with agate blue eyes as hard as stone. This one's scaled hide was an iridescent yellow-green. It stood as tall as a man, with two arms and two legs, but with a face made hideous by an absence of any Humanity. Fan-like vanes grew from the side of its nose-less face where ears should have been. They folded open and back with each breath the creature drew.

"What do you want?" I demanded.

The Thye Vessoth knew I was speaking to it. A nearly lipless mouth opened. Words came out, distorted with hisses but understandable.

"It is not I that wants. It is Vessoth!"

It lowered its head slightly as it spoke its god's name, and the verdant wand on its staff brightened for an instant.

I'd seen such wands plenty of times before. Much like the ones used by the Pilot Caste, each of these had been touched to a *toir'in-or* stone and used to siphon off and contain some of the milkstone's power. But, while Piloting wands turn a faint milky color when in use, these became as brilliantly green as cut emeralds. I had no idea why the color was different between the two types of wands; I knew only that the green ones were tools of sorcery. My hand slid down to rest upon the grip of the Colt Trooper holstered at my belt. If the Thye Vessoth tried to use its magic, I had some other magic to counter it. It was called a bullet.

"What are the spider-things doing?" I whispered to Shai at my left.

She looked around, then back. "They seem to be waiting."

I nodded, then took a half step toward the Sporns and the lizard priest in their midst.

"Est Yaal shei, Vessoth," I said slowly and deliberately, which best translates as, "To hell with Vessoth."

The sorcerer stiffened. Its broad tale quivered. "Blasphemers suffer indescribable torments," it said.

I smiled. "I guess we'll see. Now what do you *want*?"

It gestured with its wand toward the death-ornamented stakes along the banks. "A sacrifice is required before you pass farther up this holy river."

"No."

"Then one will be taken."

"Valyan," I said.

Swifter than wind, the Nakscherii warrior drew and released an arrow. The tlatel-wood shaft punched completely through the Thye Vessoth's throat and sent it staggering back in a welter of pale rheum.

The Sporns shrieked as their priest struck the ground, its sorcerous staff falling beside it. By that time we were all firing crossbow bolts and arrows into their packed formation as quickly as we could work our weapons. Insectile limbs were torn away; silver blood sprayed. The Sporns shrieked again and threw themselves at us.

I fired a copper quarrel into the face of a charging Sporn. The heavy bolt smashed through the feelers around its mouth, tore half its head away. I dropped the crossbow and drew the rune-blade.

That blade began to reap.

The Sporns swarmed around the five of us. We were rocks against the tide, the edges of our weapons all that stood between us and a bloody ending. Rence's twin kahnnas flamed. Shai's rapiers cut, slashed, stabbed. Even Valyan foreswore his bow and pulled his saber. Our enemies came against us with curved yataghans flailing. But their steel glittered no brighter than ours, and they died.

Amid the wild clamor of crashing blades, we all offered up sacrifices to the gods of war. Then it was over. The remaining Sporns fled, many with limbs missing and wounds dripping gore. They left their dead littering the ground. I turned to my companions. Smiles curved the grimy faces I saw. One face was missing.

"Where's Daik?"

We all looked for our friend, then looked toward the bend in the river around which the last of the Sporns had disappeared.

"They must have taken him," Rence said. "He was beside me but I didn't see it."

I grabbed up my crossbow and took off running. Footsteps hammered the ground behind me as the others followed. We rounded the bend in the river, and stopped. Nothing was to be seen except for the scuffing of hundreds of tracks in the channel's bed.

The Sporns were gone, taking a good man with them.

CHAPTER TWENTY-EIGHT

A PLEASURE TO BURN

We plodded now. Along the river. Like automatons. It seemed at times we'd been walking this channel forever. All of us were exhausted. All of us hurt for the loss of Daik. For me, he had been my crewman and my responsibility. He'd also become a friend.

Had there been a trail to follow, I would have taken it in pursuit of crewman *or* friend. Unfortunately there were many trails. The Sporns had split into at least a dozen small groups after the fight and had fled into the petrified forest, beneath the gray canopy of the fungus. Nowhere did we see any sign of which group might have Daik.

The Thye Vessoth had mentioned "sacrifice," and horrible as that word sounded it gave me some slight hope Daik might be alive, and that they would try to use him against us later. Maybe, just maybe, they might show him to us *before* they sacrificed him. That would be our best chance to save him. Our sole chance most likely.

Adding to our misery was the heat that continued to build around us. The air steamed; a hot mist coiled along the river bed. We were all soaked in sweat but we'd had to start rationing our water. We certainly couldn't drink the sludge that filled the many pools now dotting the channel. Most of it bubbled and stank with sulfur and other chemicals. Some of it did not look like water at all but like burnt grease caked in the bottom of an old skillet.

It did not help that the river had started to narrow again so the dead jungle pressed closer on either side of us. Not only did this shrink our view of the red sky overhead, but it placed the line of sacrificial stakes and their offerings constantly in the corners of our eyes. Those stakes stood as tall as a man now, and their cargos had changed again. Mostly we saw just heads, the heads of ghyre and reeth and taverel, the heads of horses, stugah and pigs. I wished for blinders to spare me sight of all that death.

We passed a wide hole in the river bed where a viscous, black substance bubbled to the surface. I saw a dozen more such holes in front of us. The tarry liquid filling them looked like crude oil and I couldn't imagine where it would be coming from on a planetoid that was artificial in nature.

I stopped walking, glanced behind me. The dead-river spiders still followed us and I was getting tired of that. I went down on one knee and leaned over the black pool to smell it. It stank like petroleum, though with a new idea running suddenly through my head I didn't find the smell terribly unpleasant.

The others stopped as well. "What are you doing?" Shai asked.

"I think it's time to get rid of our escort," I replied.

"How?"

I didn't answer. Instead, I slid Daik's pack, which I was now carrying, off a shoulder and rummaged inside to pull out a long coil of rope I'd asked him to bring. Cutting off a six-inch length of the rope, I soaked one end in the oily pool. From my own pack I took a small device called a "striker," which some Taleran genius had invented many years before. It consists of a small metal tube filled with highly flammable rundal oil into which a wick has been inserted. The cap of the tube contains an attached flint and tiny metal spike. To get fire, you pop the lid and it drags the spike over the flint, sending sparks onto the wick.

I clicked the striker open and held the flaming wick to the wetted end of the piece of hemp. It flamed up instantly, sending sparks flying. I quickly tossed it aside, then looked up at the others and smiled.

"Fire," Shai said.

"Keep an eye on our friends," I said to the others as I began to feed coil after coil of the rope into the noxious ink-black puddle.

"They've stopped moving," Valyan said. "They're waiting for us. Like always"

I soaked about twenty-five tahng of the rope, over seventy-five feet. Leaving a good handhold of clean twine to hang on to, I cut the rest off and stuffed it back in its pack. I handed everything except weapons to the others to carry and then started pulling the oil impregnated rope out of its pool and weaving it along the channel, making sure to dip coils of it into all of the similar pools I could reach.

"All right," I said. "When we get to the end of the rope I'm going to drop and hide. The rest of you keep going. Slowly. And ready your bows. As soon as the fire flares up, start shooting. I'd rather none of them get away."

Nods let me know everyone understood.

Now, the steaming mist that half filled the channel worked in our favor. I didn't know the limits of the spider-things' vision but I doubted they could see us any better than we could see them. I was also rather skeptical about their ability to count the difference between three walking Humans and four.

We reached the end of the rope and I dropped flat beside it, doing my best to become part of the ground. The others continued on. I saw the mass of the spiders start forward on our trail. They were ugly through the mist. I waited with the striker ready to hand.

When the first monster was a bare handful of paces away, it saw me and froze. The thing had lips, and they curled back to reveal its four stabbing fangs. I didn't wait to see what it might do but worked the striker and lit my makeshift fuse. Flames spurted up, stuttered for an instant that brought my heart rising through my throat, then raced like a whirlwind down the oil drenched twine. Wherever the rope touched one of the black pools, fireballs ignited, spraying outward in every direction.

Spider beasts erupted into flames as I leaped up and drew my sword. I heard them shriek, like wounded horses. I could feel no pity. The creatures skittered madly about, twisting and turning as they tried to escape the fiery devil that gnawed at them, and consumed.

One fanged monster came leaping through the veil of smoke and mist at me, its carapace running red with fire. I hacked it in twain. Then I heard racing footsteps behind me and arrows and crossbow bolts from my friends began sleeting into the mass of the beasts. Most died burning. A few tried to flee. My companions cut them down. If any escaped, I did not see it.

Flames continued to roar skyward from the burning pools of oil. I backed away from the heat, sheathed my sword. Unexpectedly, Rence began pounding me on the back. Valyan too. I even saw Shai grinning, somewhat of a rare experience.

I smiled, then laughed. "That felt good. Like puncturing a boil."

"Indeed," Shai agreed. "I was sick of being driven by those things." She was apparently striving for a return to some decorum but her face wasn't cooperating.

"Now," I said, with something very close to a sigh of relief. "We need to find somewhere to set up camp. The way the channel has started to narrow, I think we may be getting close to the end of the river. But we're far too exhausted to face Vessoth as we are. Even if we're running low on time, we've *got* to have some rest."

I looked primarily at Shai. I thought she might make an argument for us to continue. I knew she was worried about Chalathar as he tried to hold the sphere gates closed against Vessoth and his minions. But even her iron constitution seemed to have reached its limit. She did no more than nod.

Vessoth would have to wait a little bit longer. So, too, would the unknown bladesman whose sword had already tasted my blood.

CHAPTER TWENTY-NINE

SHAI TELLS A STORY

After our victory over the dead river spiders, our luck took a turn for the better. I hoped it would last. We rounded another bend in the channel to find a decent camp site. A flash flood must have swept through this area not too long before. It had cleaned out the noxious pools of bubbling tar and replaced them with a fine layer of silt and sand that had later dried to form a nice, smooth surface. It looked more inviting than the softest mattress I'd ever seen. Too, even though it was still very hot, the air was cleaner here so we could lower our bandanas to breathe. That was a relief.

"This place," I said, then looked around to see that everyone was already shedding their packs.

"Too bad we can't build a cooking fire," Rence said. "I could go for some tea. Something to eat besides passal."

"Maybe a fire isn't out of the question," I replied.

I walked over to the river bank where several of the ubiquitous impalement stakes had been washed out of their beds. Picking one up, I found it was made from some kind of dense wood that looked like it might be chelaquin. Using a knife, I began cutting shavings for kindling.

"This'll work," I said.

The others followed my lead and began dragging stakes out onto the sand and hacking them up for firewood. We soon had a blaze going and a pot of verhlis tea brewing. Verhlis is a staple on Talera and is consumed much the same way coffee is on Earth. I don't know if it contains caffeine or not but it does have stimulating properties. Its natural sweetness makes one think of honey.

Valyan had brought along a dozen taabers and we cut a few up to mix with some jerky and a little of our precious water supply to make a stew. A taaber is a bit like a hard potato and I suspected the name was a variation on the English word. I didn't really care. It was good to eat something softer than the travel foods we'd been gnawing on.

After our meal, I told everyone to get some rest while I kept watch. There were a few protests but none very adamant. Soon, my three companions were rolled in their blankets and sound asleep. I poured another helping of tea and got up to walk around so as to keep myself awake.

Perhaps a dhaur and a half passed when I heard stirring among the sleepers and glanced around to see that Shai had risen and was filling a mug of tea for herself. She brought it over to join me.

"You didn't sleep much," I said.

She sipped from her cup. "I don't need a lot of sleep. Between Pilot training and some meditation techniques Chalathar taught me, I'm able to get a good, deep rest in a short time."

"Sounds useful."

"I'll teach you. When this is over."

I nodded.

"You should rest yourself now," she said.

"In a bit."

We stood together on watch then, and after a moment Shai spoke again, which surprised me. She hadn't shown any evidence of being the talkative sort.

"Chalathar told me he asked you once to join him in his fight to bring peace to Talera."

"He did. I said I would. When Nyshphal was safe. That doesn't appear to be an easy task to accomplish."

I tried to make my tone light, in hopes of getting Shai to smile. No such luck. All I earned was a nod.

"How did *you* come to serve Chalathar?" I asked boldly.

Her gaze shifted to mine. She remained closed off for a long moment, but then sighed softly, as if reaching a difficult decision to trust me.

"I know quite a lot about you so I guess it's fair for you to know something of me. After mother died I became quite the handful for father. Rebellious hardly covers it. At fifteen, when we were informed that I was eligible for Pilot school, *he* decided I would go and learn some discipline. I wanted to go, but not be 'ordered' to do so. I stole a flyer and took off.

"I headed into Thresh, the only place I could think of. In the mountains north of a city called Twinegarten, I crashed. Wind currents are always treacherous among the peaks and I wasn't nearly as good a Pilot as I imagined. I walked away from the wreckage but would have died in those mountains if it weren't for Chalathar.

"A pair of hungry quall cornered me. I managed to squeeze into a crevice in a cliff but they were tearing it away piece by piece. Chalathar was out hunting. He killed them both. With a bow and arrows. I'd never seen such shooting.

"After I told him my story, he offered to take me to Twinegarten, where in those days he'd established himself as a merchant. He said he would sponsor me to the Pilot school there. I agreed. I think, in part, because I was already half smitten with him. He was so tall. With red hair and those pale eyes.

"I...." She paused for a moment and I could almost swear a blush of deeper gold crawled into her face. "I threw myself at him. One night. After we'd been alone together in the woods for several days. Somehow, he managed to turn me away without hurting my feelings. The next day we reached the city. Chalathar insisted I contact my father and tell him I was alive. He didn't insist that I go home when my father ordered me to."

"What did your father do?" I asked.

"He came to get me. We argued. But I'd learned something from Chalathar in those mountains. I enrolled at the Pilot's school in Twinegarten. After I completed training, Chalathar revealed to me who he really was and what he was doing. I was happy to join him."

"Did you ever mend things with your father?"

"Mostly. I don't see him very often. When I do we pretend it never happened."

"You know," I said, changing the subject, "I met Rence before. When he came with Chalathar for our final battle with Vohanna. I'm surprised you weren't with them then."

"I was on another mission."

"What kind of mission?"

She did smile then. "One requiring a Pilot."

I chuckled. "I take your meaning."

She shook her head. "I'm not sure you do. It's not that I don't trust you. I've learned to do so. I think such details should come from Chalathar himself. I know he would like to speak with you about many things."

I nodded.

"You should really get some rest now," she said.

I nodded again. "Two dhaur. No more."

"I'll wake you."

Feeling exhaustion lying like a fuzzy layer of wool over my thoughts, I sought my bedroll. I slept and did not dream.

CHAPTER THIRTY

THEY WHO SUFFER

A little over two dhaur later, the four of us left our temporary haven for what I hoped would be the last leg of our dead river odyssey. The channel continued to narrow dramatically, the way a snake's body does just before the head. I became more and more convinced we were nearing the end.

The stakes lining the banks suggested the same thing. They had grown taller, double the height of a man now, and their burdens soon reached the ultimate in horror. We began to see intelligent beings impaled. I noted an Ebon Llurn, a Klar, a Vhichang. Mostly I saw Sporns. Dozens of them. All these beings had clearly been impaled alive, for their fresh blood had run down like paint upon the wood. Their expressions screamed of agony, even the inhuman faces of the insect-like Sporns.

It struck me that there could be no better illustration of Vessoth's evil. Not only did he torture and murder those he thought of as enemies, but he slaughtered even the ones who served him. All life seemed but a tool to him. We had to stop him before he escaped Nimeru and brought his dark hate to every land of Talera.

There was also a third reason why I was sure we were coming to the termination of our search for Vessoth. Days ago in Nyshphal the Snake God had sent me a vision of my death and I'd felt the bite of the fatal sword through my chest. There'd been no resulting wound but there had been pain and a slick of blood on the skin after. The pain had quickly faded then. After the second vision, it had not passed so fast.

The same hurt had flared again as we first approached the dead river. I'd told myself it was a coincidence, but I could make that argument no longer. Where the masked swordsman's vision-blade had struck, my chest had begun steadily to throb. Each step we took increased the pain. It had to be because we were nearing the source.

"Ivrail!" Valyan said suddenly.

I was startled to hear him, for he called upon his goddess only in moments of the strongest emotions.

"What?" I asked, though I was almost afraid to find out.

He pointed ahead.

I saw a straight stretch of channel before us, perhaps a hundred tahng in length. A stake loaded with a sacrificed Sporn stood every ten paces or so along the banks. That was not what the Nakscherii warrior pointed at. Valyan had better eyes than I did. All I saw was a black opening at the end of the channel, and a large wheel-shaped structure upon which something hung suspended.

"It's Daik," Valyan said then. "Alive!" He began to run.

Daik! Alive!

I too began to run. Rence and Shai followed. We tore swiftly down the channel. I recognized Daik then. His arms and legs were stretched into an X against a crimson wheel fit for a giant's wagon. He writhed against the bonds that held him.

Valyan and I reached our friend at the same moment but held back as we saw what had been done to him. The wheel where he hung was of hardwood. Iron staples, like the ones I'd used on Earth to put up barbed wire fences, had been hammered in around his wrists and ankles. They'd been hammered so deep the circulation was cut off in his extremities and both his hands and feet were brutally swollen and starting to blacken. The staples were almost swallowed in his lacerated flesh and I saw no chance of prying them loose without hurting him further.

I looked up to meet Daik's eyes. They were red-rimmed and bloody, rolling with pain. His face was ghastly, sunken, and only the lips had color against his pallor. He had been stripped naked and his body was a mass of bruises. The worst thing was that he didn't look relieved to see us.

"Hold on," I said, almost choking on the words. "We'll get you down."

"Doesn't…matter," he said, his voice a dry, whispering croak.

The wheel where Daik hung stood on a small stone base and I climbed up beside my friend. Valyan climbed up on the other side.

"It matters," I said to the older warrior. "Ahrethane will be here with the ship soon. She's a healer. She'll know what to do. If we can get you down."

I looked over at Valyan: "We'll have to hack this whole structure apart," I said to him. He nodded and we both drew our daggers.

"No. Ruenn!" Daik spoke again, his voice a little stronger.

I paused. His eyes were trying to focus to meet mine but the pain must have been overwhelming.

"Look," Daik said. "Look. My…stomach."

I looked. A pattern of darkened pores stippled the flesh around his navel. It took me a moment to realize what I was seeing.

An involuntary hiss escaped my lips. "No. God no!"

"What is it?" Shai demanded.

"Krutt!" I said.

She looked confused. Rence too. Valyan had seen the same thing I had and his throat worked as he tried to swallow back bile.

"Not the curse," I said to Shai and Rence. "The insect. Those dark spots are holes made by the ovipositors of the Krutt beetle."

"Oh," Shai said. The word came out very small, as if from a child Rence turned his head and spat thickly, spat again.

"How long?" I asked Daik.

"Too...long," he murmured. "Can... Feel... The larva...hatched." His eyes did focus then. "Kill me! Ruenn. Kill...me. Please!"

I shook my head. "No! Ahrethane. She—"

"Ruenn!" Valyan said.

I glanced around at my friend's alarmed tone. He nodded his chin toward Daik's belly and I looked there again. My gorge rose. Daik's navel had collapsed inward, and through the resulting hole worms came spilling. They were an obscene pink in color and as long as a man's little finger. They were mostly head and jaws. Dozens of them rained down around the base of the wheel, and following them came a gush of black blood and other liquids. Then the bleeding slowed to a trickle as a knot of other worms dammed the hole.

I heard the sound of retching. Smelled it. Like acid. I didn't know if it were Shai or Rence, or both. I did not look to see. My shoulders slumped. There must be thousands more of the Krutt larva inside Daik. Most of his soft tissues, his intestines, liver, spleen, would already be gone.

"Kill me," Daik begged again.

He was dead already.

I lifted the dagger, placed the point against Daik's chest over where his heart would lie. "It was an honor to serve with you," I said, and shoved the blade home in one quick stroke. He spasmed; his eyes rolled back in his head. He left us for good.

I drew the weapon from the wound and stepped back.

With shaking voice, I told Valyan what I wanted. "Find one of the oil pools. We'll douse his body and the wheel with it. Burn it all!"

Valyan nodded, turned to obey. I stopped him for an instant. "Fill one of our empty water skins with oil too. We might need to bring fire along with us."

Valyan nodded again, moved away. I glanced toward Shai and Rence but they were already following Valyan to offer their help. I was glad of that a moment later, for it kept them from seeing the final indignity Vessoth forced upon Daik.

When I turned to look back into my dead companion's face, his mouth was open and filled with ruby light. Words came whispering through that light. Vessoth's words.

"Ruenn. Ruenn. I know the wounds you've taken from my servant's blade are paining you. That pain will grow. Just as with your friend and the Krutt, the wounds will eat you alive from the inside. You are already a hollow man."

I snarled and hoped the Snake God could see it. "You've made a mistake," I said. "You only get one."

No answer came. The ruby light died.

I stood alone with the corpse of my friend and a dagger wet with his blood.

CHAPTER THIRTY-ONE

UNDERWORLD

Beyond the wheel upon which Daik had been hung, the dead river reached its end. The ground dropped away as if sliced cleanly with a knife, and a series of iron steps led down into a dark, subterranean lair. We were not meant to flounder in blackness, though. As our feet rang on the steps, a dim golden light bloomed around us. By that light we made our way.

Behind us, we left a fiery signal for Bryce and the crew aboard the *Khiang*. To build Daik a proper bier, we tore up the sacrificial stakes along the banks and piled them high around our friend's body. We lay the corpses of murdered Sporns around the base of the wheel and soaked the whole arrangement with oil. We lit it and walked away, knowing it would burn for hours and smoke for days.

If I knew Cailif Ostt, he'd exceeded his expectations about how long it would take to make the *Khiang* ready to sail. Reinforcements might already be on their way to us and the smoke would guide them.

We could not wait, though. Increasingly, it felt as if time were turning against us. Vessoth was not sitting idle. I felt he would face us directly if he had too, but that he preferred to let us blunt our steel against his servants while he sought a way to escape Nimeru. The moon was still a prison to him in many ways; I doubted he'd had time to gather the resources he wanted before Chalathar closed the sphere gates. And, like his wife Vohanna, the Snake God almost surely had a bolt hole somewhere on Talera where he could build his power undisturbed.

Yet, judging from Vohanna and what we'd seen so far from Vessoth, the Asadhie did nothing in the simplest way. They'd used Talera like their own personal chessboard for too long. Or, more accurately, they'd treated this world like a vast Kyrellian [8] board, which is a highly complicated war game similar in many ways to chess. Complexity seemed ingrained in the Asadhie mind and I doubted we'd seen more than the opening moves in Vessoth's game. It would be foolish to think differently.

---

8   See the Taleran Encyclopedia entry 8 for information about the game of Kyrellian.

At the end of several hundred steps down into the gold-lit underground, we came to a long corridor stretching far out in front of us. It was six-sided, like a cell in a honeycomb—maybe twenty feet in height and wide enough for all of us to walk comfortably abreast. The walls were of some metallic alloy put together in segments. Every five paces or so we passed a small separator, like a crack in the corridor around which a flashing light traveled. I had no idea of its purpose.

The air felt wintery here after the horrific heat outside. It was also odorless and tasted clean. Our half poisoned lungs appreciated it. The cool, crispness was like a balm to our entire bodies. We all lowered our sweat soaked bandanas. I even put my duster back on.

Before we got far down the corridor, a grinding noise came from behind us. The walls vibrated and dust motes came sifting down. I thought for an instant the roof must be caving in over the underground's entrance, but the sound was too regular and then came to a booming stop.

"I think Vessoth just shut the door behind us," Shai said dryly.

I realized that must indeed explain the sound, but it didn't matter.

"We weren't going back anyway," I said. "When the *Khiang* arrives she can blow the doors apart with her cannon. If Ahrethane can't open it."

I continued on down the corridor. The others caught up and we strode side by side along that way. As with Vessoth's scarlet pyramid, the walls were engraved with symbols. Shai let one hand trail across those deeply incised marks.

"Are these the same as we saw before?" she asked.

"I don't think so," I said. "Those looked like mathematical symbols. This is more like...writing."

"If it is, it would appear to be in more than one language."

She pointed to the wall we were looking at, then gestured to the opposite wall across the corridor. I studied both sides as we proceeded.

"You're right," I agreed after a bit. "I wonder if it could be the same message in two different tongues."

"Like a bragging wall?" Shai asked.

I looked at her curiously.

"In Thresh, I've seen tombs with stories of great deeds written on the walls in a dozen different languages. Always figured the people buried in those kinds of tombs wanted to make sure everyone could read of their glorious accomplishments."

"Something like that would be a boon to translators," I said. "There'll be a lot here to study. Once this is all over."

No one responded to that.

While the corridor looked straight as we walked it, I felt sure it had a slight right hand curve to it. It also sloped gently downhill. After a while, we came upon side corridors and briefly followed two of them. Both were short, no more than a few hundred paces, and ended in diamond shaped rooms that struck me as some kind of storage area. The ones we checked stood open and empty. I imagined it was the same for them all.

It seemed unlikely to me that Nimeru had originally been built as a prison. It must have been converted for that purpose, and perhaps at one time the storage rooms had been filled with whatever strange artifacts the Asadhie found necessary for carrying out their activities. I did not wish to think of anything more than the coming showdown with Vessoth and his pet swordsman, but I couldn't help but be filled once again with questions regarding the ancient Asadhie and those beings who lived now and claimed the same title.

This moon, for example! It was a marvel of engineering. The beings that made it *must* have had powers many would judge as godlike. Yet, Vohanna had not even known the concepts of engines and gunpowder explosives. She'd had to be shown that by members of my old ship's crew from Earth. How could Vohanna and Vessoth—and yes, Chalathar—have once possessed the knowledge to build something like this moon and then lost it?

How could mere Humans such as myself and Rannon be anything more than fleas to such beings? Yet, it certainly seemed that we were. We and others like us had repeatedly been able to thwart Vohanna's plans.

Jedik had first used the term "technology" with me. I'd not even known what it meant until he explained. His culture had produced a technology capable of building ships that could travel through *space*. Yet, before his death, Jedik had admitted to me that Asadhie technology was far beyond anything his people could muster. Apparently, it was far beyond what beings like Vohanna and Vessoth could muster as well. Therein lay the conundrum. The "creators" of Talera appeared to be incapable of doing what they were credited with doing.

I was beginning to form an opinion about the Asadhie I had met. It wasn't a flattering one. I was beginning to believe they were imposters, masquerading as something they were not. Certainly they were powerful. Certainly dangerous. But they weren't even close to being gods and someone had to put a stop to their usurping of that title.

"There's a wider place ahead," Valyan said, interrupting my reflections.

We stopped for a moment when we came to that spot. It was a kind of alcove. The corridor itself ran on without alteration but there were chambers to either side of it where copper…benches were arranged as if for people to sit. Those benches had recently been used for another purpose. They were piled high with more of the sacrificial stakes we'd seen implanted along the dead river. At least some of the sacrifices themselves must have been carried out here. Blood, of various colors, had dripped and dried on the copper, and some of the benches bore nicks and scars that looked like the work of blades. I smelled old rot.

"Are those doors?" Rence asked, pointing to a pair of wide metal panels that made part of the wall behind the last benches on either side of the corridor.

"I don't know," I said. "Try the one on the right."

I approached the panel on the left side myself. It *looked* like a door but there was no handle by which it might be opened. I pushed and prodded. To no avail. Unlike the other walls all along the corridor, however, this panel had just one symbol engraved on it. As my fingers ran over it the word "exit" popped as a thought into my head. I had a feeling that answers to at least some of my questions about the Asadhie waited on the other side of this panel. They might as well have waited on Earth for all the good that did me.

"I suspect it's a door," I said, turning back to the others. "If so, it's locked."

"This one too," Rence added from across the way.

Shai shrugged. "We go on it seems."

A short distance ahead we came to a much larger widening of the way. This time, two other corridors came in at equal angles to cross the first. It reminded me very much of a switching station for trains and I began to suspect we were looking upon something similar. These tunnels were part of a transportation system, I felt sure. For people or supplies. Or both. Though what manner of vehicles might travel along them I could not guess.

"There are five possible exits from this place," Shai said. "Which one do we want?"

"I wish I knew," I responded. "Everyone have a look around to see if you can find anything to help."

The four of us spread out to search. The walls were not engraved here. Instead, near the openings of the six tunnels stood large rectangular blocks of copper. Each was densely covered in engraved script. *Almost like signposts*, I thought. Perhaps they were.

I stood looking at one, trying to make sense of it. "Anyone recognize any of the symbols on these things?"

"Here," Shai said. "I think."

I walked over to stand beside her where she was staring at another of the engraved blocks. She pointed to a mark that resembled an "S" with a bent nail pounded through it.

"This looks like the symbol we used in Pilot school to represent downward."

I glanced around. "The tunnel beyond it slants down. Maybe a coincidence. Still...."

Valyan was standing in front of a third block. "I see the name of the Goddess Ivrail," he said. "Written in the priest's tongue. I think most of the rest is in the same language but I have no knowledge to read it."

"Something a little different over here," Rence called. "You all need to see it."

We joined him, and none of us liked what we saw scraped off on the edge of another of the copper rectangles.

"Snake scales again," Shai said. "Big ones."

"Not as big as whatever we saw sign of at the dead river," Valyan added.

"Something that size couldn't even get down here," Rence said. "But this looks like it would fill most of one of these corridors. I sure don't want to meet it."

The gaunt warrior seemed to have forgotten that he'd denied even the possibility of a snake big enough to form the dead river. I wasn't going to remind him, but apparently Valyan decided the situation was worth a little teasing.

"Maybe this is the big one's baby," he said.

Rence looked startled, and I glanced over at my green Llurn friend and shook my head at his joke. He grinned. "Well, Diken would have said it. If he were here."

"Yes, he would," I agreed. "But you're not nearly as funny as Diken *thinks* he is."

Valyan's grin widened for a moment, then faded as a strange, distant echo came rolling up the corridor where we stood. The hair rose on my body; everyone's eyes widened. The sound was like children shrieking.

Another sound followed the first and quickly grew louder. It was a kind of rumbling but with strange harmonics beneath the bass throb. It registered as mechanical and organic at the same time.

"Get away from the center of the tunnel!" I shouted.

We all pressed back against the corridor walls—two on one side and two on the other. And not a moment too soon. A large...sphere swept out of the tunnel to our right and flashed by us at incredible speed. I caught an impression of glass and steel and then it was gone. It had to be some kind of vehicle, though.

"Did you see anyone in that thing?" I shouted.

"Empty," Valyan called back.

"I see something else!" Rence said from beside me.

I glanced at him, and then down the tunnel from which the machine had appeared. The first thing I saw was eyes, maybe fifteen feet off the ground. They glowed like cut emeralds. Then I saw a diamond-shaped head and knew what was coming. I didn't even have to hear the sound of scales rasping on metal as it sped toward us.

"With me!" I shouted. "Run!"

CHAPTER THIRTY-TWO

THE BATTLE BENEATH

We ran.

I led the way as we pelted back down the tunnel we'd come from; I had an idea. A short time before we'd passed through a room piled with the long stakes upon which Vessoth and his priests impaled their sacrifices.

"We'll use the stakes like pikes!" I shouted to the others.

They'd all been soldiers. They'd seen battle. They knew what I meant.

I glanced over a shoulder. I had no word other than snake to name the thing that followed us, but it was no Earthly creature. It was scaled and legless like a snake, but moved like nothing I'd seen. Segments of its body expanded and contracted in a rhythm that let it "ripple" its way forward. It was fast, though, and big. Very big. The corridor was twenty feet high and this beast filled two-thirds of it. I couldn't tell how long it was; I couldn't see its tail. There wasn't much time to look.

We reached the wide place in the corridor that was our goal. The snake-thing's great size had forced it to slow as it turned from its original tunnel into a new one. But now it was at our heels, coming like a freight train without brakes on a downgrade.

"Grab a stake! Backs against the wall!" I roared.

A stake found its way into my hands. I hardly recalled reaching for it. I leaped the benches where strange beings might once have waited for a very different kind of train. We turned. The four of us. I planted the makeshift lance's butt against the angle where floor met wall, locked my grip on the wooden shaft. The others matched me.

On Earth, in the Middle Ages, foot soldiers sometimes broke the charge of mailed cavalry using a weapon called the pike. It was a simple weapon, essentially a long, thick wooden spear with a tip of iron. When anchored solidly against the earth and held by disciplined warriors, the pikes created a bristling hedge of mighty thorns against which a cavalry charge would bleed white.

The sacrificial stakes available to us were nearly twelve feet long, and though they lacked the metal tip of the traditional pike they were sharpened to a blade's edge. We readied them—just as so many warriors in Earth's past and Talera's present had readied similar weapons against a foe heavier and more powerful than they.

The snake surged into the widened area of the tunnel. We stood at a right angle to the main corridor. The monster's head had to turn to face us, but there wasn't room for its whole body. It opened its mouth on a bellow that rattled the corridor. There was no tongue in that mouth, no fangs either, only multiple rows of teeth that looked more like straight razors than anything else.

It struck at us, quickly recoiled after getting a face full of spear point. It roared with rage, then struck again. The tip of Shai's lance broke off in the thing's jaw. It reared back, flung its head from side to side to dislodge what to it was little more than a splinter. Another coil of its body pushed into the widened area; its scales scraped on the metal walls. It lifted its head for a third strike, with more of the power of its body behind it.

The beast's head was diamond shaped, flattened so it was hard to hit a critical spot. The emerald eyes were almost rectangular and hid behind a frill of bone that protected them. Its nostrils, though. It had four of them. They were a wide, salmon pink. They looked vulnerable.

I had no time to yell that discovery to the others, but had an instant to shift the angle of my pike a bit. The snake struck with a roar. My lance went up one nostril. It went deep, ruptured through so the tip came bursting out of the scaled skin just below its eyes. Green blood sprayed. The beast roared again, with more agony than rage this time. It reared back hard, the top of its head banging the ceiling.

I couldn't hold on to the stake. It was embedded too deep. As the makeshift pike was jerked from me, I reached to draw my sword. Instead, Valyan pushed his own pike toward me. I took it by reflex.

"My bow!" the Nakscherii warrior shouted.

I nodded as he unslung his longbow and put two arrows into the air as quick as thought. Both darts struck true but pinpricks would not stop this monster. Again it pushed forward. The corridor rattled and dust shifted down upon us. The beast's head wove back and forth as it sought a way around our weakened hedge of pikes.

"Fire!" Shai shouted from the other side of Valyan. "The oil we brought."

Of course.

Valyan's yellow eyes lit with understanding as well. He grabbed the skin of oil from his belt and opened it to thrust the head of an arrow inside. It came out dripping black. Holding the pike with one hand, I pulled the striker from my pocket and gave it to Valyan, then grabbed the oil skin from him.

"I throw, you shoot!" I shouted.

He nodded, clicked the striker and lit his arrow. I flung the bladder of oil toward the snake, aiming for right above its eyes. Valyan loosed his shot. A fiery streak leaped from Valyan's bow to the bladder, cut through. The oil erupted into flame as it sluiced down over the snake's head. The monster bellowed, jerked back from the pain. But burning oil had wicked into the cracks of its scales and the pain followed it.

It bellowed again, backed farther away from us. With a shot worthy of a "Tre Khiang," Valyan put an arrow in its left eye and its bellow became a shriek. It turned in the tunnel; I don't know how because of its size. But in every creature I'd ever known, pain and fear could make the body do things anger and hunger could not.

The thing fled faster than it had come. I rushed into the center of the corridor to watch it go, its head wreathed in flames. Rence cheered as he joined me. The others were more subdued. I was just trying to get my heart to slow down.

"Nice shooting," I told Valyan after a moment.

He inclined his head.

"Quick thinking about using the stakes," Shai said to me. "We'd be dead if not for that."

"Or dead if you hadn't thought of fire," I replied. "Reckon we'd all be dead several times by now if it wasn't for each other. Let's get back on the trail. We're taking too long." I reached down and picked up a couple of the big stakes and tucked them over a shoulder. "We'll bring along a few more pikes in case we meet that thing's mother, though."

This time there were smiles all around, even if they did seem a bit tired.

CHAPTER THIRTY-THREE

A STRANGE WAY TO TRAVEL

We headed back to where the six corridors merged, to what I was mentally calling a "switching station." The monster snake was gone, although along the way we saw spatters of gore and burnt scales it had left behind. The blood spore led down the corridor I'd noted as slanting downhill. Unfortunately, that was the very corridor I believed we needed to take. I had a feeling the white sand beach beside the black ocean where Vessoth awaited us lay in the depths of Nimeru. I told my companions as much.

"So you want to follow the snake," Rence said.

"It's not a matter of wanting. It's a matter of needing."

"How much farther do we have to go, do you think?" Shai asked.

I shook my head. "I don't know. Farther than I'd like. Why?"

"Chalathar didn't know for sure how long he could keep the sphere gates closed. But we're reaching the limit of the time he thought feasible."

I nodded. "Then we better hurry."

We started off at a warrior's jog, alternated it with periods of walking. It was a pace all of us could have kept up indefinitely if we'd not already been worn down by thin rations and a lack of good sleep. Breathing came harder than it should; even in the cool air, I sweated. Still, a verlang fell behind us. Then another.

We passed other alcoves where benches waited for occupants who would never come again. I finally called a halt to rest when we found something we'd not seen before. Seemingly embedded into the wall on either side of the corridor were a dozen large glass and metal spheres like the one that had rushed past us before the monster snake arrived.

"What exactly are those things?" Rence asked.

"A conveyance of some kind," Shai said.

"An elevator," I added.

They all looked at me strangely.

"The last time I was on Earth," I explained, "they'd invented this thing called an 'elevator.' They're found in tall buildings. It's like a rectangular box that is moved up and down by a cable and pulley system.

People ride in them. Saves having to use the stairs. I think these spheres are like elevator cars. At least they illustrate the same principle."

"I'd rather take the stairs," Valyan said.

"These are much faster," I replied. "Much less work. Nice to ride when your legs are turning to lead and it's hard to breathe. Like now."

"Too bad we can't use them then," Shai said.

"Let's just see," I murmured, walking toward one of the spheres.

As I approached within a hand's-breadth of the thing, a glass panel on the side suddenly slid back with a faint whoosh. I nearly jumped out of my boots. The others didn't fare much better.

"Vhish!" Rence said, holding his chest over the heart. "Don't do that."

I shrugged, then moved closer to the sphere again and leaned to peer inside. There were no seats for passengers, only a dozen upright booths separated by thin crystal panels. Each booth was big enough to hold a person, and between them, literally floating in the air, hung a set of six blue symbols.

"Look at this," I called to Shai.

She approached warily, leaned her head beside mine to have a look at the symbols.

I pointed out one in particular. "Isn't that the one you said represented downward?"

She nodded. Then, "So?"

"So, I think these might be the controls for the sphere. I think if we get inside this thing and touch that symbol, this…'conveyance' will take us down that corridor in the direction we want to go."

She looked skeptical. "It's a rather large risk."

"Yes, but we may need to take that risk. We know time is running low. This thing could get us to where we're going a lot faster than walking."

"What if it doesn't? What if it takes us in the wrong direction?"

"Maybe into the middle of a nest of those snakes?" Rence added. "Besides. Will it even work? These things must have been here for ages."

"We may be going in the wrong direction anyway," I said. "If so, better to find out quickly than at the end of a long walk. As for them working. We *saw* one of them working. And Talera works. The sun and moons do. The…beings who built this place must be the same who constructed our whole world. They built to last. There's one more reason to try it as well."

"That is?" Shai asked.

"Vessoth has been directing us ever since we arrived at Nimeru. He always knows where we're going to be. And when. If we're to have any chance of defeating him, we need to surprise him." I pointed at the sphere. "This will surprise him."

Shai opened her mouth, then closed it. "I can't think of any more objections. We won't be able to take our pikes in there, though."

I nodded, leaned the big stakes that I carried against the wall. The others did the same. Then we all stood around looking at each other.

"What joke do you think Diken would make right now?" Valyan commented. Without waiting for an answer, he pushed past the rest of us and entered the machine.

We all held our breaths, but nothing happened. Valyan found one of the booth-like structures and wedged himself into it. I went in next, found my own booth. Shai and Rence followed, more reluctantly. Clothing rustled; weapons clinked as we got ourselves situated.

"All right," I said when everything had quietened down. "Hang on."

Feeling rather silly for doing so, and expecting nothing whatsoever to take place, I reached toward the blue symbols floating in the air and touched the one that looked like a bent nail hammered through an 'S.' It was the same that Shai had translated as "downward." That symbol immediately began to blink on and off while the others went dark.

Several things happened almost at once. First, though the walls of the booth looked like glass, they began to soften and mold themselves gently around me. Before I could react to that, the sphere shifted unexpectedly into the center of the corridor. Startled by the walls closing in, I'd begun to press back against them when the sphere accelerated straight ahead at tremendous speed. I was glad then for the cushioning of the walls and realized that must be their purpose. I tried to force myself to relax. It wasn't easy. The others didn't seem to be having it any better.

Outside our transport, the corridor was nothing but a blur. I could make out no details. The only sound to indicate any movement was a faint hum. At least we were heading downward. I could tell that.

"I am not liking this," Rence called out.

I almost told him to enjoy the journey, for the destination would likely be far less pleasant. I didn't. He knew it already. We all did. I could see it in the others' faces. We were all convinced now that when this sphere stopped we'd be left to face our final battles against Vessoth and his servants, including the disguised swordsman who hated me for reasons I could not name.

My chest throbbed where more than once now a vision-sword had cut me to the heart. I rubbed at the spot with a hand; it did nothing to assuage the ache. When Vessoth had promised me agony from the invisible wound, after letting us see the horror of what he'd done to our friend Daik, I thought he'd made a mistake. I thought he'd only enraged me and that rage would carry me through until I found and killed him.

But now, in the quiet cocoon of our strange journey, while the world whipped by outside, rage began to cool. My reflection gazed back at me from the glass of the sphere. I was not in the habit of looking much at myself, but there was little else to do now but study my mirrored form: the dry and cracked lips, the gaunt face behind unshaven bristles. My eyes were red-rimmed, and the green irises that some described as 'cold' did not seem cold to me. There was emotion there, straining to get out. I dared not let it come.

Soon I'd find the black sea and the white beach. I'd find a gray-eyed warrior who wore a mask. I would fight him. According to all the visions I'd had, I would lose. I would die.

I did not wish to die. For a moment, memories painted over my own reflection with the image of another. I saw Rannon of the dark velvet hair and blue eyes. I smelled her clean scent. She'd said: "bring yourself home to me."

I'd made a promise to do so. At that moment I'd been sure it would be true. I no longer knew if I could deliver. I wanted to. For the sake of the woman I loved, for the children we had spoken of having. And for myself, of course. I wanted to taste terval steak again, fresh and dripping from the fire. I wanted to drink the wines of Thresh and Nyshphal. I wanted to ride, a swift tasaber across the plains, a swifter sabrun through the skies. I wanted to do a thousand things I'd never done.

The pain grew in my chest. I winced and bent over slightly, but tried not to cry out so the others would not know. If Vessoth and his minions defeated those of us here in this traveling cage. If he escaped Nimeru and gained time to gather his full strength. Then surely Rannon would be at risk. So, too, would the land of Nyshphal, which I'd come to call my own. Indeed, all of Talera, this fantastic and bounteous world to which I'd been pulled, could be laid waste.

I tried to summon anger through these thoughts, anger at what I might lose and anger to combat the pain that wracked me. Anger would not come. Something else came instead.

Fear.

CHAPTER THIRTY-FOUR

DOWN TO A BLACK SEA

Abruptly, the speed of our conveyance began to drop off and my mind came back to the moment at hand. The chest pain subsided and I was able to straighten up. The thin hum I'd been hearing changed to a whoosh-whoosh as the corridor outside began to pass more slowly. Then the sphere stopped and the doors immediately opened.

I hesitated a heartbeat before climbing out. Like at the other end of the corridor, the tunnel ended at a small rectangular room with steps leading up from there. I glanced up those stairs and saw, dimly, the reddish glow I knew would have to be there.

"This is the place," I said, quietly. There was no doubt.

The others watched me as I stood at the bottom of the stairs. They did not speak, merely waited. A moment of irritation swept over me. Thoughts came unbidden. Why did I always have to lead? Why couldn't I just follow? The thoughts were false. It was the fear talking. Plenty of times I'd followed better leaders than myself. Now was *my* time to lead, and if I couldn't feel the courage inside, I still had to show it on the outside.

Steeling my spirit, I started up the steps. This time I counted them. Four hundred. This place was so precisely constructed I imagined it had been the same number at the other end. Not that it mattered. I was only trying to keep my mind occupied with safe considerations.

At the top of the stairs we came to an opening into a wide cavern that stretched farther than I could see. I studied the scene before venturing out in it. The sky was low and red, as if lit by the flames of some vast but distant forest fire. A stretch of white sand beach led down to an inky sea that tossed itself into foam against the shore. I could smell the briny water from here, with a faint whiff of tar in the mix. It might have been the image from my vision, except there was more to this setting.

Rows of sacrificial stakes ran along the beach, each bearing a dying Sporn. I heard their mandibles clicking in agony. I smelled their blood. Almost, it seemed I could smell their pain. I'd had no good dealings with Sporns. Not ever. Still, the evil of this hellish torment was enough to make me feel for even *these* enemies.

"There," Shai said, pointing at something.

I looked and saw that a narrow walkway ran between the rows of Sporns and led to a causeway that stretched out over the black sea's waters. At the other end of the causeway's stone paving waited a small island perhaps two hundred tahng across. A crimson pyramid no larger than a farmer's cottage stood at the far end of the island. In front of it I could make out a row of shadowy figures holding what looked like emerald torches.

"Thye Vessoth," I said to the others. "I can see their green power wands. They'll be protecting their god. That's where we've got to go."

"Not much of a surprise if we walk right out in the open across that bridge," Rence said.

"Which is why only two of us are going to cross it directly," I replied.

They all looked at me.

"Shai and I will take the bridge," I continued, speaking primarily to Valyan and Rence. "We'll let them see us coming. Get their eyes focused on us. You two follow. But stay hidden. Use the stakes for cover, if you can. When you get to the bridge, see if the water is safe to swim. If it is, you've got your path. Get in a position to help us. Don't act until you absolutely have to, though. If all we have is surprise, then we better make it count."

Both men nodded.

I straightened up, Shai beside me, and we stepped out on the beach and begin to walk. The Sporns moaned louder as they saw us but I didn't know what that meant. Were they begging for succor? Or trying to warn those who had done this to them? Either way, I ignored them, kept walking. I did not look back at Valyan and Rence.

The Thye Vessoth saw us when we reached the bridge. They'd been laboring over more of the sacrificial stakes, doing something to them I didn't understand. They certainly seemed surprised at our sudden appearance and milled about for a bit before regaining their composure. There were five of them, and over a hundred Sporn warriors behind them. These were not the typical Sporns but the new type of Sporn soldiery we'd fought just once before. They stood head and shoulders taller than I, and were built like granite boulders. Their eyes were green instead of white and they wore corselets of steel. Each carried two swords and a broad shield banded with iron.

Our enemies came forward as if to meet us, but then formed a solid phalanx of armored flesh about halfway between the end of the bridge and the small crimson pyramid. The five Thye Vessoth sorcerers were in front of the formation, each carrying a verdant wand that gleamed like an emerald afire. They wore tunics of fine cloth dyed purple, and one of them bore a headdress made from snake scales bigger than a man's palm. I could read nothing from their inhuman faces and dead blue eyes. I *could* smell their musk and it stank.

The beast with the headdress raised his wand as we approached and shouted, "Halt!"

We halted. For the moment.

"Where is Vessoth?" I demanded.

"He is wherever he chooses to be," the priest intoned. "He will come to this place when he is ready."

"Tell him to come now or we'll wade through the lot of you to get his attention."

"You would die then," the priest snapped.

I smiled, though I didn't feel like it. "I don't think so. He wants his pet swordsman to kill me. You wouldn't dare take that moment away from a *god* who will impale his own followers simply for the pleasure of it."

The five sorcerers looked back and forth between themselves. I couldn't read any communication that passed between them but I had a feeling they didn't want to die. Especially not at the hands of their own God.

"Then we will kill the woman," the one with the headdress said.

Shai chuckled. I glanced at her. Her braid of brown hair was dirty. Sweat grimed her golden skin. But she stood with her hands close to the hilts of her rapiers. Her head was high. She spat on the sand.

"Have at it," she said.

I was glad she was on my side.

The Thye Vessoth speaker looked again at his fellows. Strange murmurs followed in a language I did not know. Now there *was* something registering in their faces. Confusion. I saw no reason to give them time to overcome that. I started walking forward again and Shai paced alongside me.

"Halt!" the lead priest snapped again. We didn't halt. Nor did we draw any weapon. For a moment our enemies stood their ground, then began backing slowly away in front of us. Their murmuring increased. Their wands flashed on and off. The Sporns fell back with them, seeming to have no volition of their own.

We kept walking. They kept retreating. Ten paces. Fifteen. Then something stiffened their spines. The leader slashed his wand across the ground in front of us and a line of green flame cooked the sand into slag.

"You will halt!" he shrieked.

I did halt, but over my shoulder I drew a crossbow. Shai did the same. We locked and loaded bolts, then began to lift our weapons.

"I'm going to hang that headdress in the palace in Timmuzz," I said to the lead beast. "Not gonna bother keeping your actual head, though."

"Hold!" a voice boomed.

I looked up, over the heads of the Thye Vessoth and their Sporn army. I saw the crimson pyramid open and the Snake God come forth. Straining on a leash in front of him came a gray-eyed killer with the lower half of his face hidden.

CHAPTER THIRTY-FIVE

VESSOTH

Vessoth! Known as the Snake God. It wasn't clear why. Except for his viper eyes he looked nothing like a snake to me. The true form of the Asadhie seemed more like insects or mollusks than anything else. This Asadhie floated effortlessly in the air, his scarlet tendrils trailing about him and the whole of his form refulgent with the sparking of electrical discharges.

I recalled what Bryce had told me not long ago aboard the *Khiang*: "You'll need Ahrethane when you face Vessoth." He'd added: "Swords of steel cannot best an Asadhie. Not alone. No matter the courage of those who wield the blades."

Yet, Vessoth was here and Ahrethane was not.

Bryce believed I would die if I faced Vessoth as Shai and I were doing. There were two things I understood that Bryce did not. First, Vessoth was not nearly as powerful now as Vohanna had been when we'd fought her. When I looked beyond the Snake God's sparking form, I saw the small crimson pyramid from whence he'd just come. I had thought of the pyramid as being the size of a cottage. I realized now it was the size of something else—a prison cell.

Vessoth had been locked in that cell for ages and he'd come forth with his power greatly diminished. Those who had jailed him had stripped away all his milkstones save that which kept him alive. And according to Shai, Chalathar was striving to block the power of the one stone the imprisoned Asadhie retained. Time and again we'd seen that Vessoth's attacks were as much illusion as reality. Right now, he was vulnerable.

The second thing I realized that Bryce did not, was that Vessoth did not intend to kill me himself. That pleasure he had reserved, for whatever reason, for the swordsman whose leash he held. Now, finally, I had a moment to study the mysterious warrior in whose hands my fate rested.

He was perhaps an inch short than I and thinner in build, though we probably weighed close to the same considering my passing acquaintance with food of late. As before, black silk veiled most of his face below the piercing gray eyes. There were no crow's feet around those eyes, nor wrinkles on his deeply tanned forehead. He appeared young, and that felt wrong to me. His hair was dark and fell past his shoulders, and that length felt wrong to me too. I could not explain why. He glared at me but said nothing. I did not glare back, but looked again to Vessoth who drifted a little closer to us and spoke.

"Where are your two companions?" the Asadhie demanded of Shai and me. Even though I could discern emotional tone in his voice, the words themselves sounded mechanically produced and the soft white lips did not move.

"Lost in the tunnels when your snake attacked," I replied.

Vessoth's face could show little in the way of Human expressions but I heard a sneer in his words as he called me a liar.

"I doubt that. Playing sneaks and thieves more likely. Hoping to surprise us. They will not."

The Thye Vessoth with the headdress turned toward his master. Some communication passed between them for in the next instant the priest ordered forty of the Sporn soldiers to search beyond the causeway and through the corridors there for our friends. I did not think they would find Valyan and Rence where they were told to look. I did not smile at the thought.

Vessoth's whole body rotated to face me squarely then.

"The moment is here, Ruenn Maclang," he said, gloatingly.

"Why?" I asked.

A quietness fell, broken only by the lap of water against the island's shores.

Vessoth's snail-like lips did part then. A thin ribbon of pink tongue protruded for a moment, then withdrew back into the mouth.

"You are curious as to why I've chosen to end you in such a fashion," he said. "Surely you should know. You and the traitor who calls himself Chalathar killed my mate—Vohanna. You delayed my escape from this…prison. I will destroy you first, for that. It will send Chalathar a message that soon he will writhe on his belly before me. His death will not be as easy as yours."

"So it's nothing more than revenge? I find that hard to believe. From the time Bryce and I arrived on Talera, Vohanna sought to use us for her own ends. First she took my brother. Then she tried to recruit me. That wasn't revenge. She had another reason. So do you. Tell me what it is!"

A smirk was clear in Vessoth's voice now. "How sad to die with unanswered questions. In a few moments you'll be beyond worrying about it. What my loving mate could not do, I will do with a proxy."

His bulbous crimson eyes turned toward the leashed warrior who waited for the signal to kill me. I did not shift gaze to the man, as Vessoth expected. I spoke only to the Snake God, giving to my words a braggadocio I did not feel.

"What are you going to do after I carve up your little pet?"

I heard the swordsman's leash rattle, heard a low moan of rage coming from behind his mask. I did not look at him, only at Vessoth.

The god laughed. "You've already lost to him before. More than once. You bear wounds from his blade that are rotting you away from inside. You cannot defeat him. You have already admitted as much."

Now I looked at the man. "Let's fight and see," I snarled.

"Other things first," Vessoth said. "You foolishly brought a companion with you. A woman...warrior. There will be two fights. You will face my swordsman. The woman will face my legion."

"It's me you want for vengeance," I protested loudly. "Let Shai leave this place."

"No!" Shai shouted.

"Do not fear that I will be unfair," Vessoth continued. "Your...Shai will face them one at a time. Until she is dead."

"One at a time or all at once," Shai snapped. "It won't make a difference."

I glanced over at her; she looked back at me. A savage smile curved her mouth and she squared her shoulders and dropped both hands to the rapiers sheathed at her hips. We'd not expected to escape this without blood—ours or someone else's. Our expectations were about to be fulfilled. I nodded to her, and she to me. I looked back at Vessoth and his swordsman.

"How long you going to keep us waiting?" I asked, and this time I felt the sense of swagger the question was meant to express.

"One last thing first, my impatient Ruenn," the god said. "Let us reveal who it is that will kill you."

He pressed at something held in one of his tendrils and the leash and collar fell away from my eager assassin. The warrior straightened fully, reached up with one hand and tore away the cloth hiding his face.

I stared. "Can't be!" I said.

CHAPTER THIRTY-SIX

A WARRIOR REVEALED

Jedik! Jedik Ver Lha Yed!

I knew this man. But how could it truly be him?

Jedik had been the first to explain Talera's artificial nature to me. He had told me much of the Asadhie and their sphere gates. He, too, had been an outsider to Talera, from a world called "Earth," although we both believed it to be some Earth other than mine, or else one far into the future of my own world. He had been much more than a fount of information, however. As the Talerans say, Jedik had become Zay Khi-ang to me, a phrase meaning "teacher for a warrior." Mentor is the term we might use on Earth, though it is weak to encompass all this man had meant to me. This could not be him.

I stared at the man who faced me wearing the features of a friend. "Jedik is dead," I said into that face.

He half smirked and shook his head at me.

I looked at Vessoth. "Jedik is dead! I saw him killed with my own eyes."

"Where was that?" the Snake God questioned, in a tone both sweet and sick.

"On Talen. The island of the Klar. He died in battle after helping me free Rannon from chains."

"Do you recall?" Vessoth asked, "the circumstances from which you rescued your princess? And who it was that ruled the island of Talen in those days?"

"She was about to be sacrificed," I snarled, and then a razor of ice caressed me to the bone. "Sacrificed to you," I added. "By the Thye Vessoth."

"Yes," Vessoth practically hissed, and in that moment he sounded like the Snake God in truth. "There I have another reason to kill you. You stole my sacrifice. One that meant much to me."

I frowned. Rannon's death would have meant much to *me*. I did not understand how it could mean more to Vessoth than the death of anyone else. Perhaps he was only speaking in ugly metaphor about the death of a noble woman as opposed to a peasant, and right now my head was full of questions on another topic.

"We were talking about my friend, Jedik," I said.

"Indeed. Your *friend*. Jedik. My priests discovered his body after the battle. They…did certain things to it."

"What kind of things?"

"Things to preserve it. To keep further corruption from it until it could be brought to me."

"I don't believe you have the power to bring the dead back to life," I snapped.

"Yet you see that power expressed before you."

I looked again at the Jedik who could not be. Once more I noted the long hair where my friend's had been cropped short. Hair grows, of course. But there was the face. Unlined. Unscarred. Too young. And….

I looked back at Vessoth with triumph. "Jedik's nose had been broken. Had healed crookedly. There's no sign of such in this *imposter*."

"I am Jedik!" the swordsman shouted.

He started toward me, drawing his blade. I reached to draw mine.

Vessoth's voice came calmly: "Not quite yet."

The man stopped dead. His body quivered as if he were a hunting jaguar scenting its prey. I wondered when he would realize that he was no longer on his master's leash. Probably he never would. He seemed completely dominated by Vessoth's will, and that, too, was unlike the man I'd known.

"If you are indeed Jedik," I said, "why do you hate me? Jedik and I were friends."

He snorted contempt at my words. "Friends! You so easily sacrificed me for your *princess*. With not a thought about it. And I wasn't the only one. Nor did you tell those of us who accompanied you what your true goals were. To disrupt the lawful worship of Vessoth among the Klar."

I don't know if I looked as surprised on the outside as I felt on the inside at his statements. They made no sense to me.

"That wasn't how it happened," I protested. "You knew we were going there to try and save Rannon. And not even Jask the Klar himself knew about the Vessoth cult that had sprung up among his people."

"Lies!" he said, though in the next moment a frown came over his face. It lingered, started to siphon away some of his anger.

"Jedik has been shown the truth," Vessoth said suddenly.

The man's anger returned. "I have been shown the truth," he repeated.

I began to understand. Vohanna had done much the same to Bryce. Through drugs, pain, lust, and the power of the *toir'in-or* she had convinced him that he and I were enemies, that I had treated him like a worthless child—had oppressed him, tormented him, degraded him. She had grafted hate onto him like a farmer grafts the limb of one fruit tree onto another. Now, it seemed Vessoth had played a similar gambit against me with Jedik. This hate the man felt was not original with him, but an evil contributed by the Snake God.

That didn't mean it wasn't powerful. Bryce's transplanted hate of me had been powerful. I'd not been able to break through it. He had broken it himself, after much pain and suffering on the parts of many. There was little hope of that here. I'd have to kill Jedik to stop him. And he was better than I with a blade. At least the original Jedik had been, and recent visions clearly suggested this one was too.

Where had this Jedik come from? I did *not* believe Vessoth could raise the dead. Then a memory tugged at me and took hold. Jedik himself had told me once of a scientific way the dead could be brought back to life. It was called "cloning" and involved principles I did not ken. Jedik's people in the melancholy city of Emira were the product of such a procedure.

As Jedik had explained it, with proper tools an exact duplicate of the Human body could be regrown from a small piece of tissue taken from the original. It was possible also, at least for the scientists on his native world, to store memories and emotions in machines called computers, and for those characteristics to be reintroduced into the cloned body— essentially recreating a Human life.

I had seen a wrecked ship on Jedik's Isle that could only be called a "star ship." Jedik believed it had come through a sphere gate before crashing down onto Talera. In it there had been some of the cloning machines. The crash had activated them, and Jedik and his people had come out of those machines.

Was it possible Vessoth had somehow gained access to those devices? Or others like them? According to Jedik the machines had quit working. What if he'd been wrong? What if there was another ship he didn't know about? Vessoth had mentioned his priests preserving Jedik's corpse. Perhaps that was where he'd gotten the cloning tissue. Judging from Vessoth's own words, it must be. But could memories be taken from a dead brain. I suppose it depended on how long that brain had been dead.

There was something else about this Jedik who stood before me. Even disregarding the hatred of me that Vessoth had inculcated in him, he lacked…depth. His spirit—his khi—seemed empty of those characteristics the true Jedik had displayed in full. Basic emotions and skills, this man had in abundance. But humor? A sense of honor and loyalty? Love? Perhaps only a living brain could hold such things.

I looked up at the Snake God where he floated like a crimson demon in the sky. I asked him those kinds of questions. His response was terse, and directed toward his swordsman, toward the new Jedik.

"Kill him now!" he said.

CHAPTER THIRTY-SEVEN

SWORD-SONG

Jedik's sword flashed instantly into his left hand and he started toward me. I drew the rune-blade and waited. Vessoth had not forgotten Shai. From the corner of an eye, I saw her unsheathe her twin rapiers as a huge, green-eyed Sporn leaped toward her with a bellow. She cut that one down but a second Sporn immediately charged her.

I had no time to see the result of that charge. Jedik came in with a blazing attack. I'd forgotten how fast he was. Or perhaps I'd never known his true speed. We had fenced when he trained me but he wasn't trying to kill me then. I parried his first strike, backpedaled, parried his second. He had more.

He scored a cut across my chest, a near miss of my throat. The cut was a mere burn. It wouldn't slow me. I blocked a thrust in a jangle of steel and riposted. He batted my sword aside. His weapon was a rapier, thinner, lighter, and swifter than the rune-blade. But not as long. He attacked, attacked, his eyes blazing, his mouth a grim line of rage. I backed up, holding him off with my lengthier blade. Just barely.

For a moment there came a lull in Jedik's fury. I spared one glance toward Shai. She'd killed three Sporns now; their carcasses sprawled at her feet. Her legs were braced in sweat-darkened leather breeks. Her rapiers sheened with silver blood. She was smiling, but a forth Sporn soldier came charging against her. Fifty more waited behind that one. How could she survive?

Vessoth was hissing in excitement. I could hear it. He floated just above the heads of his five Thye-Vessoth priests. Their *toir 'in-or* charged wands sent sheets of emerald fire into the air as some kind of shield for their god. Even if I could kill Jedik, how could I get through that? The first bite of despair took hold of me then. Its teeth were sharp. Where were Valyan and Rence? Maybe it was for the best. What could they do but die as well in the face of such odds?

Jedik launched another onslaught. This time I did not back up. I fenced with him, our swords weaving so fast that light and sound must have been little more than a fireworks display to those who watched. My foe was incredibly quick but for a moment I held him at bay. In an instant when he paused, I even tried my own assault, earned a stinging slash across the back of a hand as payment. Jedik followed with a blistering series of movements that left one shallow cut across my left forearm, another at my chin. I backed away again.

Harshly, I breathed. Rivulets of sweat stung my eyes and wounds. I tasted salt. The air that had felt so cool before felt broiling now. I was getting tired. My legs burned. Jedik showed none of this. His blade winked like lightning as he launched flurry after flurry of attacks. Somehow I held him off, held him off. But I knew now. This *was* Jedik—at least where skill with a sword was concerned. I'd fenced with him enough to know his style, and to know I couldn't match his talent forever.

Again there came one of the lull's that are inevitable in all combat. Again I glanced toward Shai. Five Sporns lay dead by her hands now but red blood trickled down her face from a cut on the forehead and she seemed much less fresh than she had moments before. The sixth Sporn went down before her then; for an instant her shoulders drooped and I saw her gasping heavily for breath beneath her bone armor.

"Now two Sporns at a time," Vessoth called. A dyad of the monsters came charging against Shai.

"No!" I shouted, as the woman swung her blades up to defend herself.

A bright agony lanced my left shoulder. I'd paused too long. I leaped back, felt Jedik's sword slide free of my arm. I glanced down, saw the blood. The tip of Jedik's rapier had stabbed completely through the outer flesh of my shoulder, missing the muscle only by great good fortune. Crimson bubbled slowly from both the entrance and exit wounds.

A flush surged over me. With a snarl, I leaped toward my foe. For a moment I drove Jedik back. His face twisted with rage but he was retreating. Our swords met, rebounded with a discordant crash, crossed again with the friction of metal on metal. We were chest to chest. I swung a punch at him, narrowly missed breaking his nose anew. He backpedaled. I roared a curse, rushed him. This time he stood his ground and we fenced in a bright fury of sword-song, in a poetry of glinting light and clanging steel.

Such a pace could not last for either of us. One more time the lull came. I stepped back, panting for breath like an exhausted hound. Blood slicked my left arm to the elbow. The wound hadn't damaged the working of the arm but the blood loss would tell on me soon. At least I had the satisfaction of seeing that Jedik, too, was breathing hard now, and that sweat ran on his patrician's face. So, he wasn't superhuman.

"That was your last rally," Jedik snarled at me. "There's nothing left inside you."

"There was never *anything* inside you," I snarled back. "You're no more than a puppet."

A muscle jumped in his jaw but he did not charge against me. By that, I knew he needed the respite as much as I did. I was grateful, for the coin of my strength was nearly spent.

He spat. "Look at your friend now. I will withhold any attack."

I glanced toward Shai. We'd been side by side when our battles started. Now she was so far away. I could not count the Sporn corpses laying scattered at her feet, but I could see her whole body shuddering for air and the flood of sweat that drenched her. Her armor had been cut to threads and blood glistened on her from at least a dozen small wounds. She'd been driven back across the beach until the waves of the black sea crashed to shore at her back. There could be no farther retreat for her.

"Now three at a time," Vessoth called out loudly, no doubt knowing that I looked upon the scene.

"No," I whispered, and took a step toward where Shai stood. Jedik moved just enough to block my way.

"Keep watching," he sneered.

I did not want to. I groaned. I wanted to hack the sneer from Jedik's face. But my body begged for breath. My muscles shrieked for rest. The sword weighed like an anvil. And I could not look away.

Three Sporns came forward then, to face a Shai who could have little left to give them. They attacked all at once. I took another step toward them, intending to try and force a way through Jedik to help her. My heart stuttered suddenly out of rhythm. The pain of my vision-wound come throbbing to the surface so I had to clench teeth on a scream. I bent over, with chest on fire but eyes locked on Shai. She killed one of her three attackers but the blade of her left-handed rapier snapped off in its flesh as it fell.

The other two were upon her. She hacked madly at them. I saw Sporn and Human blood mixed. I snarled at Jedik and lifted my sword, took a shuffling step toward him. He backed away a pace, keeping himself between me and my companion. Then Shai went down, clubbed to her knees by the blow of a Sporn shield. She was stunned. Even if I could get past Jedik now I would never reach her in time.

Then Shai got up. I don't know how. She got up. From somewhere she found the strength to shriek a war cry. A booted foot lashed out to send one Sporn's shield smashing back into his body. Shai's remaining blade became a blur. She cut the two Sporns apart; she shredded them like meat.

Something rose inside me. I straightened my shoulders, glanced at Jedik with triumph. It could not last, of course. Both Shai and I were going to be dead soon. For the moment, though! For that moment, we were warriors. We had taken everything thrown against us and had thrown it back in our foe's faces.

Jedik growled in a frenzy of rage and hurled himself at me. Steel clamored and sang. I parried, parried again. I retreated, but not because I was afraid of him, not because I despaired. My heart had steadied; fear had fled. The vision-wound's pain was gone. Jedik kept coming.

I realized suddenly where I stood on the beach. The look of it. The feel of it. The very smell of it. In the visions, it had been at this exact spot where the masked swordsman's blade cut through my heart. It was here I died.

Jedik realized it too. His own smile of triumph leaped into his face. In my mind, our movements slowed to the flow of cold molasses. I started to step to one side, realized that in that step I had stumbled, had given Jedik the opening for the death stroke. I could see exactly where Jedik's blade lay, could see the pathway it would take into my heart.

I threw myself toward him. His eyes flashed surprise. His blade was lower than it would be an instant later and he was drawing it back to prepare for the final thrust. I felt the steel slice into my side, but his strike didn't have the power of his muscles behind it. The blade cut through flesh and struck the ribs on the lower left half of my body. The tip glanced along the bone, hung up for an instant.

Before I had time to register the pain I twisted to one side, tearing his weapon away from the wound it had made. At the same instant, I slashed the rune-sword across with all the power of my own muscles behind the heavier blade. I heard an awful thunk. Jedik's eyes went wide. On instinct he parried; his rapier knocked my sword away. It made no difference. He looked down, mouth gaping open. Blood fountained from his deeply gashed side onto the white sand. Splinters of his shattered ribs stood out from the flesh.

I spun off my left heel, came around with both hands gripping the hilt of the sword, twisting the blade downward to point toward the ground. I rose almost onto my toes, the weapon lifting high. Jedik tried to raise his arm to ward the coming blow. I ignored that feeble defense, drove the sword down as if I wanted to bury it in stone. It struck through his chest behind the sternum, carved through a lung, smashed through more ribs; it tore them all asunder.

I released the hilt of the rune-blade, for the sword was lodged in Jedik's body like the Excalibur of legend had indeed been lodged in stone. The gray-eyed swordsman fell onto his side. He was alive, but in terrible shock. His mouth opened, forced apart by gore the color and thickness of cooked raspberries. Whatever words he tried to mutter drowned in that scarlet flow.

I turned away from Jedik. My left shoulder ached; wet redness coated the whole arm beneath it. My side howled with pain. A shirt half-full of blood leaked crimson down my breeks. It did not matter.

The battlefield had fallen silent. The Sporns had ceased their attack on Shai. The Thye Vessoth stared in disbelief. I pointed toward Vessoth, whose form trembled in the air, but my words were meant for all our enemies.

"Your Snake God is no god at all!" I shouted. "And if prison cannot hold him, surely death will."

CHAPTER THIRTY-EIGHT

ONE SCARLET MOMENT

Vessoth trembled. Then he shrieked to his Thye Vessoth wizards and his Sporn soldiers, "Kill them! Kill them!" Even through the mechanical quality of his voice, I thought I heard fear. He began to back away in the air from those who protected him.

Venting their high pitched keen, the Sporns hurled themselves in mass toward Shai. Before I could even move to aid her, two new war-cries shattered the air and Valyan and Rence came surging up from the dark sea to enter the fray. The cavalry had arrived, and though their bow-strings were too wet to fire, their sharp blades reaped bodies like a scythe reaps wheat.

The Thye Vessoth were far more dangerous than the Sporn soldiery. Like emerald torches doused with gasoline, their *toir'in-or* charged wands blazed up. The stench of sorcery tingled my nostrils. A wave of heat and sound rumbled over me. Three of the lizard priests turned to confront Shai, Valyan and Rence. Two others faced me. They lifted their wands; the words of some arcane spell came twisted from their lips.

Sorcery is a fell weapon; it is not always a swift one. My right hand dipped beneath the rawhide duster I wore, slapped against the leather holster there. In one continuous move, my thumb unhooked the thong holding the revolver's hammer and the hand came back out from beneath the coat with a .357 magnum clutched tight. I opened fire, and the con-cussion of the discharging rounds sledged my ears and rolled in echoes across the water.

I wanted Vessoth most of all but he had dropped down to hide be-hind his priests. So I took his priests. The first hollow-point punched a fist-sized hole in the chest carapace of one Thye Vessoth. Green ichor sprayed. The beast went down and thrashed. A second wizard's head took the second bullet and disintegrated in a splatter of scale and bone.

The third bullet struck one of the Thye Vessoth wands. I'd seen a milkstone explode when nicked by a shell and it had been like a dozen sticks of TNT going off at once. This effect was much more modest but it knocked all three of the remaining lizard priests to the ground. Stunned, they lay there, the emerald brilliance of their wands dying down.

I stalked forward. A quick glance to the right showed Valyan, Rence and Shai mopping up the Sporn soldiers, who, with the downing of the priests, had lost any sense of organized attack. When we'd battled these Sporns before it had been as if they were controlled from outside. The green glow of their eyes had suggested the Thye Vessoth, and this moment seemed proof of that supposition. With the priests unconscious or dead, the Sporns simply flailed about with their weapons, mewling almost pitifully when my companions' swords razed them down.

I turned attention back to Vessoth's wizards. One of them shook his head from side to side as he regained full consciousness and started to rise onto his hands and knees. I stepped forward to wallop a boot into his chin, or where the chin would be in a Human. The beast's head snapped up and back and I heard the vertebrae break. It flopped down and wouldn't ever be getting up again.

The other two priests were beginning to stir and their hands groped for their fallen wands. I didn't intend for them to have a chance to recover those weapons. The two lay one on top of the other. I stood over them and fired a single bullet that tore through both bodies. That left me one round for Vessoth.

I looked then for the Snake God. He cowered against the scarlet pyramid that had once served as his prison, and which I now intended to act as his tomb. I raised the pistol, sighted down the barrel. The Asadhie pulled his tentacles in close to his body, seemed to actually shrink in size. I was not sure a bullet could kill him but he certainly seemed to fear the gun. Even if it just knocked him out of the air we could hack him to pieces with swords.

Before I could fire, Vessoth had some kind of seizure and collapsed, falling hard to crash onto the sand. The crimson sparks that continually leaped across his body flashed, flashed, faded, and failed. I hesitated, lowering the pistol slightly, then took two steps toward the now pale body of the would-be god.

What had happened?

"Look out!" a voice shouted. I recognized Valyan.

I started to spin and a spear of agony greater than anything I'd ever felt tore into my back. I was halfway around; momentum carried me the rest of the way. Then my legs gave out and I crashed down on my spine.

Jedik stood over me, the rune-blade still buried through his upper chest and down into his body. I did not know how he lived and walked. The rapier in his hand glinted with fresh crimson at its tip. He leaned toward me. I saw the thrust of the blade begin that would end my life. I fired the last .357 hollow-point up into his face. The gun boomed and smoke and flame blotted out sight of that face. The lead slug obliterated it physically. But not before I had seen and knew. It was Jedik no longer.

Crimson eyes. Crimson viper eyes. Vessoth had possessed Jedik's body, somehow wrung a last jot of strength from him, enough to get him on his feet, enough to bring him in to kill me in one last scarlet moment. He hadn't killed me. He'd died himself at the point of a gun.

No, he hadn't killed me.

But I couldn't move my legs.

CHAPTER THIRTY-NINE

DEATH'S GATE

I felt the warmth of blood under the middle of my back, and nothing below that. From somewhere came shouting, and feet rushing through sand. I realized it was my friends running toward me and in the next instant Valyan dropped to his knees by me. His yellow eyes gleamed with emotion as he studied me. He knew something was wrong but asked anyway.

"You? You're all right?"

I shook my head. "Can't move. Below the waist."

He winced, reached for my arm as if to turn me over to see the wound, but then paused, unsure of what to do. Shai appeared over his shoulder. Then came Rence. Both were bruised and bloody but Shai was much worse. A jagged cut on her forehead leaked crimson into her hair. Both eyes were swollen. What little armor she had left hung askew. She looked as if she'd been beaten with hammers. I suppose that wasn't far from the truth, though she'd done plenty of hammering back. The grimness of her face now, however, seemed mostly out of concern for me. She'd heard what I told Valyan.

"The sword blow," she said. "Must have...nicked the spine."

I didn't think "nicked" was quite the right word.

Shai's glance went to Jedik, who was missing half his head. Next she turned toward Vessoth where the Asadhie's body lay on the ground like a swollen dead slug. The Snake God's tentacles were coiled tightly around him; all color had fled from his form, leaving something wan and glistening behind.

Shai looked back at me. "What happened to Vessoth?"

"He possessed Jedik. That's how a nearly dead man got up to stab me despite the sword I'd put through his chest. I saw Vohanna possess people before. Every time, the possessed ones showed *her* black eyes. Jedik had crimson eyes at the last. Vessoth's eyes."

Shai looked startled, then scared. Her response instantly ignited my own fear. I twisted around to where I could see Vessoth's quiescent form. A rasping sound came as Shai tore her rapier from its sheath. I suddenly knew why.

Vohanna didn't die when a body she possessed died. She simply moved.

"Kill it!" I shouted. "Quickly!"

We were too late. Vessoth's waxy form flushed with crimson, and as Shai leaped forward with her rapier, the Snake God spasmed into life and soared into the air out of her reach. Shai dropped her sword, grabbed for the crossbow normally hanging over her shoulder. That weapon had been torn away in her fight with the Sporns. Valyan and Rence's bows still had wet strings.

I had the Colt. I fumbled the revolver's cylinder open and punched out the empties, then grabbed for a cartridge from the gunbelt. It was awkward on my back, trying to look over a shoulder at the same time to keep Vessoth in sight.

Strange laughter shrilled the air, like the screech of a train's brakes against steel rails. Vessoth's electric tentacles vibrated like sonic whips. The laugher shut off and I heard the Snake God speak clearly then:

"You can't kill me but you've all killed plenty of others. Enough others to grant me a new pathway out of this prison. These last deaths. The Sporns. The Thye Vessoth. Especially Jedik Ver Lha Yed. These were the final offerings I needed."

To punctuate his words, a roar of sound built suddenly from nowhere. The whole island juddered. Vessoth backed into the opening of his scarlet pyramid and a caul of clear tissue sealed over that opening. Sand began to rise up from the ground in thick streamers. Next, it spun into a cyclone around the pyramid. *No!* It spun around some core of purple-black light at the center of the pyramid.

I'd seen that purple color before. I'd seen it along the dead river when Vessoth had tried to convince me I was contaminated by the fungus and should cut off my own arm. This was immensely more powerful, as if the other had been nothing more than a dry run for this moment.

Shai and Valyan and Rence all leaped toward the Asadhie with blades drawn. The purple and black vortex shrugged them away, sent them sprawling like children. I managed to get one cartridge into the pistol, flipped the cylinder shut and started pulling the trigger. Two clicks came, and on the third the boom of a shot. The vortex pulsed and I heard the whine of a ricochet.

I cursed, but there was nothing I could do. I could not even get to my feet.

"Do not worry, Ruenn Maclang," Vessoth called from within the terrible light. His voice sounded tinny and distant. "You'll not be a cripple long. Death is still coming for you."

The storm-dark vortex pulsed one more time and a wave of energy spread out from it that stung every fiber in my body. The ground juddered again, more violently. I saw Vessoth framed in the middle of nothingness. Then he was framed no more. He went…somewhere. And took his pyramid with him.

"No!" I shouted. "No!" I tried to rise, only managing to flop over onto one side where agony found and punished me.

"No," I said again, softly and with despair. "The sphere gates are closed. Chalathar had them closed. How could Vessoth open one?"

Shai had struggled again to her feet. "That was no sphere gate," she answered, despair in her own voice. "It was a death gate. Not bound by the same rules. I should have known. Chalathar told me of them. Now all the sacrifices make sense. The impaled Sporns. Daik. Even the animals. The insects. A death gate works through the accumulation of khi energy. Every living thing has some. Some living have much. You have to kill them to liberate it."

Shai's words explained many things all of a sudden. "That's why the Thye Vessoth tried to sacrifice Rannon years ago when she was a Klar prisoner," I blurted. "Her khi is powerful. Even I can sense it. That's why they *did* sacrifice so many others. Why Vohanna sought so many deaths in the war. It was to build this gate for Vessoth."

"Yes! I'm such a fool. I saw it! In front of me!"

"I saw it too," I snapped, out of anger at myself rather than Shai. "I knew beings like Vessoth and Vohanna never do anything without a purpose. I assumed the sacrifices were to scare us. I never seriously considered any other reason."

"We could all find fault in ourselves," Valyan said as he returned to my side. "It isn't helping us now. Is there any way to figure out where Vessoth went?"

"A death gate can't be traced like a sphere gate," Shai said. "At least not by Chalathar. Vessoth could be anywhere on Talera."

"Or off Talera?" I asked.

Shai shook her head.

"No. Death gates don't work that way. They're much more restricted than sphere gates. He's on Talera. Somewhere. Or maybe one of the other moons."

I fell silent, looked down. My legs didn't appear any different than they had before. But no matter how hard I strove, they would not obey me. Wherever Vessoth was now, others would have to track him down. I was no longer capable of that. The taste of failure filled my mouth like a cud of ashes.

The island we were on shook again. For an instant, I believed Vessoth was returning. I glanced up, expecting to see the Asadhie's death gate reform from nothing. Then a bellow came from off in the distance, from what sounded like the throat of the world beast.

All three of my companions looked toward the sound and suddenly called upon a god of some kind. An instant later, a wave smashed against the beach, threw up foam across my legs. The gargantuan bellow came again.

"What is it?" I shouted. "Sit me up. Let me see!"

Valyan knelt behind me. He was shaking but he lifted me up by the shoulders with his chest supporting my back. It hurt horribly, but I had to see. Then I did.

"You have to run," I said. "All of you. You have to run. Get into the tunnels. Leave me here. Run!"

CHAPTER FORTY

GOD OF BEASTS

I looked out over the black waters of the underground sea and saw the thing coming. In the tunnels, when we'd first found sign of the alien "snake" that attacked us there, Valyan had quipped about it being a baby. I had later joked about running into the baby's mother. I doubted any of us had *truly* believed such a massive creature could exist. Now the joke was on us.

At last I understood why Vessoth must be called the Snake God. It wasn't that he looked like one. It was that he controlled one, controlled, in fact, the god of such beasts. The monster storming toward us in a welter of foam looked much like the snake we'd set on fire in the gold-lit corridors we'd left behind us. But it was far, far bigger. Bigger than any whale I'd ever seen in the seas of Earth. Bigger than any ten whales. Vessoth must have called it up before fleeing. He'd promised death was still coming for us. Here it came.

Another wave crashed the beach, swept all the way to me in a splash of white froth.

"It can't follow you into the tunnels," I said to my friends. "You can escape it."

"We won't leave you," Valyan said.

"I'll bury myself in the sand," I added desperately. "It won't find me."

"It's marked us all," Shai said. "It'll find us all."

Rence looked at me; his lips quirked into a strange smile. "We wouldn't make the tunnels anyway."

Shai tightened her grip on her rapier. Rence crossed the blades of his twin kahnnas in front of him. The gestures were almost laughable against such a monster. I did not want my friends to sacrifice themselves for me, but any further arguments would be met with silence. They'd made their decisions. I could but honor them, even while my heart felt dismay that they'd die because of me. I snapped open the Colt's cylinder and began rapidly stuffing shells into it. We'd fight, even if it was surely futile.

"Prop me up with some of those stakes," I told the others.

I didn't want Valyan to have to try and hold me up when the beast came upon us. At least if he could move he might avoid the thing. For a while. Nor did I want to die lying flat on my back.

Rence sheathed his kahnnas for a moment and grabbed up two of the sacrificial stakes the Thye Vessoth had been working on before we surprised them. Between him and Valyan, they got them stabbed deep into the sand to support me. Then both men rose and palmed their blades.

Four of us waited then, three on their feet, me leaning against a framework of wood with legs stretched out dead in front of me. I lifted the pistol, squinted along the barrel. I had no hopes bullets would do anything to stop the monster smashing through the black sea's waves to kill us. Nor could we use the pike maneuver that had been successful against the small version of this thing. We were in the open here, and the twelve foot stakes would be less than splinters to such a beast.

Fifty paces out from the shore now, the thing came on. Wave after wave of salt water hit the beach and came frothing across my legs. The beast's flattened head was the size of a locomotive. Its eyes were like shields carved from jade. Teeth the size of an elephant's tusks clashed together as it opened and shut its red-lined mouth.

Rence wiped his own mouth with the back of one hand. "Dahh!" he cursed.

Valyan muttered quiet prayers to Ivrail.

Shai's hand squeezed and squeezed at the hilt of her rapier.

I opened fire.

The Colt .357 banged out fire and lead as fast I could pull the trigger. There was no effect. I was sure I hit the thing; it was too big to miss. It gave no sign of any reaction, not even a twitch. I clicked the revolver's cylinder out again, punched clear the empties, had time to reload three shells before I knew our last moments were upon us.

Twenty paces from us now, the thing started to lift its head, arching its neck to gain power for its strike. Up and up went that head. I raised the pistol to match. The wave riding in front of the monster struck the shore, broke white. Water surged halfway up my chest. The beast gave another bellow, a roar so big it dwarfed the sound of the Colt as I emptied three more bullets into the thing's snout.

The roar almost covered another sound too. My ears recognized it dimly. My eyes saw it clearly. A swirling mist burst into existence from nowhere as a sphere gate opened right in front of us. Just as Shai, Rence and Valyan vented war-cries and started forward on the attack, Ahrethane stepped from that mist to stand before us.

The fire-tressed woman wore a linen gown of deepest green, and the bell-shaped sleeves fell back from her wrists as she raised her hands above her. The waves smashing across the beach divided to flow around the spot where Ahrethane stood. And it was as if the titanic snake hit a wall.

The enraged beast bellowed one more time. The world shuddered with the sound. It tried to strike but smacked against something invisible in the air and recoiled to shake its head. Now, Ahrethane took a step toward it and "pushed" with her hands. A pulse of energy leaped from her fingers. It, too, was invisible, but I saw the ripples it left through the atmosphere. A blow hit the snake like the slam of a giant's mallet across its face. It shook its head again and backed up. It vented a different kind of cry, confused, plaintive. Then this monstrous thing bigger than any building I'd ever seen fled from a woman who stood barely five feet tall.

Ahrethane turned to face us where we all four gaped in awe. She made a sweeping gesture with her hands and another sphere gate opened behind her. Bryce and Diken Graye and two dozen more of the *Khi-ang*'s crew came rushing through, blades and bows at the ready. Both Bryce and Diken looked wildly around for foes to smite, and when they found none they rushed instead toward me where I lay propped up on the sand. Everyone tried to ask questions at the same time. Shai's voice cut through the babble.

"Ruenn was stabbed in the back. He can't move his legs. Perhaps the...efrinore can help."

The...efrinore looked *through* us instead of at us. Her silver and jade eyes glittered with light. A flow of brilliant copper hair fell across her shoulders and framed a face as pale and expressionless as alabaster. But when Bryce—who knelt beside me with a look of deep concern—turned to glance at her, her expression and posture immediately softened.

"Of course," she said, and her voice was Ahrethane's voice. Almost. Only faintly did I hear a deeper timbre to it than I'd known before.

In the aftermath of rage and terror, as Ahrethane moved quickly to my side, exhaustion began to catch up to me. The Colt revolver slid from suddenly numb fingers. My heart began to labor and I wondered how much blood I'd lost.

Ahrethane knelt at my shoulder in a soft rustle of cloth. A feather light touch brushed my back above the wound and warmth spread upward from there. The agony of the injury eased and I sagged against the stakes upon which I leaned. I'd not realized how tense my body had been as it fought the pain.

Ahrethane remained kneeling, one hand at my back. She must have probed the wound itself then, though I could feel nothing of that.

"Well?" Bryce asked anxiously after a moment.

"I've helped his pain but I cannot heal such a wound. It requires more than sorcery to knit a spine together again." There was a long pause before I heard her say, "I'm sorry." I think it was meant more for Bryce than for me.

"We need to get him to a phoros quickly," Diken said.

"We can use another pair of these stakes to make a litter," Valyan added.

I saw Bryce look at Ahrethane. "Can you open a gate to Timmuzz?" he asked. "We should take him there."

She nodded and stood up again.

"How did you…. How did you open a gate at all?" I asked, glancing up at the sorceress. "I thought Chalathar had them all shut down."

She shrugged. "The gates were locked. Then they weren't. I told Bryce and he bade me find you. I came to the place where I'd sensed the death gate. It is good I did."

"Yes," I said, trying to smile. "We would have been dead ourselves in another moment."

"That beast is like Vessoth's avatar," she said, gesturing toward the dark sea. "Your deaths beneath its teeth would have strengthened him further."

"I—"

A sound burred the air. Another sphere gate opened some ten paces from us. I heard weapons being drawn and grabbed reflexively for the empty pistol lying beside me. Chalathar himself stepped through this gate. A sigh of relief passed through those of us who knew him.

The Asadhie wore the Human form I'd seen him in when we fought Vohanna. In that body he was a tall, broad-shouldered man with a ruddy complexion and long, red-gold hair. Normally, Chalathar exuded health and vigor. He stood stooped and wan now, his hair sweat-soaked and lank around his face. A growth of beard roughened his chin. Only his eyes shone brightly, like gin over ice, but the whites were shot through with broken blood vessels and the lids were swollen. The chain mail he wore looked too heavy for him to carry. Holding the sphere gates closed so long must have leeched much strength from him.

Shai moved quickly toward her mentor, a look of concern on her face. For his part, I saw Chalathar wince at the extent of the woman's hurts and bruises. He put a hand on her shoulder. Their fondness for each other was apparent, though I did not think Chalathar was in love with Shai. The opposite was clearly true.

"Vessoth opened a death gate," Shai told the Asadhie. "I should have guessed that was his plan. We all saw the sacrifices being made to him."

"I know of the gate," Chalathar said in a voice that sounded immensely tired. "That's why I'm here. Do not blame yourself. It is my fault more than any. We have long been afraid he might try something of the sort. I had no idea he'd caused so many deaths and collected their energy."

I wondered who the "we" was he spoke of.

Chalathar's gaze turned toward me then. "You are hurt, my friend."

"I'm paralyzed," I responded. I did not think there was bitterness in the words, though I felt it in my heart.

Chalathar started toward me, then halted as his gaze suddenly took in Ahrethane. His pupils widened. His mouth snapped open, then quickly shut. He returned his gaze to me, very deliberately it seemed. I was quite intrigued by what he must see with his Asadhie eyes in our new Ahrethane.

Continuing over to me, Chalathar knelt. His fingers spidered down my back and again a pleasant warmth flushed through me. He glanced up once at Ahrethane, a speculative light in his eyes.

"The efrinore has done all that can be done here," he said to me after a moment. "But I would ask that you travel back with me to my home. There is something I would like to think upon."

"You cannot heal such a wound either," Ahrethane said.

Chalathar shrugged, without looking at her. "Perhaps not. But all problems need careful study before one admits defeat."

Ahrethane licked her lips as if they were dry and seemed about to speak further. Bryce moved to stand beside her and she held her silence.

"I'll go," I said. I tried to smile. "If I return to Rannon like this she'll be mad I wasn't more careful."

Chalathar smiled too. He rose. Valyan and Diken quickly made a litter from some of the remaining stakes and from tunics they stripped from the dead Thye Vessoth. They eased me on to it and stood up beside Chalathar.

"I can take those who wish to go with Ruenn," the Asadhie said.

"Someone has to inform the ship of what's happened," I said.

"I'll do it," offered one of the crewmen who had come with Bryce and Diken. Most of the other crew members murmured similar sentiments. I suspected they were a little afraid of Chalathar. That was understandable.

"I'll open a gate to send the crewmen back to the *Khiang*," Ahrethane said. "I will remain here." We all looked at her. "This place will be mine now," she added, gesturing as if to encompass all of Nimeru.

A shiver caressed the parts of me that could feel.

Bryce touched Ahrethane's hand. "I'll go with Ruenn," he said. "I'll come back here later. If you want."

She smiled, with redder lips than I remembered. "I do want."

Chalathar awaited no further discussion. He blew out a breath and a large sphere gate came spinning into existence. Shai and the Asadhie stepped through it. Rence followed. Diken and Valyan carried me toward it, Bryce pacing beside me.

I glanced back once. I had walked into this place. I was being carried out. I may have been born in 1888 on Earth, but I had been to a much more modern Earth where such weapons as Colt .357s could be manufactured. I'd seen medical advances far greater than any my own age had known. Even those couldn't repair a spine. I did not think Chalathar would be able to do so either.

So, perhaps my last battle had been fought on this small stretch of sand. If so, it was a battle I'd lost. Even if I'd managed somehow to beat the greatest swordsman I'd ever fought, his master was free.

Vessoth was still free. Soon he'd be hunting.

CHAPTER FORTY-ONE
RISKS

I lay beneath clean, soft linens on a bed built from bansul wood. The blood and sweat and dirt had been sponged from my body. The air smelled of healing herbs and poultices. I felt very little pain.

Chalathar had taken us back to his "home," but I'd seen nothing of that home. During the transition through the sphere gate I'd passed out, and awakened here. Bryce and Diken Graye kept me company. Bryce looked miserable. Diken japed continually to try and keep my spirits up. I pretended it was working.

Chalathar had a phoros serving with him. She was a Kaldi with red fur, by the name of Tuunshin. She and her assistants had cleaned me and bandaged my lesser wounds, of which there were many. Then she'd taken Shai, Valyan and Rence off for similar treatments. They would live, though all three were hurting after what we'd been through.

Chalathar came through the door into the room. His chainmail had been replaced by rawhide breeks and a buff tunic of cotton. His sword had been put away. He looked a bit fresher than he had earlier, but fatigue revealed itself in the lines of his face. He nodded to Bryce and Diken and requested a few moments alone with me. They left reluctantly.

Chalathar paced for a moment, then came over to stand beside me. His pale eyes concealed his emotions. "These will never work again," he said, gesturing toward my legs where they lay paralyzed under the sheets.

A muscle jumped in my jaw. Dryness filled my mouth.

"I did not think they would," I said finally.

"As king in Nyshphal, you will have many servants to aid you. A chair with wheels can even be made. Rannon is a strong woman. Fine and good. She will not stop loving you. Much is left that you can do."

I nodded.

"There is…a gamble you could take."

"A gamble?"

Now, he nodded. "You could gamble the future I've described for a chance to walk again. To fight again. To…love again."

I frowned. "You said the legs were finished."

"If you walked again it would not be in this body."

I did not understand his meaning, but my heart pounded. "How then?"

"You know we Asadhie can change forms."

My heart pounded harder. "I know. I've seen it. With Vohanna."

"I have other bodies as well." He smiled. "Did you know that you first met me as a Nokarran?"

"What?"

"In Andertalen. When the freed slaves stood against their former Klar masters at the battle before the Lava Mines, [9] do you recall a Nokarran warrior with reddish fur and eyes the same color as mine?"

I blinked. "Yes."

I did recall such a Nokarran, a member of that race who look like humanoid lions without tails. I recalled his scars and his fighting prowess.

"His name was Chaiden," Chalathar said. "Few knew it. Perhaps you never heard it."

"I don't believe I did."

"Also," Chalathar continued. "Once on the Shauval River. When the flyer carrying you and Rannon crashed. [10] Was there not a red-headed bargeman who offered his help?"

"I remember," I said. "I'd only seen eyes like his once before."

Chalathar smiled again.

"You were...watching us?" I asked.

"Yes. I knew even then you and Rannon were going to be involved somehow in the war against Vohanna. Though I did not understand exactly how."

I nodded. My mind tripped back to those days of which Chalathar spoke. I saw my blue-eyed Rannon. I stroked her dark hair and kissed her lips. I heard her say she loved me. Hand in hand, I *walked* with her.

"The point for us now," Chalathar continued, "is that you've met me in three different forms. I have many more."

"I don't think I'm quite understanding the point."

"Vohanna and Vessoth were interested in you and Bryce because of your powerful spirits, your khi. And because you both have certain... abilities."

I suddenly understood what he was talking about. "Sorcerous abilities, you mean."

"Yes. Bryce assumed the mantle of his. Through Vohanna's intervention. Yours are deeply buried. I do not know what it would take to bring them out, but they are there."

---

9   See *Swords of Talera.*

10   See *Wings Over Talera.*

"You're not going to turn me into a bane-thrall?" I asked, only half joking.

He chuckled. "No. But because of what lies inside you, you *might* survive what almost no other Human *could* survive."

"You want to transfer my soul into one of your Asadhie bodies," I said.

"It depends on what *you* want," he replied. "First, there is much more to discuss. As I knew you before, I also knew Jedik. I learned much about him. His history. I know he spoke to you of the concept called 'cloning.'"

"He did."

"Jedik thought the cloning machines in his ship were broken and dangerous. I wasn't so sure. I brought two of them here. For study."

"You have two cloning machines?"

"I have one. The other was stolen."

"Stolen? By who?"

"A traitor among my own people. I do not yet know who. I'm quite sure, though, that Vessoth used the stolen device to create the Jedik you just fought. He had all of the original Jedik's physical skills, his ability with a sword. The *khi* was corrupted, however, because Jedik was dead when it was taken."

"The khi exists within the brain, does it not?"

Chalathar looked surprised at the question, but that did not stop him from answering.

"To some extent at least, yes. As I understand it, the cloning machines take an impression of the brain that is restored to the cloned body when it is fully grown. Sort of like a mold can be made of a person's face to create a likeness. Whatever…character exists within the brain at the moment when the impression is taken, that is the character the clone will exhibit. A brain begins to deteriorate rapidly after death, however. I do not know how badly Jedik's brain was decayed when Vessoth took his impression, but I imagine that is why the Snake God was so easily able to twist your friend's mind."

"Vessoth spoke of having his priests 'preserve' the original Jedik's body. Some time would certainly have passed, though. Damage would have been inevitable. What does this have to do with my particular situation?"

"I can use the machine I have to take tissue from *you* right now and begin the cloning process. When the body is ready I can take an impression of your brain and copy it to the clone. However, although the clone grows at an accelerated rate until it reaches the age of the tissue donor, it will be about a year before the body is ready. It will result, though, in a new Ruenn Maclang, one with legs that work."

I had started to realize what Chalathar was getting at but to hear it in plain words stunned. Hope flared, then took another battering as I understood the full implications of what he was saying.

"You mentioned 'copy.' You mean there'll be *two* Ruenn Maclangs. One with legs that work. One without."

"Yes. Unless we do things a little differently."

"How differently?"

"I brought the cloning machines here to examine because I thought, perhaps, they were a model for how our, how my, surrogate bodies were originally produced. But they work by a different process than what happens when I change forms. There's only one me. If I switch my khi into Chaiden, the body known as Chalathar loses consciousness and remains no more than an empty shell until I switch back. Our.... The 'Asadhie' process results in transference. Cloning results in duplication."

"That means?"

"It means that if we use the Asadhie process to transfer your khi into one of my surrogate bodies, then the Ruenn Maclang body. This body," he pointed at me where I lay on the bed, "will be emptied. When the clone is fully grown and I transfer your khi from the surrogate into it, the surrogate will be emptied. There'll be only one Ruenn Maclang."

"If I survive the transfer?"

"That is a rather large question."

I had many large questions. What would Rannon want me to do, was one. I suspected she'd not want me to risk the transfer. But if I did. And it worked. How would she react to the surrogate body carrying the khi of her husband? How would others around us react? How would the people of Nyshphal respond to me as a product of Asadhie sorcery so soon after they'd dealt with the horrors of Vohanna's sorcery?

I couldn't lie to Rannon, or to Bryce and Valyan and Diken. I supposed I could keep the secret from Nyshphal's people. That would mean Rannon and I would never be able to show our love for each other while I lived within the surrogate. A year apart! I didn't know if I could handle that.

As for the clone. Rannon would probably say she didn't want that either. Yet, to help her govern Nyshphal...to be able to fight by her side in a world where conflict made the difference every day between life and death...I needed working legs. The clone would *be* me. It would be a duplicate of me—at least until the moment when the impression of my brain was taken. The problem was that *I* would also still be here, trapped in this body. I could not present Rannon with two husbands. Nor make her choose between them.

I knew men and women who lived without legs, or without a hand or an arm. Or eyes. I'd seen their toughness as every day they made a life for themselves without those things most people take as a given. But none of them were being offered the opportunity I was being offered. If they had the possibility of getting back what they lost, wouldn't they try for it? What would they not risk for such a chance?

There was another thing. *Vessoth*! He'd escaped Nimeru but was left weakened. We'd taken allies from him. We'd hurt him. We needed to find him again now and strike before he could build his strength and recruit armies to his side. I did not doubt that Chalathar and Shai, and Diken and Valyan and others, would hunt Vessoth with everything they had. Selfishly, though, I wanted another chance at the Snake God myself. Because I knew in time he would come for Rannon and everyone else I loved. I couldn't let that happen if there were any way to prevent it.

I looked at Chalathar. "I've made my choice."

EPILOGUE

I lay on an altar of obsidian, in a circular room somewhere in the heart of Chalathar's domain. Around me in the walls, upright in glass-fronted cases, stood bodies. I recognized the faces of Chaiden the Nokarran, and of a bargeman I'd met once on the Shauval River in Nyshphal. There were many others. Male. Female. Human. Non-Human. They all looked as if they were asleep.

Chalathar had explained to me that he did not know which of his surrogates would be most suitable to house my khi. We had to let the khi itself choose. I did not really understand it. But I believed him.

"It's time," Chalathar called from somewhere behind my head.

"All right," I said.

There came a rattling, as of marbles vibrating in a wooden cup. It was the sound of milkstones in a matrix as Chalathar the Asadhie began to manipulate them. A lassitude coated me. I closed my eyes, feeling sleep steal upon me. I chose not to fight it, even though I had no idea what I'd find when I awoke.

If I awoke.

COMPLETE CAST OF CHARACTERS
MAJOR CHARACTERS

Ruenn Maclang: An Earthman who has made a place for himself on Talera. An American born in 1888. Tall. Lean. A swordsman with green eyes.

Bryce Maclang: Ruenn's grey-eyed younger brother. Although he was once corrupted by Vohanna's sorcery, he seems to be recovering his original self.

Rannon Jystral: Queen of the island empire of Nyshphal, and Ruenn's wife.

SUPPORTING CHARACTERS

Ahrethane: A beautiful forest druid who has helped Ruenn more than once. However, since the events chronicled at the end of *Witch of Talera*, she has begun to change.

Arca Heskern: Tall, gray-haired and gray-eyed. She is head of the scientists (alchemists) of Nyshphal.

Chalathar: A mysterious warrior who was revealed in *Witch of Talera* to be an Asadhie, supposedly a member of the race who created Talera. Unlike most Asadhie, Chalathar wants to end the constant strife that torments the planet. For more information, see "Races of Talera" in the Taleran Encyclopedia section of this work.

Diken Graye: Once a mercenary. Now a close friend of Ruenn's. Dark eyed.

Horlis Kazhian: Whipcord lean and sharp featured. He is head of the Nyshphalian navy, which includes both ships of the air and the sea, as well as the saddle bird cavalry corps.

Jask: A member of a reptilian race called the Klar. He and Ruenn fought together in *Swords of Talera* to free his people from tyranny. He became High-Council of the Klar kingdom of Talen.

Kreeg: Once a fighting slave, now Ruenn's self-appointed bodyguard.

Kuurus Jystral: Younger brother of Rannon. He allied himself to Vohanna in an attempt to gain control of Nyshphal, but was arrested for his crimes at the end of *Witch of Talera*.

Rajan Critus: Commander of the Nyshphalian Imperial guard, which also serves as a kind of police force. He is one of Ruenn and Rannon's most trusted lieutenants.

Taskin Bhent: Short, stout, blunt-featured. A soldier who commands the Nyshphalian army.

Valyan Tiersal: A member of a variant Human race called the Llurn, who were genetically modified in the past to have emerald skin and yellow eyes. Also a close friend of Ruenn's.

Vohanna: (Deceased). An Asadhie sorceress. She hoped to conquer Nyshphal and make it the center of an empire. Her evil was brought to an end in *Witch of Talera*.

NEW CHARACTERS IN WRAITH OF TALERA

Cailif Ostt: Pilot for Ruenn Maclang's air battleship, the *Khiang*. Pilots are hired as members of an independent Caste and are generally not citizens of the nation that employs them.

Daik, Oleg, Taren, and Vohn: Members of Ruenn's crew aboard the *Khiang*.

Munt: A young war-orphan who serves on Ruenn's battleship. His name, which he chose himself, is taken from a term meaning monkey.

Rence: A Human warrior who has joined Chalathar's fight to bring peace to Talera.

Shai: A warrior woman with light brown eyes who has also joined Chalathar's effort to bring peace to Talera. The faint golden color of her skin suggests some possible variant ancestry.

Vessoth: Another Asadhie, the husband of Vohanna.

Volek: A Kaldi warrior who fights for Chalathar.

TALERAN ENCYCLOPEDIA

(1). RACES OF TALERA

An alien race known as the Asadhie condensed Talera from the heart of a gas giant planet so it would be hidden from the outside universe. They constructed an artificial sun to warm the planet. They then used a type of worm-hole technology, called "sphere gates," to bring plants and animals and intelligent races from many other planets to populate their newly created world. They also genetically modified some species, including Human populations, and even created artificial biological races in some instances. In the following list of races that have appeared in the Talera series, the "Natural" races are those that evolved on their own. "Modified" races were altered by the Asadhie. "Artificials" were created by the Asadhie.

Asadhie: Very little is known about the Asadhie, and much of what is known is mixed up with myth. Supposedly, the Asadhie constructed Talera and then some of them stayed on to make it their private playground. Ruenn Maclang knows Talera is indeed an artificial construction, but none of the Asadhie he's met seem to have the technological mastery to have built it. In fact, there are very large gaps in their scientific knowledge.

The Asadhie are known to use the *toir'in-or* milkstones to work sorcery and are supposedly the creators of the stones. Again, however, Ruenn has seen no evidence they are still making the stones. Ruenn *has* seen that the Asadhie can inhabit artificial bodies, and under certain circumstances can even possess another being's body.

In Taleran mythology, there were originally twelve Asadhie, generally referred to as the First Gods. They treated Talera and its nations like a giant chess game. Eventually, a war is supposed to have broken out among the Asadhie and their followers. It was called the God's War and spanned most of the planet, destroying over half of Talera's civilizations at the time. According to legend, the Asadhie who were not killed in the God's War fled the planet, but Ruenn has already met at least three beings who claim to be Asadhie: Vohanna, Vessoth, and Chalathar. Below is a list of the "First Gods" and what legend has to say about them.

1. Amenophor: This the Asadhie name of the being known in the Talera series primarily as Chalathar. He was named in *Witch of Talera*, but appeared in both the earlier books in the series as well. Although he most frequently appears as a Human male, he seems to retain red or reddish-blond hair and gin-colored eyes no matter what body he inhabits. He has told Ruenn that he is now working to help Talera recover from the centuries of strife created by the Asadhie.

2. Heshval: Chief God of the Klar. Supposedly a twin brother to Vessoth.

3. Ivrail: A goddess. She supposedly created the Nakscherii, the Green Llurns, and is considered by them to have been kind and loving. They still call upon her in prayer.

4. Sidian: A goddess. Known as a loner.

5. Thanamaud: Supposedly the creator of the Black Llurns. Legend claims that he dwells in a sky city.

6. Theris: Another goddess. Legend claims she was killed by Rhanyhn, an evil force she conjured. Rhanyhn then took her place among the First Gods.

7. Toghrul: Said to be evil.

8. Urthrik: According to legend, he became permanently trapped in a surrogate body and in that form is known as Kamrack the Bull.

9. Vessoth: The snake god of the Thye-Vessoth. Husband and lover of Vohanna. He was supposedly imprisoned inside the moon of Nimeru by an alliance of other Asadhie. Part of Vohanna's goal in the Witch's War against Nyshphal was to try and free him.

10. Vohanna: A goddess. Considered very evil. In ancient times, she ruled the area of Nyshphal and the Rosjavik Peninsula as her empire. Ruined Vohan, on the island of Nyshphal, was the capital. Wife and lover of Vessoth.

11. Yaal: God of the underworld. He supposedly carries the smell of corpses with him wherever he goes.

12. Yashand: According to legend, he was seen by most other Asadhie as a weakling.

Darzuna: (Naturals? Artificials?) Worshippers of Vohanna. Not known to be found on Talera. Ruenn Maclang met this race on another planet to which Vohanna tried to exile him. He described them as centaur-like. They are four footed and hooved, but with bodies built more like bighorn sheep than horses, and not as big as horses. They have tails like cattle. They have a very Human appearing torso at the front of their bodies, with Human-like shoulders, arms and six-fingered hands. Their heads are described as being like those of bighorn sheep as well, with flat noses stretched out along a muzzle, thick lips, and curling horns. Both sexes have horns, although males have larger ones. Their whole bodies are typically covered with white hair or fur. Male fur is typically curlier than female fur.

Kaldi: (Naturals.) Bear-like, with reddish or brownish fur covering their bodies. Males are quite a bit larger than females; the latter are near Human size. Male fur is coarser. Bipedal humanoids. Their features look very Human. Common on Talera.

Klar: (Naturals.) Reptilian humanoids with either green or black skins, and with bullet-shaped heads. They are generally hairless and have scales. They have a rat-like tail. Very militaristic. Common on Talera.

Koro: (Modifieds.) Modified from basic Human stock. Dwarvish in build, averaging around five feet for men and quite a bit shorter for women. They have short, squat trunks, barrel chests, and broad shoulders, with jutting jaws, thick lips, and heavy lashes. Most males are bearded. There are two primary subgroups, the highlanders, who tend to be taller and blond, and the lowlanders, who are shorter and with reddish or brownish hair. Common on Talera.

Llurn: (Modifieds.) Modified from Human stock. The main differences are in hair, skin, and eye colors. Llurns can intermarry with Humans and often produce offspring but the offspring are almost always sterile themselves. Relatively common on Talera. Subtypes include:

1. Green Llurn = also called Nakscherii, green skinned, with black hair and yellow or green eyes. Valyan is a Nakscherii.

2. Black Llurn = Ebony skinned, with silver hair and eyes.

3. Golden Llurn = Golden skinned, with violet eyes and fiery red hair.

4. Indigo Llurn = purple or dark bluish skin with purple-tinted eyes.

Minotaur: Bull-men. (Modifieds? Artificials?) Described as having bull-like heads and hooves, but otherwise resembling large and muscular Humans. Not typically found on Talera. Brought to the planet by Vohanna to attack Nyshphal. See *Witch of Talera*.

Nokarra: (Naturals.) Bipedal humanoids. Typically larger than Humans. They look somewhat like upright, tail-less snow leopards. Their fur is most commonly reddish or golden. Their eyes are generally gold or green (less commonly gray, blue, or black). Common on Talera.

Phylari: (Naturals?) This race has almost translucent skin and generate their own natural light internally. They also have extremely melodic voices. They are about Human sized, with gossamer wings and long, very thin legs. They are intelligent but have no arms or hands and manipulate everything with prehensile toes. They have no technological culture. They are extremely beautiful, almost like living creations of glass. Very uncommon on Talera. Ruenn suggested that sightings of these creatures might have inspired the concept of angels. See *Wings Over Talera.*

Reploids: (Naturals.) A reptilian race brought to Talera by Vohanna to attack Nyshphal. There are both winged and non-winged versions. Not typically found on Talera. See *Witch of Talera.*

Sporns: (Naturals.) An insectoid race. They have eight limbs, four they walk on and four they use like Human arms. Approximately seven feet tall on average. They have silver blood with mild acidic properties, eight eyes, a bundle of "feelers" around the mouth, and a chitinous exoskeleton. Most have antler like structures made of chitin on their heads. Eyes are typically whitish. Very common in some areas of Talera. There is a second type of Sporn that is quite a bit bigger and has green eyes. These are rare and may be modified from the original Sporn stock.

Ss'Korra: (Naturals.) Often described as looking either wolf-like or baboon-like. Bipedal humanoids, though somewhat shorter than Humans. They have muzzles and are mammalian in nature. They are furred, except on their bellies. Fur color is usually black or gray, or both. Their feet look much like paws, although they have Human-type hands. Many have blue or green eyes. Primarily carnivorous. Common in some areas of Talera.

Syber: (Naturals.) Generally humanoid, with four arms and two legs. They have a tufted tail that is prehensile and contains a poison barb to which Humans are not susceptible. Genitalia are hidden inside the bodies and extruded only when they mate. Their faces resemble vampire bat faces, with ribbed ears, upturned noses, dark beady eyes, and needle teeth. Rare on Talera.

Toibel: (Naturals.) Small, fox-like beings with a black stripe across the nose. They are bright-eyed and can move on all fours like a kangaroo, or on hind feet alone. They are generally not considered highly intelligent and have no civilization. They live in small family groups, generally in dry burrows, and possess a musical language. They may be partially telepathic. Some people keep them as treasured pets. Relatively rare on Talera.

Thye Vessoth: (Naturals? Artificials?) Reptilian. They have two Human-like legs and arms, but have grossly distorted faces with stone blue eyes. They have only slits for a nose, and a wide red mouth lined with yellowed fangs. Their skin is typically an iridescent green and gold, and they have large vanes at the sides of their heads that resemble bat-wings. These are not ears, though, and their purpose is unknown. While most Thye Vessoth have broad, thick tails, some lack them. They are primarily sorcerer priests serving various Asadhie, most notably Vessoth. Relatively rare on Talera.

Trolls: (Modifieds? Artificials?) These look like how trolls are usually described, with warty bodies and tusks protruding from behind the lower lips. Not commonly found on Talera. They, too, were brought to Talera by Vohanna during her war against Nyshphal. At that time they were accompanied by creatures called "Man-hounds," which look sort of like a cross between a hyena and a hound with a pair of Human arms added. See *Witch of Talera.*

Vhichang: (Naturals.) Avian in appearance. Bipedal humanoids that vary widely in height. Most are somewhat shorter than Humans. They give birth to live young but do not suckle them. Their faces are beaked, with the tip cruelly curved. Above the small beak are small eyes, described by Ruenn Maclang as being like "wicked yellow rosary beads." A pelt of downy feathers covers their bodies and their shoulders are humped with the muscle that is a legacy of their flying forbearers. An occasional baby is even said to be born with vestigial wings on its back. Vhichang legs are curved almost into the shape of an unstrung bow, built more for perching than striding. Very warlike. Common on Talera.

Vlih: (Naturals.) They are generally humanoid, with two legs and two arms. They have a cat-like tail that is prehensile. They also have two tentacles below the arms, which they use in battle. Typically, they have dark skin and extremely course hair, which is generally black. Their hips are articulated more like a bird than a Human, which leads them to walk leaning forward with a stalking movement. They generally fight in all male bond groups called Vlih-Nha. Relatively uncommon on Talera.

(2). LANGUAGES

Ruenn Maclang's journals, which are the basis for the Talera series, are written in English. However, many local Taleran words and names creep into his writing, and below is a brief dictionary of some of the more common ones. Many of these come from the language of the Koro traders, which is a common "trade" tongue. There are, of course, many different languages on Talera and apparently a substantial sharing of words among them.

GENERAL WORDS

Ahy — Greeting. Basically "hello."

Dihn — A small coin of little importance.

Dhu — Hundred.

Efrinore — Druid-witch-shaman. A magic woman of the forest. Herbalist.

Gleene — Blade.

Hyr — Half.

Jaikil — Raptor.

Jhesan — Lord (or sometimes Prince).

Jhesana — Lady (or sometimes Princess).

Khi — This is an important concept on Talera. It means, among other things, soul, spirit, psychic energy, charisma.

Khiang — Warrior, in the Nyshphalian tongue.
  1. Ahy Khiang — a greeting to a warrior.
  2. Tre Khiang — a great feat of arms.

Khisan — Warlord, one who rules by the Khi.

Kyr — King.

Lehr — Outlaw.

Mercredi — A mercenary who serves as infantry.

Mordai — The name for the 1st hour of the Taleran day, the hour after midnight when the veil between the living and the dead worlds is said to be thinnest.

Munt — Monkey.

Nex — Place.

Phal — Island.

Phoros — Healer or Physician.

Phorosnex — Hospital.

Phrer — Priest or monk.

Rha — War.

Rhath — This also means warrior, but in a different Taleran language. "Rath" is a variant spelling.

Rhahn — battle.

Rhanvin — Fighting slave, gladiator.

Saar — Gesture of polite title, like Sir.

Saaress — Gesture of polite title for a woman. Madam.

Saysa — Term of endearment, equivalent in English to "baby" or "honey."

Sendaht — Term meaning telepath.

Sendahtia — Telepathy.

Vin — Slave.

Ver — Of.

Verdredi — Mounted mercenary.

Zay Khiang — A teacher for a warrior. Mentor.

COMMON CURSE WORDS AND PHRASES

Dahh — Generally translated as Damn.

Dihmus vishka — Possible translation is "god in heaven."

Krutt — Used as a curse because the habits of the insect of this name are so disgusting to many.

Lart — Rodent. Generally considered a mild curse meaning, "you rat."

Ruck (Ruckers) — Worthless (Worthless ones).

Vhish — Usually translated as Shit or Piss.

Est Yaal shei — go to hell.

Ivid Yaal shei — What the hell?

Sae Yaal shei — Oh hell, or, by hell

COMMANDS FOR SADDLE BIRDS

Haih Kerang — "Let's ride." Used to signal a saddle bird to take off.

Jehas — An order that means for the bird to vent a loud cry.

Rish — An order to the bird to fold its wings and dive straight toward the ground, which is generally used as an escape maneuver.

(3). MEASUREMENTS OF TIME

There are many ways of measuring time on Talera but this is a common method. It is the one used in Ruenn and Rannon's homeland of Nyshphal.

Shri — 2.34 seconds. (100 shri = 1 dhorrin)
Dhorrin — 3.9 minutes. (20 dhorrin = 1 dhaur)
Dhaur — 78 minutes.

There are 20 dhaur in a Taleran day, which, strangely enough, equates to exactly 26 Earth hours. The 10th Taleran dhaur is noon and the 20th is midnight. First gray dawn light comes around the 4th dhaur, sunrise itself around the 5th, and sunset around the 15th.

(4). MEASUREMENTS OF DISTANCE

This is a common method of distance measurement on Talera. It is the one Ruenn uses most often.

Koen = 1.15 inches. (8 koen = 1 heka)
Heka = 9.18 inches. (4 heka = 1 tahng)
Tahng = 1.02 yards, or 36.72 in. (2500 tahng = 1 verlang)
Verlang = 1.449 miles.

(5). EARTH SPECIES TRANSPORTED TO TALERA

The Asadhie borrowed liberally from many planets in populating Talera. They didn't neglect Earth. Below is a partial list of some of the Earth plants and animals brought to Talera.

Animals — horses, deer, pigs, elephants, cattle, sheep, chickens, dogs, rabbits, wolves, panthers, monkeys, birds of various kinds (hawks, vultures, cardinals, jays, wrens), reptiles of various kinds (cobras, rattlesnakes, pythons, lizards, crocodiles), insects of many types (ants, moths, butterflies, honey bees, dung beetles, spiders, flies, scorpions, praying mantis), and many more.

Plants — rice, wheat, oats, hops, sage, blackberries, grapes, beans, peas, potatoes, onions, leeks, cotton, lilies, roses, bananas, cacti, trees of various kinds (oak, pecan, walnut, willow, sequoia, pine, cedar, mahogany, maple, thorn, apple, persimmon, pear) and others.

(6). THE TALERAN CALENDAR

Because Talera is a constructed world, it has extremely regular temporal characteristics. Although there are some variations in how times are measured across the planet, the majority of nations and races follow a standard calendar as indicated below.

A Taleran Year = 400 days

A Taleran Day is called a Dhorn = 26 Earth hours.

A Taleran Week is called a ten-day (tenday) = 10 days

A Taleran Month = 30 days

There are a number of conspicuous similarities between Earth and Taleran calendars, including the 30 day months. The Taleran Year also contains 12 months. Every three months there is a "Passage." This is a 10 day period in which the sun changes colors to alter the seasons. These ten-days are celebrated as feasts. There are 4 "Passages," generally referred to by Ruenn as the Spring Passage, Summer Passage, Fall Passage, and Winter Passage.

(7). NOTES ON TALERAN PLANTS AND ANIMALS, AND PRODUCTS MADE FROM THEM:

Aestor: A flying mammal that looks something like an arctic fox.

Ahmbr: A relatively short tree that makes beautiful shade.

Arquaal: A small, four legged winged reptile. Primarily an insectivore.

Bansul: A blonde wood tree that provides a sturdy wood much used in making furniture.

Bhurl: Both a type of tree that grows commonly in Taleran forests, and the small nut of the tree, which tastes much like black beans and is frequently served in similar ways.

Bittergrass: A tough, Bermuda-like grass with creeping roots that generally grows low to the ground.

Carbaxus: A huge tropical/semi-tropical tree with a wide trunk and smooth bark. It makes up the bulk of the major wood in the jungle of Vohan on Nyshphal. See *Wings Over Talera*.

Cenboth: A sea monster that looks something like a mixture of octopus and lobster. They normally live deep in the ocean but come to the surface when giving birth. The young are considered delicacies. Ruenn faced one in *Swords of Talera*.

Chelaquin: A rough barked tree of medium height but with a very thick trunk. Grows in marshy areas. Very resistant to rot. Used for building in wet climates.

Chirik Root: Chirik grows mainly in warm climates and in low hilly areas where it is not too wet. The root is cylindrical and is sliced into buttons and chewed to produce two types of drug effects. It is a stimulant in small doses but in larger doses the user becomes rigid and enters a kind of coma where they experience hallucinations of form and color. Mildly addicting. Used like caffeine at low doses. Cheap.

Collex: A saddle animal. Large, somewhat splay footed. It is not the easiest gated of beasts but is prized because of its extreme loyalty. The collex can be imprinted on a rider at birth and will then remain loyal and close to that rider for life. It will always recognize its master and will usually die if its master dies. The collex has six legs, accounting for its uneven gait, and a long flat tail that it holds stretched out behind it when it runs.

Cymer: A yellow grain grown on Talera. Grows in fields like wheat but is taller and has very thin, spearhead shaped kernels. The kernels don't develop just at the top of the plant but in tiny pods all around the shaft of the plant from just above the bottom to near the top. The top has a flowering yellow head full of pollen. The grain is used in making fine breads and the kernels can also be eaten pretty much as is.

Ghyre: Sometimes described as a tiger/dog. Very aggressive. A predator. Also called the "Stalking Cat" because of its walk. There are a number of subspecies, including plain and mountain ghyres.

Goldenswords: A flowering plant with blade-like blooms.

Gret: A vicious, rodent-like beast roughly the size of a small dog. It lives mostly in swampy lands and often travels in packs, made up mostly of females. The males tend to be solitary and less aggressive.

Hanris: A bush with small, red, decorative berries. The foliage of the plant is a bright blue. The berries are weakly poisonous to Humans but are eaten by some non-Earth birds.

Harsupex: A kind of ferret/cat that has the habits and intelligence of a raccoon. Looks mostly like a ferret.

Heen: Rat-sized predators that hunt in huge packs. They look like miniature monkeys with big heads, but have the teeth and feeding habits of piranha. They are notorious for their rapid reproduction rate. To "breed like heen," is sometimes used as an insult.

Hespern: A very large saddle-bird, often used to transport freight.

Honey Grain: The plant produces three commercial products. First is its well known seeds, which give the plant its name and from which sweet breads and cakes are made. Second, so called "Spice Mead" is also made from fermented Honey Grain and is much in demand. Third, the pollen of the plant, located on the husks surrounding each ear of the grain, is used as a cinnamon-like spice when dried. The grain is very rich in vitamins and high energy nutrients and is sometimes mixed with other materials and used as journey rations.

Honey whisper: A kind of long and intricately knotted moss that grows in strands of black and silver with tiny silver pods on it that taste sweet when eaten. The pods are also rich in energy.

Hyr-Quall: A saddle lizard. A larger and more even tempered version of the quall. May be used as a war beast or a draft beast. They are predators, though, and sometimes go insane in battle once they scent blood, which makes them double-edged weapons. They are often trained to attack anything that is not on their back. They have a pounding gait but are very powerful when used as shock troops. Not many cultures have mastered the hyr-quall.

Hysis: Several varieties of flowers with brightly colored blooms. Crimson Hysis is the most common but there is also Blue Hysis, Ivory Hysis, etc. An herb, also called hysis, is made from the plant.

Ironwood: A type of tree with very dense wood. Often used in the making of staves and spears.

Iskit: A small, hard blackberry that grows wild over much of Talera.

Jergal: A large, slab-sided river fish. Mostly a bottom dweller. Its meat is used in making passal.

Jit-leaf: a Taleran "chew," which is used somewhat like tobacco. It consists of a mixture of jitter grass leaves and shredded Verhlis leaves, both of which have stimulating properties.

Jitter Grass: A plant whose leaves are rolled and smoked. A mild stimulant.

Juujum: A low bush with a round broad trunk about three feet high and very large, spear shaped leaves. The leaves are thick and strong and are used sometimes to construct roofs. The plant grows mostly in tropical environments.

Kahurra: A plant that may produce a kind of natural steroid. It is used by gladiators and assassins. It increases strength and aggressiveness but sometimes creates violent, uncontrollable rages.

Kellet: A bivalve common in Taleran waters.

Krell: A flying reptile with a ten foot wingspan. They are carnivorous but rarely attack people. Their hides make a durable and lightweight leather.

Krutt: A beetle-like insect that lays its eggs in living animals. After the maggot-like larvae hatch, they eat their way out of the animal from inside. There are treatments for the infection but if the treatments are prevented the resulting death is horrible, prolonged, and very painful. This is used in some places as a means of execution.

Kryll: A swift, fast saddle-bird that is highly predatory and dangerous.

Kryshawk: A flying bird of prey.

Laith: A large, water-dwelling reptile with a head something like a moray eel, large front limbs like a lizard, and a tapered body like a snake. It does have tiny hind limbs and a whale-like fluke for a tail. The laith is just one example of a Taleran "sea serpent." It primarily dwells in salt water but is often seen in rivers when small. Blood Drug, which is named for its color, is made from laith venom. The venom is highly toxic to organisms from the same planet as the laith, but with Humans and many other species the primary effect of the substance is to produce powerful hallucinations. It is sometimes used in religious ceremonies.

Blood drug is quite rare and expensive. It is addicting, but because of the prohibitive cost people seldom use it frequently enough to become addicted. A full grown laith will produce several quarts of pure Blood Drug, and a man who is able to kill one can become rich. They are not regularly hunted because of their size and viciousness. Stories are told of sailors finding dead laiths floating on the surface of the ocean and retiring to live like kings as a result of harvesting the beasts' venom.

Lart: A type of rodent. Much like a rat in behavior, but larger and more vicious, and with even more disgusting habits. They often infest sewers and feed on corpses. They have red or pink eyes, webbed toes, and no tail. Their fur grows in thick clumps between patches of bare, scaly skin. The term "lart" is used as a gesture of contempt on Talera.

Moonrose: A very beautiful, rose-like flower that combines all the colors of the four moons in delicate pastels—light blue, light turquoise, pale gold, delicate red. Its petals are sometimes used as an herb in cooking.

Needle Cane: A type of cane that is very thin and sharp. It is sometimes used to inject drugs, such as Blood Drug.

Nightrose: A beautiful, night blooming flower that is deadly poisonous.

Ninjam Weed: A plant used to make a narcotic. Although the drug is concentrated primarily in the roots, some is found in the leaves and most people prefer to chew or smoke the leaves to get the effect.

Passal: A kind of travel food, sort of like pemmican. Made from ground up fish, fat, berries, and nuts—particularly the jergal fish and the iskit berry—and usually walnuts or pecans. It is then allowed to "set" in rawhide containers, producing a light-weight and high-energy food source. Not known for being tasty, however.

Porphit berries: Although these are called berries, they are more like muscadine grapes. They are purple in color and of medium sweetness. They grow well in thick forests and jungles where the light is relatively dim. Their juice is used to make dies and paints.

Quall: A predator of Talera. It is lizard-like but warm blooded. They are most often found in the foothills of mountains but there are types that live in forests and deserts. Qualls are vicious and quite willing to eat a Human. They vary greatly in size, with some types being no bigger than lions while others grow as large as a ton or more. They are incredibly fast. They have four legs and a tail. The eyes are generally yellowish-green and reflect light because the creatures are primarily nocturnal. The quall has a crocodile shaped snout with teeth angled back into the jaw.

Quattle: A large, mantis-crab like creature from the same planet as the Sporns. The Sporns use it as a brooder for their young. They have two hooked front claws, like a mantis, and six pincered side claws like a crab. They have a fluke-like tail. Their carapaces are very tough and virtually impossible to penetrate with a sword.

Redbriar: Thick growing briars that don't make much in the way of fruit. Sometimes used as protective hedges.

Reeth: A jaguar-sleek, lean, dangerous predator. Sometimes called the harlequin-wolf for both its mocking smile and its white on black patchwork coat.

Rithk: A saddle flier. A bird/reptile mix. Very large. Artificially bred. Very aggressive, very powerful, very fast.

Rundal: A common, large fish that lives in coastal waters and often ventures into the mouths of rivers. It produces a clean, bright burning oil.

Sabrun: A sleek, light-boned, very fast, very hawk-like saddle bird. They have violet eyes but can have varicolored feathers, ranging from gray through brown.

Safweed: A thick, woody-stemmed weed.

Samphur: A rare wood, often used in decorative furniture.

She-ashin: A type of grape from which fine wines are made.

Silver Nyxe: A flower with silver blooms.

Stugah: An ox-like beast, not very smart, but strong. Very large, standing seven or eight feet at the shoulder. There is a wild variety and a domesticated variety, the latter of which are commonly used as draft animals. Stugah are generally mild mannered. The exception is during the rutting season when the wild bulls can become quite uncontrollable. This aggression has largely been bred out of the domesticated stugah. Their hides are very thick and are often used to make boots and other articles of clothing, as well as sword sheathes and bow quivers.

Taaber: A small, hard, potato-like vegetable, often carried for travel rations. It may be derived from the Earthly potato, or at least the name is likely to be a corruption of that English word.

Tasaber: A hoofed saddle animal. Horse sized. It looks vaguely like a cross between a horse and a mule deer. Tasabers have horns and stand 15 hands high on average. They have long necks and fine looking heads. The males have a thick, unruly mane, which females lack. Both sexes have a long tail similar to a horse's. The legs are long and lean and appear fragile, but are sturdy and strong. They are prized as riding animals, with fire, spirit, courage and loyalty. Coat colors vary from red through gray, to white and black in the same way horses do. Their eyes tend to be brown or black, but gray or even blue are not uncommon.

Taverel: A goat-like creature. Often domesticated. A common source of cheese and milk.

Terval: A short horned type of cattle. They are domesticated and often kept in great herds. They are large but tough and can survive with relatively little care.

Tharspa: A thin, fine wood, often used for shutters.

Tipit: A tree with bright orange fruit of the same name. It usually grows in tropical and semi-tropical climates. Although not highly palatable to Humans, it is nutritious.

Tlatel: Also called the gourd tree. A large tree with yellowish wood, averaging around thirty feet in height. Each tree produces several hundred gourds a year, which are used for a variety of purposes. The wood is supple and strong, prized for bows and arrows.

Traen-tha: Another yellow-wooded tree. Also used in bow making.

Traepa: A water plant that grows thickly in lakes and ponds. The plants begin as seeds that take root near shore, under water. Each plant produces twenty to thirty hollow bladders filled with a light and expensive oil that burns a long time and has a pleasant smell. The oil is lighter than water and as adults the plants breaks free of their roots and become free floating.

Trenkil: Eagle-like bird of prey.

Tris: Also called candle-bugs. Small, light giving insects. They live in many underground places, such as sewers. They are smaller than a lightning bug but their turquoise light is pretty much constant, only occasionally dimming or brightening slightly. They are also flightless and move in large masses.

Tull: A forest bird whose feathers are used to fletch arrows and whose eggs are eaten. There are several species, most of which have brilliant plumage that is used for artistic and decorative purposes.

Turex: A large, mussel-like creature that dwells in fresh-water rivers in jungle or tropical areas of Talera. It periodically sheds its shell as it grows, but after the shedding the new "undershell" remains soft for a good long time. If harvested at that time, the shell can be worked into a very durable, flexible material from which boots and other items of clothing can be made. Highly expensive.

Vashok: Also called Howlers. These creatures have short, squat bodies with bristle fur. They are usually three to four feet tall, with baboon-like faces. They have huge curved claws on all four paws. They are primarily ground hunters and are very vicious. They also run in packs of thirty or more. Ruenn faced a pack of these beasts in *Wings Over Talera*.

Verhlis: A bush whose leaves are used to brew tea. Its roots can be used to make a much stronger version. The tea has mild stimulant properties and is used much like coffee. It has a naturally sweet, almost honey-like taste.

Vimen: A gigantic deep-ocean fish.

Vull: A smallish sea bird.

Vullwing: A saddle bird. It has an eagle shaped body, massive wingspread, elongated neck, and is usually indigo in color.

Wax Cane: A small variety of cane that grows thickly along rivers and in marshy areas. It is often used for thatch and can be worked to produce a rough, linen-like cloth. More extensive working produces paper of varying qualities, depending on how it is treated.

Wine-grapes: A collective term for grapes that are intended for wine making

Wurstid: A sort of pig/rabbit. A small varmint that roots in gardens.

Yellow Angel Hair: A type of flower.

(8). SOME DETAILS ON THE GAME OF KYRELLIAN

Like chess on Earth, Kyrellian is also called the game of Kings, and Kyr means "King" in one of the Taleran tongues, probably one originally derived from Earth. There are two versions of the game. The long version is called Kyrellian and the shorter version Kyrel. In Kyrel, there are only two sides, called Crystal and Obsidian. The board has four parts, a central piece of 100 squares called the "War-Board," two smaller pieces of 20 squares each called "Lands," and two rectangular pieces called "Bridges" that attach the Lands to the War-Board. The Bridges consist of 10 squares arranged in rows of 5. Each player's pieces are initially placed on their own "Land" and must move across the bridge to the War-Board. The object of the game is to capture the opposing player's Land, which means control of at least 15 of the 20 squares.

The rules of Kyrellian are the same but it is played with four Lands and four Players, and the capture of one player's Land turns over the remaining pieces of that player to the Conqueror. In addition to Crystal and Obsidian, there are Argent and Vermilion. Both Kyrel and Kyrellian are played with 20 pieces per side—five "Major," ten "Minor," and five "Lesser." The pieces have various names in various cultures but below is an English translation of the most common names for the pieces in Kyrel.

CRYSTAL	**OBSIDIAN**

MAJOR PIECES

Crystal Prince	Obsidian Prince
Fire Rider	War Rider
Air Rider	Winged Rider
Earth Rider	Death Rider
Water Rider	Iron Rider

MINOR PIECES

The Owl	The Raven
Priest	Priest
The Wolf	The Beast
The Falconer	The Piper
The Sword	The Dagger
The Shield	The Stone
The Lance	The Thorn
The Angel	The Lady
Wind	Cloud
Mage	Sorceress

LESSER BEINGS

Slave	Slave
Trader/Merchant	Trader/Merchant
Singer	Singer
Child	Child
The Peasant	The Peasant

ABOUT THE AUTHOR

CHARLES ALLEN GRAMLICH grew up on a farm in Arkansas, near the foothills of the Ozark Mountains, then moved to the New Orleans area in 1986 to teach at a local university. He's since sold several novels and numerous short stories. His tales, while mostly in the genres of horror, science fiction, and fantasy, have also included westerns, children's stories, mainstream fiction, slipstream works, and experimental pieces. He has also published poetry and nonfiction, the latter ranging from scientific reference works to articles on writing.

After Hurricane Katrina smashed up New Orleans, Charles and his wife, Lana, an award winning photographer, moved to Abita Springs, Louisiana, where they live in the woods with many birds. Charles has an adult son named Joshua.

Charles is an editor for *The Dark Man: The Journal of Robert E. Howard Studies*, and is a member of HWA (the Horror Writers Association). He is on facebook as Charles Gramlich, and blogs regularly at: http://charlesgramlich.blogspot.com